BLOOD'S SHADOW

LYCANTHROPY FILES, BOOK 3

CECILIA DOMINIC

ABOUT BLOOD'S SHADOW

The disease has teeth...but the cure could be deadly.

As Investigator for the Lycanthrope Council, Gabriel McCord went above and beyond his official title to keep werewolf kind out of the public eye. Now he has a new challenge as the liaison to the Institute for Lycanthrope Reversal, advocating for humans turned werewolf against their will.

The Institute's controversial "treatment" is nonetheless generally accepted – until one of the project's scientists is found murdered at his desk.

The suspect list is long: purists who believe lycanthropism is a non-returnable gift; wolf-borns who want the cure for their own; and the ethereal Selene Rial, an Institute psychologist who's lost her most precious possession to a secret society dedicated to the annihilation of werewolves.

If Gabriel fails to solve this case, the fragile peace between wizards and lycanthropes could shatter, and his friends' lives could be ruined. But even if he succeeds, he has to face the consequences of his heart being pulled in a dangerous direction – a woman whose secrets could destroy them both.

AUTHOR'S NOTE

Thank you for picking up *Blood's Shadow*!

I really enjoyed writing this book because it brought back so many of the memories from the trip to Scotland that Hubby and I took several years ago. Writing first person from the male perspective was also a lot of fun, and I appreciated the opportunity to explore the ins and outs of Gabriel McCord, a character that my readers and I have found fascinating since his first appearance in The Mountain's Shadow.

Look at the back of the book for a chance to sign up for my newsletter list, and as a thank-you gift, I'll send you a short story or novella (selection varies).

Thanks again, and happy reading!

Cecilia

LOOK FOR THESE TITLES BY CECILIA DOMINIC

Urban Fantasy Books:

The Lycanthropy Files
The Mountain's Shadow
Long Shadows
Blood's Shadow
A Million Shadows

The Fae Files
The Shadow Project
Shadows of the Heart
The Shadowed Path

Dream Weavers & Truth Seekers
Truth Seeker
Tangled Dreams
Web of Truth

Steampunk Books:

The Aether Psychics
Noble Secrets
Eros Element
Light Fantastique
Aether Spirit
Aether Rising

The Inspector Davidson Mysteries
The Art of Piracy
Mission: Nutcracker

Blood's Shadow

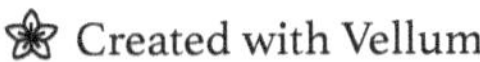 Created with Vellum

DEDICATION

If someone had told me two years ago that I would have three books out in thirteen months, I would have told them they were crazy, and if they could make it happen, I would owe them big. Well, it happened, and I need to thank several people.

First, to the readers who took the chance and picked up a brand new author in the crowded urban fantasy/paranormal world, thank you! I couldn't have done this without you. Whether we interact online or in person or only through the characters who inhabit my imagination and now yours, I'm so grateful you've allowed me to share this experience with you.

Second, if I have anyone who's been a fairy godmother in this process, it's my wonderful Samhain editor Holly Atkinson. She challenges me and makes my work the best it can be. Kudos also go out to my critique group—Amy, David, Kimberly, and Susan—who help me get my words right and make sure I'm not missing any bodies by the end of my books. Thank you all for your patience and feedback!

Third, to Amber my awesome adminion who keeps me sane and organized at the office, I couldn't have done all this without you.

Fourth, I have to thank my family, especially my husband Jason for his caring and support. Whether it's due to me stressing out over proposals, meeting deadlines, or marketing, he's always there with a big hug and an appropriately calming beverage.

Finally, I would like to dedicate this book in loving memory of my Italian grandmother Cristina Rose, an avid reader who wrote a book once upon a time but never pursued a writing or publishing career. I'm grateful for the genes, the support while you were still with us, and the continued prayers from Heaven.

1

I noticed the blood first. Earthy and metallic, its scent wove over and under the olfactory texture of the clinic, a red ribbon among the blues and greens of antiseptic and rubber glove. If it had been any other clinic, and I had been any other type of man, I might have dismissed it or processed it with only mild curiosity. But here among my fellow predators at the Institute for Lycanthropic Reversal, the spilling of blood in the quantities I sensed meant someone had made a deadly mistake.

As Lycanthropy Council Investigator, I was accustomed to fixing mistakes, and I thanked whatever gods may be watching that I had come on this official Council visit instead of one of the others.

"Mister McCord?" The woman's voice startled me and brought my attention back to the human part of the brain, mostly ruled by the visual.

I was glad to be back in the realm of sight, and my impressions resolved into a lovely picture. The voice came with high cheekbones with a dusting of freckles, large gray-blue eyes, and long dark red hair pulled back in a ponytail. I could even forgive the flat American accent—which stood out to me no matter how often I heard it here in my home country—particularly as it came through pale pink lips pursed in inquiry.

"And you are?" I turned on all my Scottish charm, mindful that, as a former colleague had said, "American chicks dig the accent."

"I am Doctor Selene Rial, one of the psychologists." Her tongue rolled the *r* just enough to make me focus on her mouth and her full lips before she took my outstretched hand. She leaned in and again surprised me, this time by giving me the customary sniff of our kind's greeting. On our *facial* cheeks, lest you think I'm being crude. Her scent brought to mind a vivid image of a waterfall in the humid twilight of the American Southeast in summer and a lithe red wolf watching its broken reflection in the ripples of the pool below. I wondered, as usual, what she caught from mine.

Whatever she saw, amusement and concern flickered across her face when she stepped back. "It is an honor to have you here. We haven't seen much of the Council since the Institute's ground breaking ceremony."

I inclined my head. "I am pleased to be here. But tell me, has there been an accident? I smell blood."

Her eyes widened. "Do you? I don't think anyone has spilled any today. We fired the tech who dropped the sample tray last week." She bit her lip. "I wasn't supposed to tell you that."

I would have been charmed by her guilelessness had I not been distracted. "Perhaps we should investigate," I suggested, struggling to hold on to my patience.

"Follow me." She led me through the door and to a stairway on the left. The smell diminished to just the barest hint such that I wouldn't notice it if I wasn't looking.

Lonna Marconi-Fortuna, the Institute's co-director and another werewolf, met us in the hall with her husband Doctor Max Fortuna, wizard and other co-director, at her side. The tension eased in my chest when I saw them. They had been my main concern.

"What is it, Gabriel?" Lonna asked when she saw my expression.

"Can you not smell it?"

She shook her head. "No, but your senses are better than ours—just one of the many ways how those of us who were changed by the vector differ from those of you who were born with CLS." She wrinkled her nose. "But now that you mention it, something smells off."

"Interesting." I moved ahead of them, not wanting to lose the faint blood scent. I chased it down the corridor, its ribbon thickening as I ran down another staircase and through a maze of hallways until all that stood between me and full-on assault was the door to an office. Max caught up to me and wrinkled his nose, telling me how strong the odor was since he was a wizard, and therefore limited to human-level senses.

"I told the ladies to stay back," he said.

I nodded. "Whose office is that?"

"Doctor Otis LeConte. He's one of our geneticists. He's a human."

I raised my eyebrows. "You have full-blooded humans working here already?" As soon as I said it, I recognized how ridiculous it sounded. Of course I knew they hired humans, and the scientists would have started with the others. My attention was only half on the conversation. I wanted to help the poor bugger, but I listened and smelled for signs of an assailant to avoid potential ambush.

"He was the first we hired. It was one of the items we had on our list to talk to you about today." He cocked his head. "Do you hear anything in there?"

"No, nothing's moving."

He moved forward, then stopped and looked at me. "At your command, Gabriel."

Not sure why he deferred to me, I said, "Go on."

He opened the door and stumbled back, his hand over his nose and mouth.

"Come now, you're a physician. It can't be that—" But it was. LeConte lay splayed out on his desk, his lab coat dripping with the contents of his circulatory system onto the dark brown carpet. Both wrists had been gashed open, as had his neck, and his eyes stared at the ceiling in horror. Files had been turned out on the floor and had become a Red Sea of paper.

As I recoiled in horror, my mind catalogued observations to sift through later. There was a laptop computer on a shelf to the side and several little statues and knickknacks that looked to be made of precious metal also stood in front of books on the bookcases. *Not a robbery, then.* I would have to wait and see what the coroner said—he was one of us as well—but the wounds didn't look like they had been made by werewolves. Perhaps someone pretending to be one of us, but definitely not us. Also, the window stood wide open, which allowed the air to circulate. It had likely kept any of the younger ones from smelling the blood, although I still didn't understand how *someone* didn't notice something.

"Oh my god! Otis?"

I caught Selene's arm before she barged into the room. "There's nothing to be done for him. You'll only interfere with evidence now."

Her face had gone white, even her freckles, and she wobbled. I pulled her to me so she wouldn't fall should she faint, and I found she fit perfectly against my chest. I filed that impression away for future consideration as well, turned, and guided her to a chair in the hallway. She slumped forward, her head between her knees, and took deep breaths. Truth be told, I felt woozy as well, and the hand I placed on her trembling shoulder might have been as much to steady myself as her. I hoped my father wasn't looking down from wherever werewolves went after they died and shaking his head in shame at his weak-stomached son. It seemed unfair I could eviscerate animals with ease, and I could even handle the usual murder victim, but the sight of such brutality always got to me. I blamed childhood trauma.

"I don't want to know, do I?" asked Lonna. She stood with her arms crossed and looked down at Selene, but her face had also gone pale, and her nose wrinkled. Max had closed the door and gone to call the police. Not the human ones. Lord knows we didn't need them mucking about in here.

"You're going to need to find a new geneticist," I told her. "He's been exsanguinated."

She arched an eyebrow. "You and your big words. Someone sucked his blood?"

I started to shake my head, but then stopped. A man LeConte's size—and I was pretty good at guessing heights and weights—would contain about five liters of blood. What I had seen looked like a lot, but after a certain point and with the element of surprise, any amount over about a liter would seem excessive. His neck and wrists had still been dripping, which told me the deed was recent. I stood, commanded my knees to stop their schoolboy knocking, and said to Lonna, "Can you take care of her? I need to see if I can find the trail of the perpetrator."

Lonna nodded and sat next to Selene, whose breathing deepened and lengthened into quiet sobs.

I FOUND Max outside LeConte's window, which was on the first floor. I half-expected to see him performing some sort of spell or doing something else wizardly, but instead, he shone a light on the ground.

"Ultraviolet with a little magical help," he said. "If there was blood on the bastard's shoes, it'll show, but the sun is too bright for me to see. Can you stand there and cast a shadow for me?"

"I can't imagine how there wouldn't be anything on the killer's shoes unless he'd covered them with something." I moved to the spot he indicated.

Unfortunately, it hadn't rained in days—an unusual state of affairs for Scotland, even in the summer—and the ground was dry, so there were no impressions to be found. Between the two of us, we detected some blood splotches on the mulch under the bushes outside of the building and some bent grass blades. Of course, the traces petered out, but at least it was along a straight trail leading directly toward the woods.

"I'm going to change and go after him," I said.

Max nodded and turned to give me some privacy. To his credit, he didn't say that would have been the thing to do in the first place, although I cursed myself for not thinking of it sooner. Finding LeConte's body had shaken me, as had the implications. My mind raced with what I would tell the Council and how they would react.

It occurred to me that someone inside the building may be watching, and the thought made my skin crawl, but time was too precious to waste on privacy concerns, and Max was there in case someone decided to take advantage of that moment of disorientation when the change was almost complete. I divested myself of my garments and left them in as neat a pile as I could, and took a deep breath. The life force of nature of the woods and trees nearby reached out to me, and I to the wild energy. It enveloped my limbs, traveling down my nervous pathways to blood, bone, and sinew, drawing everything to the center. I simultaneously folded inward and outward, gritting my teeth at sensations that, although they had become familiar, were never comfortable—like hands molding and rearranging me with no regard for the limits of my tendons and muscles. I understood the change differed for everyone, and I envied those for whom the transition went smoothly. Some legends held that werewolves wore their animal skin on the inside when they were human. Turning inside out would have been easier.

Finally, after I had physically rearranged myself, I panted for a few breaths and then took off. The path that had been illuminated by the UV light now showed itself to me with the scent of LeConte's blood, heavy and fatty and crying out for vengeance. The dim light of the woods barely registered as my nose directed me to turn right, left, over, under, squeezing between. Whoever had murdered the scientist had his own interesting scent, a combination of pipe smoke and kerosene.

The trail ended at a stream, but there was still enough scent in the air to figure out which way the murderer had run. From what I could recall, there were busy roads on either side of the woods where a getaway car and driver could be waiting.

I chose the direction my nose told me to go and found the trail about forty meters north. The blood was gone, but the kerosene-pipe smoke smell was there along with sweat. That scent disappeared along the side of a road, where a small pull-off could have hidden a vehicle behind some trees, and I noted where it was so the police could come look for tire tracks. Not that they'd likely find anything of any help in the dry gravel.

I TROTTED back toward the Institute, and a lithe red wolf surprised me in the woods on the other side of the stream. She smelled familiar.

"Selene?"

"Gabriel?" She sat back on her haunches and regarded me with a concerned look. *"Did you catch them?"*

"Obviously not. And what are you doing out here? They could've been armed."

In spite of lacking human facial muscles and their range of

expression, we lycanthropes can express our emotions adequately without speaking, and her glare told me she was pissed even without her baring her teeth.

"Otis was my friend. I wasn't going to let them get away." She turned and walked in the direction from where she'd come.

"I wasn't either," I told her.

"Obviously not," she tossed over her shoulder at me.

I ran to catch up with her. *"Look here, there's no reason to get sarcastic with me. You've had quite a shock, but I'm only trying to help."*

The tears came through her mental voice. *"Don't you think Otis's murder could have something to do with your visit? The timing is odd, isn't it?"*

Her question would've floored me had we been near a floor. Here I had gone chasing after a potentially armed villain—yes, I could acknowledge my own bravado and stupidity here—and she had started sorting through the facts like a scientist. I blamed the surge of attraction I felt toward her on my current animal state, my tendency to fall for smart women, and our situation. We'd faced death and now strolled, albeit briskly, through lovely woods on a summer day. I'd learned two years previously not to fall for scientists. They'll stick with their own every time.

"You're quiet," she said. *"I apologize if I offended you."*

"No offense taken. I was just pondering what you said, and I sincerely hope my visit today had nothing to do with your friend's death."

"It would be a coincidence, and I don't believe in those. All I know is that a dear friend has been killed in a horrible manner."

I wanted to dissect the manner in which she'd said "dear friend" so I could quell the jealousy that blossomed in my chest. Had she and LeConte been lovers but covered it up to avoid a workplace scandal?

Stop acting like a pup, I scolded myself. *What the lovely Selene does on her own time is her business.* Still, I couldn't help but feel a pang of regret when we left the woods, walked into the sunshine of the Institute grounds, and once again became Lycanthropy Council Member and scientist.

"I see the cavalry is here," she said.

Indeed, the yellow-and-blue marked car, just similar enough to the human police vehicles, had arrived, its lights whirling. When I got close, Lonna's mental voice came to me: *"The police are here, and the detective wants to see you first."*

2

<hr>

Selene changed in her office, and I in Max's, and then Detective Garou met me in the conference room. He rubbed his close-cropped beard and studied me with narrowed eyes.

"Sorry to be presumptuous sir, but aren't you...?" His accent held a hint of French, definitely more continental than English or Scottish.

"Yes, I'm Gabriel McCord, Investigator for the Lycanthrope Council."

"Oh. Dreadfully sorry to trouble you, sir. You may go."

"No," I said and stopped myself from snapping at him, choosing instead to patiently explain. "I was there when the body was discovered. Question me like you would any other witness on the scene."

"Right, then. What was the nature of your business here today?" He glanced at the clock. "And when did you arrive?"

"That's better. I was here on official Council business, mostly to see how they've been progressing with starting up and to help determine whether they're ready for the first batch of applicants."

"I've heard of this place, sir, but I don't know what it's about. The Council has kept it all hush-hush, calling it merely 'The Institute'."

"The full name is The Institute of Lycanthropic Reversal. It's a sanitarium for the newly turned werewolves in the United States and elsewhere tainted vaccines were used as part of a horrible pharmaceutical experiment."

"So that's why there's so many Americans here. Why not just build it over there?"

"The method is still experimental. Some of the substances have been approved for study here, but not by their Food and Drug Administration."

He nodded. "And the time you arrived, sir?"

"About nine o'clock."

"And when you discovered the body? It was you, correct?"

I told him how I smelled the blood and about the discovery of the body, my run through the woods, and where I think the getaway car had been stashed.

"Had you any contact with the deceased, sir? When he was alive, I mean."

"None whatsoever. I imagine I would have met him today had circumstances been different."

"Thank you, that is all."

I gave him my card in case he had any further questions but doubted I'd hear from him. The Lycanthrope Police were creatures of the Council, which I disagreed with, but which had been well-established by the time I came on. He surprised me by stopping me before I left the room.

"Sir, since you're the Investigator, and all this will be going to the Council anyway, would you like to sit in on the questioning?"

I raised my eyebrows. "Thank you, Detective. I had not thought to ask, but that would be helpful."

He gestured for me to take the seat beside him and walked into the hall to have his deputy summon the next person.

WHEN LONNA ENTERED THE ROOM, she pressed her lips into a line and nodded to me. It occurred to me that I knew this group of people's secrets except for the lovely Selene, who had intrigued me by following me. There were things I had not shared with the Council, and I knew I'd have to be careful not to betray I knew more than they did. In that context, the detective's invitation no longer seemed so friendly.

"When was the last time you saw Doctor LeConte alive?" Garou asked once Lonna sat.

"This morning at staffing at eight o'clock," Lonna said, her lovely light green eyes filling with tears. I waited for her to add something and then remembered her background as a social worker and private investigator. She would be careful and only answer what was asked.

Garou seemed to come to the same conclusion. He leaned forward and said in a gentle voice, "Any information you can give us will be helpful. Was there anything unusual about the meeting?"

"No. We were mostly preparing for Mister McCord's visit."

"Yes, he told me that he was here in an official capacity. What was Doctor LeConte's task to be?"

"He and Doctor Rial were to give him a tour, and then we were all going to have a meeting and then lunch."

"And what was LeConte's role here?"

"He's our associate geneticist." She sniffled. "Or he was."

"I see. You have another one, then."

"Yes, Iain MacPherson, a human. He's out of the country currently."

"And where were you between when you last saw Doctor

LeConte and when Mister McCord and Doctor Fortuna discovered him?"

"I was in a meeting with Doctor Rial and Doctor Fortuna, finalizing the details of the visit."

Garou made a note in his pad. "Why was Doctor LeConte not present?"

"He was working on a project, but I can't say more," she said. "It's confidential Institute business."

"I see." He dismissed her with an aerial downstroke of his pen and said, "That will be all."

She gave me a pleading look before she rose from the table and stalked to the door.

"Excuse me," I said to Garou. "Please continue without me."

I caught up to Lonna in the hall and followed her up the stairs to her office. Max had been called in next, and Selene had been instructed to stay in her office until summoned, so Lonna was alone.

"Come in," she said. Her office fit her title of Institute Director with a large desk, windows overlooking the lawn and woods, bookshelves, and even two wingback chairs in front a fireplace. Their clawed feet rested on an oriental rug.

"Nice," I said. "It's *Masterpiece Theatre* meets University President's office."

"Thanks, I think."

"Sorry," I told her. "I'm a little off, so my jokes aren't working like they should."

"Oh." She gestured for me to take a seat in one of the chairs by the fireplace, which was, of course, not on. She went behind the desk, opened a drawer, and pulled out two bottles of water. "My fridge isn't here yet," she said and handed one of the waters to me.

"I was hoping you'd offer me some Scotch."

"Not while the police are still here. Max has some rum in his office if you want to get into something later."

"I might."

She plopped into the other chair and took a deep drink of the water. "This isn't how I'd hoped your visit would go." She tucked a stray dark curl behind one ear. "I was looking forward to showing our facility off and walking you through the reversal process, or at least our planned method for it."

"Yes, I imagine you had a different agenda. We can discuss other things if you like, but I am interested to know what LeConte was doing while you met without him."

"He was the one who excused himself," she said. "We didn't kick him out."

"That's not what I asked."

"He was excited because Iain had sent him the files and blood samples for the first batch of applicants for our program recently, and he wanted to review and organize them so he could tell you we'd made progress on that front."

"Where are the files now?"

"Good question. Since the Council still requires us to do everything with paper, probably in the mess in his office."

"The Red Sea," I murmured.

She covered her eyes and groaned. "Gabriel..."

"I know, I know. I told you, I'm off today. Would Iain have kept copies?"

"Yes, in case the ones he sent were lost in transit. We can tell him the bad news and ask about the files in another couple of hours when he checks in. It's still early there." She looked at me sideways. "Go ahead and ask, Gabriel. You know you want to."

"Ask what?"

"Where Wolf-Lonna was and why didn't she go after the perpetrators once y'all discovered Otis."

"It hadn't crossed my mind." Indeed, her odd situation hadn't even occurred to me until now. Whereas most of us could not access certain parts of our spirit, Lonna had a sort of spirit guide or guardian who was simultaneously part of her and capable of independent action and thought.

"I sent her to watch over Abby." She gestured to a photo on the mantel of a baby girl with light green eyes and hair the same reddish color as Max's. "I was so afraid, not sure who might have been attacking us or why, but I might have ruined the opportunity to catch the murderer."

"You did what any mother would have done," I said. "And we were all shocked."

"I know, but now I'm afraid the whole thing will tempt Max to push his boundaries, and I can't lose him."

These were the secrets we couldn't discuss in front of the detective. "Has he said he wants to use blood magic to investigate LeConte's murder?"

"No, but I know him. It will only be a matter of time, and if he uses it outside the narrow parameters we know are safe..." She shuddered.

"Your husband is a smart man. He won't do anything that could hurt you and Abby."

As if our words had summoned him, the door opened to reveal Max with a bottle of rum in one hand. He looked from me to Lonna, and the ease with which we had been conversing disappeared. By this point, she and I had moved past our brief but significant history, but I could see awareness of it in her husband's eyes every time he looked at me.

"They're almost done," he said, his tone weary. "The detective wants to talk to you again, Gabriel."

"Thank you. I may be back for a nip of that." I gestured to the bottle in his hand.

"I brought it to share."

I found Detective Garou in the reception area, talking to Selene.

"I'm sorry, but I'm not available on Friday night," she was saying, and I quickened my stride.

The disappointed look on Garou's face confirmed they weren't speaking about the case.

"The detective was kindly offering to bring me to a Solstice ceilidh," Selene told me, "since I'm obviously not from around here. However, I'm not free that night."

"You needed to speak to me, Detective Garou?" I asked, moving to stand between them so as to give Selene a buffer should she need it.

"I'll be in my office," she murmured and excused herself with a thank you smile, which she seemed to direct at me.

"I may have some follow-up questions for the doctors and Mrs. Marconi-Fortuna as well as the rest of the staff, whom Doctor Fortuna said would be reporting soon," he said. "If I do, I will let you know so you may stay involved with the investigation."

"I would appreciate that, as would the Council. I would also remind you that Doctor Rial is a potential witness and a suspect."

He narrowed his eyes. "As I would you, Investigator."

"I would say something, but there is nothing to defend myself against. I only met her today, and I'm not the one who just asked her out." I fixed him with a glare that told him he needed to focus on his work. "Anything else, Detective?"

"That is all."

"Good. Please keep me apprised of your progress with the investigation and let us know when someone can go into LeConte's office and see what could be missing."

"Yes, sir." With a slight bow, he left to supervise the forensic team as they cleaned up outside. I had no doubt they would follow the same trail I had with the same result, but they had the equipment to get paint flakes off tree branches and other tiny pieces of evidence that even our wolf senses could miss.

. . .

With the detective and his crew gone, quiet stuffed the reception area. I stood by the window and plotted my course of action. I would have to make a report to the Council, of course, but I didn't feel I had all the information. What could LeConte have been doing or have known to be the target of whoever had done that to him? Why such a brutal murder when something like poison in his coffee could have been as effective and much less messy? No, the way in which he had died—and I forced myself to shift through the details of what I had seen in spite of them turning my stomach—was meant to send a message.

Max's voice startled me out of my reverie. "Lunch is here if you feel like eating."

I turned to see him watching me from the door to the back hallway. As it had earlier, my nose picked up faint smells, this time of roast beef and potatoes. My stomach, fickle thing, growled.

"I suppose I do." I followed him back up to Lonna's office, where Selene sat in one of the wingback chairs, a plastic cup in her hand. The sweet smells told me it was rum and soda.

"What are you drinking?" I asked. "And where can I get one?"

"Rum and Coke," she said and waved the glass at me. "Tastes like home."

Lonna handed me a drink. "Sorry we don't have any Scotch. I looked."

"Thank you." Lunch sat in chafing dishes on a long table against one of the bookshelves, and I made myself a plate and sat in the other chair by the fireplace. Lonna and Max sat at her desk. Although we didn't face each other, it was easy enough to talk.

"You're not eating," I told Selene.

"Don't feel like it." She looked at me with tears in her eyes. "I just keep going back to this morning and wishing I'd insisted Otis not go back to his office, that the applications could wait."

"He did seem very excited about something," Max said.

I checked my watch. "Is it late enough to call Iain?"

"He's normally up early," Lonna said. "Might as well try." She picked up her phone and dialed out.

I crossed my right ankle over my left knee and tried to appear at ease. I was not Iain McPherson's favorite person, and the feeling was mutual. I hoped we could keep our conversation cordial for the sake of those grieving in the room.

3

———

"Iain," Lonna said. "Good morning. Did I wake you?" She pressed the button to turn the speaker feature on, and Iain's cheerful voice came through.

"I was already up. Had the oddest feeling something was wrong."

Lonna opened her mouth but covered it with her left hand to stifle a sob.

"Bad news," Max said and covered Lonna's other hand with his own. "Otis has been killed."

"Killed? Are you sure?" Noises came through the phone as though he rearranged its positioning against his ear.

"Well, yes," said Max. "He was quite dead."

"At the Institute? Could it have been an accident?"

"Yes, here, and no, that's not possible. Look, I don't want to give you the horrid details over the phone, but Gabriel McCord, the Council Investigator, is here, and we need some information from you."

"Gabriel." Iain's tone was cool, as it always was when he dealt with me. I was working undercover for the Council when

I'd assisted him with his research, and he hadn't taken the revelation well when I finally came clean.

"Iain," I said, trying to keep the impatience from my voice. He'd always treated me as an intellectual inferior, so it was as pleasant for me to talk to him as it obviously was for him to hear from me. "Look, I apologize for having to interrogate you when you've just found out about your colleague. Would you like me to call you later?"

"Why? He's going to be just as dead then. Ask your questions."

"Iain," Lonna said, "I know this is a shock…"

"It's fine," I told her. "What had you sent to Doctor LeConte, Iain? I understand it was all on paper."

"Yes, because you've done such a fine job of dragging the Council into the twenty-first century. I'd mailed him the first six applications for the Experimental Adjustment and Reversal Program along with the blood samples and other material data."

"Was there anything unusual about any of them?"

"It depends on your definition of 'unusual'. They're all Americans who were infected with CLS by vaccines and who experienced the full change. Four males and two females, all of Scandinavian or Celtic descent."

"Has anyone on your team there been threatened?" I asked.

"I'll check with Joanie and Leo, but not as far as I know."

"Thank you, Doctor. I'll be in touch if I need anything else. Oh, could you send an encrypted file with the information to the team here? We're still looking for the blood samples."

"Yes, it will take a few hours to get it all encrypted and uploaded, but I'll get right on it."

He rang off, and we all sat and looked at each other. The dead man may as well have been in the room with us, we were so somber. I was the only Scot, but the others easily matched our stereotypical grimness.

I stood. "Thank you for lunch, especially under the circumstances. I'll let you know what the Council says with regard to proceeding."

"Otis wouldn't have wanted us to stop," Selene said. "He would've told us to keep going without him. It's important to the mission that we do."

Her Southern US heritage had become evident in her vowels, likely an effect of the rum.

"I will do my best to make sure you can proceed soon."

"I'll see you out," Max said.

Selene wobbled to her feet and said, "I'll take him. I need to get something out of my car."

"Are you sure you're okay to do that?" Lonna asked. "You've just had a strong drink on an empty stomach."

Selene looked at me, her eyes imploring, and I interjected, "I'll watch her and ensure she gets back into the building safely."

"Thank you," she said once we'd left the room and were out of earshot down the hall. "I just need a few minutes to breathe and be alone."

"Shall I leave you, then?"

She looked up at me through her lashes, where tiny crystal-like tears clung. "No. God knows I shouldn't, but I feel comfortable with you." She sighed as if she wound up to say more, but she shook her head.

"You can tell me whatever you need to. Is there something about this morning?"

"No, nothing important." But she looked away.

We reached the side door that led outside, and I held it open for her. She glanced around before stepping into the watery sunshine. I couldn't blame her—after the events of the morning, I definitely felt like peeking around corners before I turned them and snarling at shadows. Although I knew she must be strong if she was one of us, her cautious gestures made me want to protect her. And find out what she might be hiding.

She's a scientist and she might have just lost her boyfriend, I told myself, although my instincts told me she and LeConte hadn't been lovers. *Still, she's off limits.*

I watched her as she fetched a small bag from her car and went back inside. Still, my mind wouldn't let her go as I drove away, although I wasn't sure if I was more interested in her as a person or in the mystery she seemed to hold. Either way, I'd enjoy finding out.

WHEN I RETURNED to my offices at Lycan Castle, the seat of the Lycanthrope Council, I found a stack of files on my desk and a blessedly welcome pot of coffee. Less welcome was the message slip my assistant Laura handed to me.

"Lady Morena wants you to phone her as soon as you get settled."

"I'm going to have to delay getting settled, then, aren't I?"

"She didn't seem in the mood to be pushed," she told me and looked sternly over her thick rectangular glasses.

"Yes, mum."

"Cheeky," she said as I walked into the inner office.

"It's a good thing you make such good coffee. You can be replaced, you know."

Now she took off her glasses and squinted at me. "You've met someone. You haven't threatened to replace me since you phoned to tell me you were close to finding Charles Landover's secret laboratory in Arkansas and his granddaughter was delightful."

"Yes, and we remember how well that turned out. Please fetch me the personnel files on the Institute staff."

"Morena. Call her."

I gave a noncommittal shrug and closed the door. Once I

was safely out of Laura's line of sight, I tossed the message slip into the unlit fireplace. Although nothing burned due to the warm early summer weather, the small act of rebellion gave me momentary satisfaction. I wanted to *do* something, not waste my time writing reports and waiting for the waffling of the Council to determine that Lonna, Max and Selene could proceed with their plans. Frankly, I didn't think the Council should be involved in the Institute, but it hadn't been my decision, and even though one of their own was an integral part of it, the Wizard Tribunal hadn't pushed back. Likely they waited to see how it all worked out so that if it failed, they wouldn't have to take any responsibility for it. They'd just throw poor Max under the bus. Coldhearted bastards.

Laura brought the personnel files in, and I tossed aside Lonna's, Max's, and the lower staff members'. The first one I looked at was Selene Rial's. A health psychologist who'd been educated in the States and turned after a flu shot introduced the viral vector into her system, she had been invited to join the team when Iain had been impressed with her. He observed that she took everything in stride and while she appreciated the challenges of being a lycanthrope, she could step back and look at the situation objectively, or at least more so than any of the other candidates he'd interviewed—both human and werewolf. He'd written that she had a "unique and sympathetic perspective" on the difficulties CLS sufferers faced, even beyond her own experience.

Meanwhile, Otis LeConte, a geneticist, had worked in the same lab as Joanie Fisher, now Joanie Bowman, prior to her being fired and turned. When I closed my eyes, I still saw Joanie standing on the balcony off her bedroom at Wolfsbane Manor, watching me change, her eyes burning with curiosity and—

"Lady Morena has arrived." Laura's voice startled me from the memory.

"Right," I said. "I didn't call her."

"She said she couldn't wait, and she expects to be seen immediately or she will fire me and every other staff member you depend on so that your lazy ass will have to learn to do things for itself."

A headache started in my right temple, and I massaged it, hoping it wouldn't flare up into a full-blown migraine. Although modern science had given a name to my "sick headaches," the medicines didn't work for me. Losing my staff wouldn't help it, so I said, "Send her in."

Morena glided in without picking her feet very far off the floor. She wore her customary navy blue pantsuit and flats. She'd adapted well to this new era in which women could dress like men. When she and I had worked together in the fifties, the skirts and heels of the time had always looked like they enjoyed being worn by her as much as she enjoyed wearing them. Her yellow eyes took in the details of the office, specifically the message slip in the fireplace, but she didn't say anything about it.

I bowed. "What a pleasant surprise, Chairwoman."

As always, she got directly to the point. It was one of the few things I liked about her. "I understand there's been some unpleasantness at the Institute."

I gestured for her to take a seat in one of the chairs in front of my desk. She sat with spine straight. I could count the number of times I'd seen her relax on one hand.

"So you've spoken with Garou," I said and sat in the other one. My office wasn't as cozy as Lonna's but still held a fair number of volumes, and my eyes strayed to one shelf of books from the original Wolfsbane Manor. They were all I managed to rescue before the fire found the library, and I had dreamed of presenting them to Joanie when I returned for her. Alas, by the time I had made it through all the bureaucratic nonsense of the Council, she had been claimed by another.

"He filled me in on the obvious details. I want to know what you think he missed."

"What did he find in the pull-off where the getaway car was?"

"What makes you think I'm going to tell you?" She leaned forward. This was our game.

"Because I'm the Council Investigator," I said, "and even if you don't tell me, I'll get the report from Garou later. Might as well save me some time."

"Insolent pup," she growled. "I should have voted against making you Investigator. You were too young."

I arched an eyebrow. "As I recall, you did, and yet here we are. The question is whether you're going to help me do my job."

"You never did respect your elders like you should," she told me. "And no, the question is whether *you're* going to be able to do your job. Remember, you're not a full Council member yet. You can be replaced."

"I see no reason why I shouldn't do my job, and yes, I do recall my position. You remind me of it every chance you get."

She stood and walked behind the desk to where I had the files laid out. "Yet perhaps I do see potential areas of conflict for you, even beyond your friendship with the directors. What do you know of the dead man?"

I moved to close the open file, that of Selene. "He was a full human and a geneticist." I grabbed for his file, but she held it away from me.

"And what else?"

"He'd gotten a batch of applications from Iain MacPherson, the CLS specialist and the other geneticist."

"Do you know about a wife? Family? Even his nationality?"

"No, no, and I suspect American. As you know, I only just arrived when you barged in. What are you getting at?"

She flipped Selene's file at me. "Only that you might be letting your small head overrule your big one."

I winced. No matter how modern we got, I couldn't get used to women speaking crudely. "I just received the files."

"And see which one you opened first." She slammed both fists down on the desk, which toppled an antique inkwell. I righted it before it could spill. "Dammit, Gabriel, this case goes beyond anything you've looked into for us, and it's got more diplomatic pitfalls than you can imagine."

"Oh?" Now she had me intrigued. I could forget the insult.

She ran a hand through her short gray hair. "We've been fighting the press away from the Institute for months now, basically since we started building it. Now we have to be careful that the human press doesn't get hold of this story. It's bad enough our community will know."

"So we deflect the humans. Business as usual. What else?"

"I'm getting to it. After months of silence on the issue, the International Wizard Tribunal has come forward to say they do not support the project, and they want to pull Maximilian Fortuna off the staff. We're trying to negotiate his staying."

A low whistle escaped my lips. "If we don't have him, we don't have an Institute."

"Right, and that's why the wizards want to pull him. They haven't come out and said it, but they're on the side of the Purists. They believe this thing is a gift, and no one should take it away, especially not using a forbidden form of magic."

"Blood magic is only part of the process. They haven't told me the whole procedure. It's proprietary, at least until they perfect it and can share it with the world."

"No one knows it, and it makes the wizards antsy because they can't study it and the lycanthrope Purists unhappy because they see it as reversing something that they have a birthright to."

I ground my teeth. It was an argument that just wouldn't go away. "We're not taking anything away from them."

"No, but they're afraid nevertheless."

"What does this have to do with LeConte's murder?" I asked. "Do you think he was killed for trade secrets?"

"That, dear Investigator, is your job to figure out as quickly and quietly as you can. I'll stall the Council, but keep in mind that they'll want a report very soon." She tapped a finger on Selene's file. "And just remember that in our world, it's rare that something is exactly as it seems."

MORENA'S cheerful visit left me with difficulty focusing. Her words swirled around my brain, especially what she hinted about Selene. As much as Morena frustrated me, she did have the admirable trait of not interfering in others' personal lives. On the other hand, I knew next to nothing about hers. Although our rules of coupling and mating were looser than the pure humans', and therefore she would see nothing wrong with me having a dalliance with Selene, I still had to worry about conflict of interest. And Morena's warning about the wizards made this an even higher profile case.

With a growl, I stood and strode out of the office.

"Don't forget your ten o'clock tomorrow morning," Laura called after me.

I waved to acknowledge I'd heard and then headed straight for the pub.

"Straight" is a relative term in the hills of Scotland. Of course leaving the castle was never direct since my offices were in a turret, and I had to negotiate a set of winding stairs. Then I had to cross a minor hall, then the major welcome one, and another minor one to the side door to the Council and employee parking. Visitors valeted so they couldn't leave quickly. That was mostly in place for the rare wizard who showed up.

The thick carpeting muffled my steps in the welcome hall. No matter how many times I passed them, I couldn't help but slow to admire the vividly drawn, albeit fading, battlefields on the tapestries.

"Ho, Gabriel!" The booming voice stopped me just as I reached the door.

4

I turned to see David Lachlan, one of the Council members, waving me down. His broad stomach stretched the fibers of his sweater vest, and his curly salt and pepper hair seemed to be giving in to the force of gravity, in that more of it now clustered around his ears than the top of his head. Although some might perceive him as ridiculous, I knew his true age and abilities, and I always treated him with wariness and respect.

In spite of his girth, he approached quickly and with more grace on his feet than one would expect. It was how he hunted both politically and as a wolf: making the prey underestimate him.

"David," I said and inclined my head to acknowledge his superiority in our little hierarchy. We all liked to pretend we weren't subject to the British crown.

"Gods, lad, I haven't seen you in years." He clapped me on the shoulder and propelled me toward the exit.

"Respectfully, sir, I think it's been months."

"Right, you've been busy with that Institute, eh? Well, I was just headed down to Marley's for a pint. Care to join me?"

My right temple throbbed again, and I continued to ignore it as my mind rearranged the pieces of this puzzle. I had no doubt that running into him was more than coincidence. David rarely appeared at Lycan Castle, usually only when there was a Council Meeting, and the next scheduled one wasn't until following week.

"I was just going there myself," I said and opened the door to outside. "After you."

"Ah, beautiful day, isn't it?" he asked. "I ran here this morning, so I'll let you drive."

His admission made me raise my eyebrows. To run to the castle was to do so in wolf form, and we all had fully appointed bathrooms with showers and changes of clothes in our office suites. Something must have gotten him excited to go through the trouble, and I worried it might have been my meeting at the Institute today. It also made me wonder if and how he had heard about the murder.

I unlocked my convertible BMW and allowed the top to open. "I would have, but I had an appointment before coming."

"So I heard. We can discuss that mess at the pub."

He leaned back and put on his sunglasses, obviously not willing to talk about it further in spite of us being less likely to be overheard in the car. I wondered again what game he was playing.

Sometimes all you have to do is be seen and not heard.

I lowered my own sunglasses. My father's voice intruded into my memories whenever I felt the tangled web of politics tighten around me, and I always wished he hadn't died when I was so young so he could have guided me through this inherited position and the crazy games that went with it. Once I had achieved adulthood, David had appeared occasionally in my life to give me a nudge in the right direction, but like Morena, he tended to be hands-off.

The side drive to Lycan Castle had once been a hunting trail into the thick forests around the hill and its base. Not that the forests spread too far these days, but there were still animals there to be chased and eaten as well as streams with cozy bends and stone outcroppings where one could take a certain red lady wolf...

"Keep your eyes on the road, my boy."

I jerked aware from my reverie and corrected my steering around a sharp curve. The car handled beautifully, and David didn't seem to notice. He didn't move, and his hands remained relaxed, one tapping on his thigh along to the Celtic music on the radio, and the other draped over the side of the door. I gripped the wheel, which had gone slick under my palms. The desire for a pint left me, replaced by the need for a shot of whiskey and then the thought that either might not be advisable since I was about to have intoxicating beverages at the pub with a potential enemy. My mind was already slipping since my father's voice sounded like it came from the backseat instead of inside my brain.

"You look ill, Gabriel," David said once we got out to the main road and the shadows of trees alternated our path with light and dark.

"I'm fine," I said. "We can talk about it at the pub."

He nodded. "Sometimes I can't help but see your father when I look at you."

"Why? Was he often ill?" I tried to make it a jest, but I couldn't keep the bitterness out of my tone since the portly man next to me had known my father for decades, and I for barely one.

"No, he was one of the healthiest men I knew. One of the smartest too. It's too bad he had to get himself killed."

"Not everyone has your knack for survival, David."

"Thankfully I was born after Culloden, we didn't have money for an army commission, and I'd allowed myself to age to the point where I couldn't be drafted by the time the first

Great War broke out. Otherwise, I might not have. Your father could have done the same, but he had his vanity, handsome bugger. You seem to have gotten his looks and his smarts but not the ego."

I tried to listen for the meaning behind his words, but this was the first time he'd opened up to me about my father.

"He's warming you up to say more than you would otherwise. Thankfully he still can't talk about me without insulting me."

I pulled the car into a spot in front of Marley's and took a few deep breaths to clear my head. The rearview mirror beckoned me from my peripheral vision. Should I look in it and see if my father's ghost sat in the backseat, glowering back at me? Did my hope make me a fool? Or did my avoidance of doing so make me a coward?

I got out of the car without looking and joined David at the front door, where a pretty blonde girl in a short kilted skirt smiled at him.

"Careful, you look old enough to qualify as a dirty old man," I told him once we'd been seated in a booth in the corner. It was the most discreet booth in the place, and I immediately went on guard, even more than I had been on the drive with just David to worry about.

"I'm old enough to qualify as one many times over," he said. "Just because I have a couple of centuries under my belt and haven't taken a wife for a while, it doesn't mean I can't enjoy a good flirt."

I couldn't say anything considering how my thoughts kept straying to Selene.

"So is the Institute ready to go, then?" David asked once we'd put in our orders for two Lagavulins—neat—and two Scotch eggs to absorb the alcohol.

"They've had a small setback," I said and leaned back.

He arched a bushy eyebrow. "Aye, do tell. And don't leave anything out. I'll be getting the report tomorrow."

I heard what he didn't say, that if something major had occurred, it would require a majority vote on the Council to allow the Institute to continue, and he liked to be the first to know.

"One of the geneticists died."

"Oh, is that all?" He waved his hand in a dismissive gesture. "Find another one. They're both human, right?"

"It's not that simple," I said. "The way he died was rather unpleasant."

This time both eyebrows went up. We didn't typically minimize things. "As in he's a full-blooded human who is no longer in possession of his full volume of blood."

"Yes," I said, relieved I wouldn't have to describe it in a public place in spite of the low likelihood that someone would overhear.

"Any leads yet?"

I shook my head. "It only just happened this morning. I'm waiting for the report from the detective, and I'll go from there."

"That's not like you, Gabriel. I know you as a man of action. You're not one to think too much."

"I've grown up," I snapped and would have said more except our drinks and snacks arrived.

He held up his Scotch. "To those departed, both long and recent."

"*Slàinte*. So would you care to tell me why you brought me here? We could have discussed this at Lycan Castle."

He leaned forward and cradled the square Scotch glass with both hands. "I have my own concerns that may not be those of others. I've heard rumors that the Wizard Tribunal wants to pull Maximilian Fortuna from the Institute. From what I understand, he does his own thing, but they're willing to do anything to make sure he doesn't continue. Something about bad blood or some such."

"Blood magic," I said and mimicked his posture. The peaty smell of the amber liquid wafted around me, giving me its familiar comfort. "It's a forbidden art, but necessary for the CLS reversal, or at least that's what they think. We trust that Doctor Fortuna can handle the ability without any bad effects."

"Have they actually tried it yet? Has he?"

"The first batch of test subjects was just recruited. As for him, I don't know. He seems a smart man, so I would imagine he would know his limits. And if he didn't, his wife would." Lonna's concern flashed into my brain, but I pushed it aside for now.

"It seems like you're building your case, not to mention a multimillion dollar Institute, on a lot of what ifs."

"We have to try, David. Lycanthropy isn't for everyone, and those who have been turned against their will deserve a shot at returning to a normal life."

"And what about those who were born with it? What if they want to give it up?"

My jaw dropped. "David, are you...?"

He shook his head. "Not me, but I know of some who are unhappy that the reversal process is only being offered to those who were changed through pharmaceutical means."

I'd heard rumors that some born lycanthropes would want to give it up. "How desperate are they?"

"Desperate enough that they've been lobbying certain Council members hard that if they don't get a shot at reversal, no one should."

Now I understood his motivation in bringing me here: others would know he stood with me, and I with him, but I still didn't understand his agenda.

"So why do you care so much?"

He leaned back. "I see potential for other applications of this process, or parts of it. I won't say what here, but I have my reasons for being behind you."

"And who isn't?"

"As much as Morena likes to talk progressively, she's on the fence. Keith is also waffling now. He has a lot of young wolves in his district who want the choice even if they wouldn't take it. Dimitri is firmly in support of the genetic wolves who want the reversal option, and Cora, being who she is, is against reversal for anyone at all. Finally, Tabitha tends to go with Morena, as you know."

"But the establishment of the Institute was a unanimous vote. I remember it clearly. How have we lost so much ground?"

"Word of what it is and what it will do got out. You know how that goes."

"Aye." Annoyingly, I did. The Council liked to talk a pro-human game because it ran counter to the Wizard Tribunal philosophy, but when the chips were down, it was every lycanthrope for himself and their biggest influencers. I'd long wondered if we'd gotten Cora's vote because her husband had been out of town at the time. He ran the closest thing we had to a cult, and the only reason it had been allowed to continue was because his wife was on the Council. As for the others, they liked to appear altruistic, but I knew they had their own agendas.

David's knife cut through his egg with ease, and he poured H.P. Sauce over it. The image of LeConte's blood dripping on to the floor came to mind.

"So you think the incident today was an attack from one of the dissatisfied factions," I said to keep the conversation going and prevent my mind from wandering toward uncomfortable memories.

"Or a wizard or something else." He took a big bite of egg, sausage, and sauce, and some of it dribbled on his chin. Or maybe that was drool because his eyes widened at something behind me, and he licked his lips. "Now that's something you don't see every day," he mumbled once he'd swallowed most of his bite.

"Let me guess, it's a pretty girl." I twisted around and saw that, indeed, it was. Selene Rial had just walked in the door, and she scanned the pub with an anxious expression on her face. I swung my legs to my right to exit the booth and go to her, but I felt an invisible hand on my arm.

"Just wait," the voice from the car said in my ear. Every single one of my hairs stood on end, and the room spun. I clutched the table for support.

"Now you really do look ill," David said. He pushed my Scotch toward me. "Or like you've seen a ghost."

"I haven't seen one yet," I managed to say. I caught a glimpse of red in the mirror at the back of the pub and observed Selene's movements that way. She met up with a man with dark hair and followed him outside. I took a deep breath, the warmth in my chest at seeing Selene at war with the cold warning in my ear.

"I never knew you for a fan of redheads," David said. He'd abandoned silverware to swipe the egg through the sauce on his plate with his fingers, and I could picture the little boy he'd been. He likely hadn't had such treats growing up under the oppressive thumb of the English in the late eighteenth century. I cut a sliver from my egg and tasted it, but it might as well have been fried sawdust. I pushed it away.

"There's something magical about them," I said. "Hang on, she shouldn't be here. I'm going to try and hear what they're saying."

I pretended I had a phone call so no one would bother me on my way out and wandered outside. I hid behind a large shrubbery and closed my eyes. My wolfish senses increased. Some would say they came online, but I'd had them long before the computer age. My human ears might have wiggled, and psychically my wolf ears swiveled to and fro, picking among the sounds of the pub, parking area, and road like a child searched through pebbles on the ground to find the perfect, shiny one he'd glimpsed from above.

There, I found it—her voice. She sounded distressed, and I once again had to resist the urge to go comfort her.

"You weren't very careful," she said. "There were traces in the woods. It's a good thing he was hot on the other trail so he didn't find them, and I had to make sure he missed them on the way back."

"Well, he's a handsome enough bloke." The accent was English, the voice mocking. "I'm sure it was such a hardship for you."

"Stop kidding around. I can't stay long. Lonna is having a gathering at her and Max's place this evening so we can all 'process' the day."

"Get shitfaced drunk, you mean?" Again, the guy sounded amused in the face of her distress.

"Have some respect," she snapped. "Otis was a brilliant scientist. He didn't deserve what happened to him."

A gasp nearly brought me from my hiding place, and I felt a hand on my wrist, warning me to stay.

"Just remember whose side you're on, love," the voice said. "And what you're risking."

"I have never given you reason to doubt my loyalty." She sounded like she spoke through clenched teeth, and I imagined his hairy thumb and fingers digging into her arm, marking her pale skin with bruises. I nearly shook with the effort to not jump to her rescue.

"You know better than to do that." Now his tone was low and sinister. "What do you remember about the scene? Or did you manage to get any kind of impression before you allowed them to strong arm you out of the way?"

She described it as I remembered it with one exception. "The wounds at Otto's wrists were puncture marks, and the skin was raised around them, like something sharp had been inserted and pulled out."

I would have to check that once the good detective had processed the body for autopsy.

"So it seems he lost some blood before he lost some blood, but let us not say any more about it here. I've heard rumors that members of the Lycanthrope Council hang out here. Buggers have crazy sharp hearing."

"Well, Crickets is closed for renovation, and I couldn't go farther out. I need to be at Lonna's by six. The least you could do is buy me a drink."

I raised both eyebrows. Yes, I would definitely have to talk to Selene again and in more depth. I opened my eyes and looked to see who had grabbed my wrist. The sensation disappeared. No one stood with me, but cold air swirled around me before disappearing. With a look to make sure Selene and her companion wouldn't see me, I exited my hiding place and returned to David's and my booth.

5

———

The mirror showed me Selene and her companion, a lanky-looking guy with a scar on one cheek, walking to the bar. She didn't look comfortable in the role of co-conspirator. Nor did she look like she enjoyed his company, and I wondered what she had gotten herself into.

"Learn anything?" David asked.

"Only that Selene might have seen our victim before I discovered him." I remembered the wrists had been torn, not punctured. "Or there's another reason she remembers it differently than from what I saw. I hope to the gods she didn't tell the detective that."

David popped the last of his egg in his mouth, and I looked at the rest of mine.

"Do you want this?" I asked. "I'm not feeling up to it."

He switched our plates. "Got no wife currently," he mumbled with his mouth full. "This is going to be dinner."

"I don't either, but I've learned to cook."

We chatted about the advantages and disadvantages of marriage versus hiring someone to cook and clean, but I kept one eye on the mirror to see when Selene and the bloke she was with left.

"Would you mind it if we tailed the guy?" I asked David once we paid up and sat ready to go. "I want to find out who he's working for, or at least where he lives." I didn't mention that apparently he'd been at the crime scene or at least around the Institute when it happened. I wanted to get him alone and question him.

"Fair enough. It's been a long time since I played spy."

Selene and her companion moved toward the exit, and we slid out of our booth, careful to stay as out of sight as possible. The pub had gotten crowded with the after work regulars, so our primary difficulty was with evading others' attempts at conversation. Some—our fellow lycanthropes—knew who and what we were. Others – the regular humans – thought we were friendly bureaucrats who worked for some government project at Castle Lycan.

Once we exited the pub, I looked around for Selene's red hair and saw a flash of it in the white car down the row she and her colleague had spoken in earlier. I ducked back into the doorway and peered around for her companion. A dark-haired figure disappeared down the sidewalk.

I handed my keys to David. "Start the car and drive slowly behind me, keeping me in sight, but try not to draw attention to yourself."

"When I was playing this game, it was with horses and carriages," he said with a grin. "It's harder to be subtle when you're clopping."

I clapped him on the arm and walked quickly down the sidewalk toward where I thought Selene's companion had disappeared. The urge to chase down and vanquish my prey blossomed in my chest, and I had to suppress it so I wouldn't change and ruin my clothing. My hearing remained extra sharp, although not wolf sharp, and I followed the sound of the man's footsteps.

He crossed at a light, and I darted after him, keeping to the late afternoon shadows. He looked over his shoulder, and I caught a glimpse of the red line running down his cheek. The tone of his rhythmic stride changed when he entered the old part of town and concrete transitioned to cobblestone. I glanced over my shoulder—it would be harder for David to follow us quietly. He stopped just short of the west port gate, and I nodded to him.

My quarry's steps quickened, so mine did as well, and I followed him into an alley beside the West Port Inn. He turned, and it occurred to me that cornering a suspicious person in an alley might not be the smartest idea just before a strong arm collared my neck. I clutched at it instinctively. It tightened, and spots swam in front of my eyes.

"Think you're so clever, don't you?" the Englishman asked. "I knew you were behind me the whole time."

"Congratulations, you caught me," I told him. "Now get your ogre to let me go, and we'll talk."

"Consider this a warning, mate. Leave us alone, and we'll do the same for you. But if you keep poking your nose into our business, then next time it won't end so well for you."

"But I don't even know who you are."

"Good."

A sharp pain blossomed on the back of my head, and every-thing went black.

I WOKE to a bright light in my eyes and shoved it away. It turned out to be David shining the torch app on his cell phone in my face.

"Not your smartest moment," he told me and helped me sit up.

My stomach heaved, but all that came up was acid. It took me a moment to find the right words to tell him, "I think I have a concussion."

He raised his eyebrows. "Someone managed to rattle the brain inside that thick skull o'yours?" He helped me stand, and I leaned on him.

"Trust me, it occurred to me that I shouldn't have rushed in, but at least I got a good close look at the guy. At least I think I did. It's fuzzy now."

"Right, then. We should get you back to your flat. Or to a doctor."

"No." I tried to shake my head, but pain lanced through my brain. "Okay, maybe, but not the hospital."

"There aren't any clinics open this time of night. I could call the NHS nurse line. See what I should look for or do for you."

"Take me to the home of Maximilian and Lonna Marconi-Fortuna," I said. "Max is a physician. Do you mind driving my car? I'll pay for your cab ride home."

"I'll figure out a way back to Laird Hall. Don't worry."

He helped me to the car, and every little bump over the cobblestones jarred my brain. I felt like sleeping when we got to the smooth pavement but remembered something about that not being a good idea, so I told David, "Keep me awake until we get there."

"I canna hit you while I'm driving. I'd put this prissy German car of yours into a tree."

I laughed. "No, just talk to me about something interesting."

He snorted. "Like what?"

I hadn't felt whatever it was—my father, a ghost, something else—since the pub, and as much as it had perturbed me, I wished it would return. Maybe it would have kept me from following the scarred Englishman into the alley. No, I couldn't blame some phantasmal force for my own mistake.

"Tell me about my father. I was only a boy when he was

killed and don't remember a lot about him."

In the waning light—the sun set so very late during the summer, which always threw me off when I returned from my travels—I saw his hands tighten and relax on the steering wheel. "What do you want to know?"

"Anything." I closed my eyes against the perceived movement of the road and trees outside but then opened them again when I got dizzier. "Whatever you remember."

"He could hold more Scotch than any other lycanthrope I knew," he said. "He had a laugh that boomed throughout any pub, no matter how small or large. That's how he and your mum got together—she was a university professor, one of the few female ones, and she was at Marley's one night with a group of colleagues."

"I know her story," I grumbled. "Get back to his."

"Well, he was also grumpy when he lost a fight," he said with a smirk. "Couldn't stand it. Not that it happened often."

"They caught me from behind."

He laughed outright then. "He'd take responsibility for his mistakes. That's how he usually lost the fights—something stupid or showing off. He could never resist an audience."

"How long did you know him?" We were almost to the house Lonna and Max rented, and I almost asked David to circle around so I could continue to take advantage of his talkative mood.

"I met him in 1800 when he came on as the Council Investigator. I'd just come out of hiding myself. The Order had shifted its attention to the American Colonies and their conflict and got stretched too thin to keep after us effectively."

"The Order? I remember something about them in Council records, but it's been a long time."

I couldn't tell with certainty, but he seemed to shudder. "And here we are, then. I'll just leave your car here so you're not blocking anyone in."

"Thanks." I made a mental note, addled as it may have been, to ask him about the Order later. We'd always maintained a cordial tone with our Council dealings, but this was the first day he'd decided to open up, and he'd only whetted my appetite for information.

We got out of the car, and he held me steady with one hand as we made our way up the front walk.

"Be careful," he said. "You remind me more and more of him as you get older." With that comment, which could have been a warning or compliment, he disappeared into the night.

I rang the bell and leaned against a post. Lonna opened the door.

"Gabriel?" Her eyes widened when she saw my face. "Come in. Max!"

I stumbled forward, and she and Max caught me and brought me to a sofa. The house smelled of Italian comfort food—lasagna, garlic bread, and the clean scent of salad with vinaigrette along with them. I guessed there was a chocolate cake somewhere. And of course, alcohol.

Selene walked out of the kitchen, and I bit back a snarl. Her friend had done this to me. She stepped back when she saw my expression, so I tried to make it more neutral. My head throbbed, and I grimaced instead.

"What happened?" Lonna asked. "You look awful."

"I did something stupid and got whacked on the head," I told her. "I may have a concussion."

Max, a medical doctor, came in with an old-fashioned doctor's bag. "I knew this would come in handy sometime." He took out a light and shone it in my eyes, then felt around my head. "For bone fragments," he explained, "although it's definitely possible to get a concussion without any damage to the skull."

I hissed when his fingers found a very tender spot.

"It's just a bump, but no fracture," he said. "Happens all the time in sports—poor kids' brains just get rattled around. Did you lose consciousness?"

"For a few minutes."

He continued through a long list of questions and finished with, "I think you'll be fine, but I want to get a CT to make sure there's not any fluid buildup. We've got one at the Institute."

"I'm aware of that," I said. "Bloody expensive machines."

Selene had been watching, and I couldn't read her expression. Did she suspect I'd had a run-in with her friends? I wanted to tell her not to go anywhere, I needed to talk to her, but I didn't want to spook her into going into hiding. I didn't have enough to arrest her, so I'd just have to be patient and corner her later. Once I got rid of this damned headache.

"I'm really sorry, but I need to go," Selene said. "Gabriel, I hope you feel better." In what seemed like a flash, she left.

"Interesting," was Lonna's comment. "Y'all go ahead. I'll stay here and clean up."

MAX DROVE me to the Institute. Once we cleared the woods around the drive, I couldn't help but think it looked like a sinister castle looming above the lawn, its stone walls lit with yellow semicircles from the spotlights. Dim lights shone from within the building. I noticed the difference between when I'd approached it earlier and now, both with regard to how it looked and how I felt. This morning, I had been confident, a little impatient, and curious on my official visit as the Council member who had advocated for it and wanted to make sure it was, indeed, almost ready to start its mission. I thought I had the backing of my peers. Now I felt wobbly and uncertain, both physically and with regard to the politics around it. I would say meeting Selene was a bright spot, but not since her friend had bashed me on the head. At least David had demonstrated a crack in his armor, and the shadowy figure who had been my father took on more definition in my foggy memory.

"Here we are," Max said and pulled into one of the Co-Director parking spots.

Steadier than before, I got out of the car on my own this time. "I'm getting better."

"Let's take a look just to make sure."

He opened the side door with a key and flipped on the lights. We both squinted against the glare. The blood scent still lingered, although not as strongly.

A bump from upstairs drew our gazes to the ceiling.

"Someone's in Lonna's office," Max whispered.

"Are you sure?"

He nodded, and we moved toward a door marked Stairs. "We're directly below the office, and as I recall, we left her at home. There's no reason for the security guards to be in there."

"Do you have a cleaning crew?" I followed him to the door.

"We told the cleaners not to come tonight. I'll check it out. Stay here."

"I'm fine," I said. Adrenaline and that extra push from the dopamine that activated when we were about to change cleared the fog in my head. "I'm going to change."

He put a hand on my arm. "Not until I can scan you. Rearranging yourself may cause further damage."

"I'm still coming with you."

He nodded. "There's a second stairwell at the other end of the hall. I'll take that one."

The darkness in the stairwell seemed total as my eyes adjusted from being in the light. With my hearing attuned for any sound that might indicate someone coming down, I felt my way up the railing. The stairwell itself smelled like paint, new rubber and cleaning agents, which blocked out the blood.

By the time I emerged onto the second floor, my eyes had adjusted back to the darkness.

Max came out of the stairwell on the other end of the hall, and we both closed in on Lonna's office. I listened for the faintest sound, but the only noise in my ears was my own heartbeat and Max's breathing.

"Anything?" he mouthed.

"No."

The door stood slightly ajar, which indicated someone had been there, and he nudged it completely open. Light from the waxing moon poured through the windows and over Lonna's desk. As with LeConte's office, paper was strewn everywhere, but thankfully, no body lay on the desk.

Max indicated he would go around the desk and look underneath. I stayed by the door in case the intruder hid elsewhere and decided to make a break for it. He shone his cell phone torch app under the desk, and I saw its light flicker in the little space between the bottom of the desk and the floor.

"Nothing," he said out loud.

I walked around and checked other possible nooks and crannies, even checking the wingback chairs to make sure no one sat curled up in them.

"Is there another way out beside the hallway and stairwells?" I asked.

"Only the windows, but there's nowhere to go once you're out, not even a ledge."

"No secret passages?"

He gave me a doubtful look. "It's a new building."

"Hey, it's Scotland," I said, but then my attention returned to the mess. "Can you tell if anything's missing?"

"No, only Lonna would be able to." He ran a hand through his hair. "I suppose we should call her. And Garou. And find the security guards."

"I'll have the detective post twenty-four hour surveillance on the place," I said. "Twice in one day is twice too many. Damn, I wish I could figure out where the perp went."

"What if no one was actually here?" Max asked.

"What do you mean?"

"You know about Wolf-Lonna and my abilities to create an astral projection."

I arched an eyebrow. "True, but you've set up wards around the place to ensure none but you and she could get through, right?"

"Yes, but those are not always foolproof."

He walked to the door, and I followed him into the hallway. He locked the door behind him.

"It will take me some time to test them and see if I can determine whether they've been breached," he told me. "Meanwhile, let's get you scanned to make sure you don't have any edema from your head injury."

I felt the back of my head where they'd hit me. The tender bump had decreased in size and painfulness.

"I'm healing. We should find the security guards first and make sure they're not hurt."

He led me into the stairwell, down the stairs, and to a vacuum-sealed door. "If there was a breach, they're likely downstairs."

"Why?" I asked.

"We keep the most important and expensive equipment in the basement," he told me. "It seems excessive, but in case of some sort of chemical or biological warfare, it's also someplace we can hide if necessary. The ventilation system has its own generators, and there are emergency provisions down here."

"Are the English going to invade again? I thought we'd been pretty well defeated two hundred and fifty years ago."

"If not the English, then maybe someone nastier. We've gotten threats."

When he opened the door, the smell of shed blood hit me full-force the second time that day.

6

When we walked into the room where the CT scanner resided, we were met by a nasty surprise: the security guards tied up, their throats slit. However, there wasn't much blood, at least not enough for two grown men.

"Not again." Max groaned and staggered back.

"Again?" I asked and reached to steady him. I took in the details of the scene, which almost seemed ordinary compared to LeConte's odd murder that morning.

"LeConte and now this. I'll call Garou." He dashed out of the room, and his speed gave me pause because I'd not known Max ever to hurry. Yes, the matter was urgent, especially since these chaps were very dead, but there was something odd about his reaction.

I'll talk to him about it later.

I shook my head and investigated the corpses. These two didn't make my stomach turn like LeConte had, but they also didn't resemble a certain picture a young boy shouldn't have seen of his mutilated father. I pushed the memory away and closed my eyes to bring my wolf nose into play and focus on the scent trail, faint as it was. There was the same kerosene-pipe smoke smell and another one that smelled vaguely of dust and mold. I sneezed.

Ah, so he had an accomplice. I opened my eyes and took off my jacket—doctor's orders or not, I was going to change. I walked into the hallway and looked around for a room I could secure against someone walking in on me.

A petite black wolf appeared in the hall, and I knew Max had called Lonna, who had sent her psychic double. It always threw me how the spirit-wolf didn't have a scent.

"It's the same one as this morning," I said.

"I wonder if their intent is to intimidate or if they're actually looking for something."

"I don't know. Let me change and I'll join you."

"Not so fast," Max said and came through the door. "Wolf-Lonna has this. She can travel faster than any of us."

Indeed, she'd left, head low, following the trail.

"Amazing how she does that. Does Abby have a double?"

Max grinned ruefully. "Like any nine-month-old, she babbles when no one's in the room with her but it's impossible to tell who or what she's talking to. It's early to know what her talents will be."

After about twenty minutes, Garou shuffled into the hallway. He looked exhausted and irritated.

"I take it you have already been in there," he said.

"That's how we discovered the bodies, yes," Max said.

"What brought you to the Institute so late?" Garou asked and checked his watch.

"Investigator McCord sustained a concussion today," Max told him. "I was concerned and decided to check him out."

Garou looked at me with narrowed eyes. "How did this happen?"

No way was I telling him about Selene and the scar-faced Englishman. Obviously she had a reason not to go to the police in spite of being involved in something dangerous, and I needed to speak to her before spilling her secrets. "I cannot say, as it impacts my own part of the investigation, Detective."

"Were you attacked? If so, you need to make a report, particularly if it concerns *our* investigation."

"Once I'm feeling coherent enough, I'll be happy to talk to you about it. Meanwhile, you have two more corpses to check out." I stepped aside and gestured for him to proceed into the CT lab.

A quick tour of the building didn't yield any more clues, at least not to my tired brain. I figured if Garou picked up anything, he would include it in a report, which I would get soon, anyway. Plus, I counted on Lonna to tell me what her double found.

After convincing Max I was feeling better and enduring another round of him looking in my eyes and poking and prodding my skull, I left without getting scanned. He had me promise not to do any changing for the next twenty-four hours, and definitely not if I had any headache, dizziness or nausea, in which case I needed to come back and see him for that CT. It was after two o'clock in the morning by the time I fell into bed and dreamed in fragments of battles and death.

LAURA'S WORDS "Don't forget your ten o'clock!" rattled through my brain at about nine-fifteen. I jerked awake with the sense I had been running through fields all night from an enemy who pursued me with relentless determination through my dreams. In spite of my fatigue, I rushed to get ready in time. This was an important appointment, one I shade every year, and the only one I'd delay investigating a triple homicide for.

The community knew that the school for poorly behaved children was called the Council School, but they didn't know why, exactly. It was another example of how lycanthropes had managed to live in human communities with only the barest of awareness. Like many of our institutions, including Lycan Castle, the name had long ago passed into the status of, "I never really thought about it much, saw no reason to." Even when it touted its expertise in treating the symptoms of Chronic Lycanthropy Syndrome, no one made the connection. Perhaps a rare lycanthrope-wizard collaboration had instituted some sort of memory spell around it so people would acknowledge it and move on.

My head throbbed when I walked into the sunlight, but briefly, and my driving was steady. I pulled up to the school, a large gray stone building with gargoyles perched on the corners of the crenellated roof. No one knew when it was built or the gargoyles added, likely sometime during the Victorian era when Queen Victoria fell in love with Scotland and decided to make the country pretty. I always liked to think of the architect adding the Gothic elements to make it more appropriate to the setting.

I waved to my favorite, a dog-like creature I'd long ago named Harry. He didn't wave back, but to me, he represented my ancestors back in the murky time of legend before everything had to be documented in minute detail for the world to see. The others represented other magical species, most of which had died out long ago or perhaps had never existed. The wizard gargoyle clung to the roofline with clawed hands and peered down with iris-less eyes set in a gaunt face with fangs. I always felt it leered at me.

Headmistress Corinne Reid met me at the door. We embraced and sniffed, and I got the image of a warm breeze sweeping across green fields dotted with purple and white heather. She stepped back and studied me with bright green eyes. As usual, her blonde hair was pulled back in a bun, but it didn't make her high-cheeked face severe or unfriendly.

"Welcome, Investigator," she said. "We always look forward

to your Solstice visit. But there's something different about you."

"It must be my current investigation," I said and gestured for her to lead the way.

"No, there's something else. Oh, well." She stepped into the gloom that was the front hall of the Council School.

I maintained some skepticism regarding the pagan feasts and their effects on us, but I respected the tradition of seeking for truth in the waxing light of the year, with the presumption being that most would be found at the time when light was most abundant. This included interviewing the children who attended the school to see who might develop into a full were-wolf and who merely had the behavioral symptoms. Those who would bloom into true lycanthropes were then invited to attend special classes and training. It was in the interest of keeping our kind out of the light of human awareness, or at least on the very periphery of it, so this "chore" fell under my jurisdiction. Although I would end up spending several hours with sullen preteens, the children often surprised me in a good way.

Today was no exception. Corinne led me to an office over-looking the wide lawn in front of the school and left to fetch the first interviewee. Thankfully, we'd left the shadows behind. Sunlight poured through the windows, and specks of dust floated through the beams. I couldn't help but note the differ-ence in smell between the synthetic new building odor of the Institute and the must and paper scent of the older structure.

"This one insisted on talking to you," she said when she returned, a piece of paper in her hand and a small white-blond boy in tow. "He's not one of our CLS kids, but he has some interesting abilities that have been getting him in trouble."

"And what does this have to do with me?" I asked.

"He saw you come in and said he has something to tell you about a soldier. Alexander, come tell Mister McCord what you need to say." She ushered the child into the room and left us to speak privately.

The child sat across from me and studied me with serious brown eyes that flicked from me to a space over my left shoulder. The office chair with its red leather cushions dwarfed him.

"Good morning, Alexander," I said and resisted the urge to look behind me.

"Good morning, sirs," the child said.

I looked up, startled, and felt a draught. "There's only one of me here."

He shook his head. "No, there's the chap standing beside you too. Bit see-through, but he's there."

The hairs on the back of my neck stood on end, and I glanced down at the summary sheet Corinne had handed to me. The boy's diagnosis space had a question mark in it followed by the words, "suspected clairvoyant or psychotic."

"What is he wearing?" I asked.

"He's got on brown pants and a big jacket."

"Describe him to me."

"He looks like you, but with more wrinkles and shorter hair." Alexander leaned forward, and light flashed through his eyes. "And he's trying to tell you something, but you don't want to listen."

"I see." I didn't speak further, just listened, and heard a sound like the wind blowing through dry autumn leaves. "Do you know what he's trying to say?"

"He says he tried to talk to you last night, but you were hurt on your head." He sat back and rubbed his temples, a surprisingly adult gesture for such a small boy. "Why does talking to him make *my* head hurt?"

"Sometimes that happens when you're doing things too much before you get used to them," I said. "It's like building a muscle. If you use it too much before it gets strong, it hurts so you'll stop."

"Do you know why I'm here?" he asked and waved his hands around, "at this school?"

"No, tell me."

"I know things I shouldn't. Like I know that you have a lot of secrets that you keep from others."

"Most grown-ups do."

He shook his head and winced. "Not all of them. The soldier is worried you're going to get hurt because of some of them."

The soldier's uniform sounded like my father's in the pictures I'd seen of him just before he shipped off to the continent to get killed in the Second Great War. I knew that no matter how desperately he felt the need to communicate with me, he wouldn't want to hurt the boy.

"Take it easy there, Alexander," I said and stood. "I'd like to come back and talk to you more in the future, but only if you promise you'll be careful and try not to talk to the see-through people too much."

His eyes widened as he scrambled out of the chair to stand. "I will, sir." He lowered his voice. "I don't want to talk to most of them, anyhow." He left the room without making much sound, and I suspected that was how he did most things—as unobtrusively as possible. It made me wonder how many secrets he'd spilled in childish innocence before he learned less attention was better than more.

I unclenched my left hand and forced my jaw to relax. When to demand attention and when to shy away from it was a lesson learned harder by some. And some of us were better at avoiding the limelight than others.

The rest of the morning passed in a stream of twenty-minute interviews. None of the other children had anything interesting to offer or say, and I noted which ones I suspected would manifest the full CLS spectrum of symptoms. I wished I could tell Corinne exactly what I saw or how I did what I did, but my determinations were based on instinct rather than logic. I only knew my father had had the same ability, one of the few tidbits I'd learned about him in his official capacity. Of course I felt like I was being watched or that he was there, but he didn't communicate with me, and I wondered whether he was, indeed, there, or if he had left when Alexander did and my mind was playing tricks on me.

"Tell me about Alexander," I said when I sat down for lunch with Corinne in her office. "How did he end up here?"

"Right now, most of our boys are here because of being born with CLS into human families, but he's the exception. His father is a lycanthrope, but he's puzzled with him—Alexander has these strange abilities and no CLS symptoms."

"So has he had behavior problems? He seems inclined to stay under the radar."

She shook her head. "His father wanted him to come here to be exposed to children with CLS to see if it would 'toughen him up'. As you can probably guess, he doesn't really fit in with the bad boys."

"Poor lad. What about his mum?"

"Died when Alexander was a baby. What did he have to tell you that was so important?" She paused with a forkful of salad in her hand.

"I'm still trying to make sense of it," I told her. "You know how it is with clairvoyants."

"Right, sometimes they're clear and sometimes not, and when you want them to be one way, they're usually the opposite."

"Exactly."

"What did you want him to be?"

I thought about being told there was a ghost following me and then how it resembled my long-dead father. "I'm not sure."

. . .

THE AFTERNOON PASSED QUICKLY with two more possible lycanthropes emerging from the group of preadolescent CLS sufferers. That brought me up to four, a typical number for the full phenotypic expression. I gave their names to Corinne before I left.

"Watch these especially closely," I told her.

"When will you be checking on them again?" she asked and opened up her calendar to August. "They'll be going back to their homes this weekend but will be back end of the summer."

"It will likely not be until September. I have a major investigation going on right now."

Wrinkles creased her otherwise flawless brow. "Is that the one about the Institute? The murders there?"

"You know I can't tell you that. It's an ongoing case."

"Right. Just let me know. I'll continue to watch over young Alexander as well. He's a local."

"Thank you."

As I walked out of the front door, I felt the weight of someone's gaze on me and turned to see Alexander standing in one of the second floor windows. He held a hand up to me as if to wave farewell, and rather than sweet, the gesture struck me as creepy. The hair on the back of my neck didn't stand down until I got well away from the Council School.

7

My interviews had ended at the termination of the school day, and although I typically used that as an excuse to knock off early, the investigation beckoned. I wanted to peek at Garou's preliminary report as to what he'd gathered, although I knew nothing would be back from analysis yet. I also wanted to get a sense of the atmosphere around Lycan Castle to prepare myself for the inevitable backlash from the previous day's events.

The first scent that came to me when I walked into the castle was that of candle smoke, which wasn't too unusual, but the green bite of sage caught my attention. Typically the only time we burned sage along with the candles was to smudge the Council Chamber before a meeting, a tradition dating back to the days when the Council met in secret and needed to clear magical energies from spying wizards. But we weren't supposed to meet until the following week.

The look on Laura's face confirmed my suspicions that I was not expected to be at Lycan Castle that afternoon.

"Got any live ones this term?" she asked and handed me a stack of messages. "None of these are urgent, by the way."

I gave her the file with my notes on my visit to the Council School. "Please type these up. And yes, a few. Nothing unusual except a little clairvoyant chap who's ended up in the wrong place."

"I can only imagine the secrets that child knows. Ghosts do love to talk." She took my jacket, and for the first time in decades, I reached for my hat, which I hadn't worn since they went out of fashion.

The appearance of my father's ghost must be dragging me into the past.

"Ah, yes," I said and pretended to scratch a spot above my left ear. Her lips quirked.

"It is a pity gentlemen don't wear hats anymore," she said. "I'll make you some tea. Will you be here long?"

"Right, thank you. I imagine I'll be here long enough."

As soon as the door closed behind me in my office, I sat at the desk and turned on my super listening skills.

"Yes, he just arrived," Laura said, presumably into the telephone. "No, I don't know exactly when he came into the building... He said 'long enough.'"

Who is spying on me through my secretary?

She hung up, so I brought my attention back into my office. Her duplicity didn't surprise me considering I wasn't the one who signed her paychecks—Morena was—but it did disappoint me. I thought she was more loyal to me.

When I opened my eyes, I found that she'd stacked the Institute personnel files on the corner of the desk so I'd have them within easy reach. There was also a file with Garou's initial report, which I pulled out once I'd sat and made myself comfortable with my cup of tea in front of me. What had started out as a relatively warm day had turned chilly and cloudy toward the end, and even with the thick castle walls and deep-set windows, I could feel it. I hated it when my body reminded me I was older than I looked.

As I expected, the report only contained a list of what had been gathered with generic descriptions and locations, but I was pleased to see they'd found something that looked like paint flakes on the trees in the pullout I'd directed them to. It would take time to match fingerprints, analyze fiber samples and paint chips, and do the other forensic tasks. It occurred to me that with crimes of this nature being so rare in our community, we wouldn't have the resources to do all that ourselves, so that meant Garou would have to send everything off to the human labs, where our items and requests would likely be in a long queue.

"Brilliant," I mumbled and pushed the button on my intercom. "Laura, set up a status meeting for me with Garou for tomorrow morning."

"Time preference?"

"Early so I can get it out of the way."

I then took out a notepad and pen so I could jot down thoughts about the personnel files. Dutifully, I pulled Otis LeConte's to me first with Selene's next in line. I flipped through the basic demographic stuff, noting only that he was in his early thirties, although his picture showed he was balding prematurely, so he looked older. He'd had a round face with a goatee and mustache, and he stared into the camera with a grim expression, like he was determined to accomplish something if it was the last thing he did. No wife or children, which was a relief—it always depressed me when a victim left behind a young family—but one brother and elderly parents. I noted the contact information for them, sure they'd been notified of their son and brother's death. I studied his picture again. There was something about his eyes, something angry I couldn't come to terms with. He looked more likely to commit murder than be the victim of one. There were no disciplinary actions listed, not that I expected any since they'd just gotten started. Nothing else struck me as remarkable in the rest of his file aside from the fact that he'd been a genealogy nerd from a young age and had started tracing his friends' family trees during adolescence. From there, it made sense he'd gotten into genetics.

That reminded me—they should have gotten the application files from Iain.

I called Lonna, conscious I only had a small piece of the picture of who Otis LeConte was. Her Institute number went straight to voice mail, and I suspected she'd left early since there wasn't much to do with all operations suspended by the Council. I hung up without leaving a message and shot her a quick email requesting a meeting for the next day so I could ask her some more questions and get a peek at the applications. I also wanted to know what Wolf-Lonna had found the night before.

Selene's file came next, and I found my lips curling in answer to the smile she'd given for her personnel and badge photo. She looked very excited to be there. She, too, was single, with only a younger brother Curtis Rial listed as family. As for hobbies, she'd left the line blank. I found that omission frustrating.

The other files passed in a blur of names and paper, but no one had anything interesting that said, "Yes, I am your murderer!" Not that I'd expected it to be that easy, but one never knew when something would pop up. When Laura poked her head in to tell me she was leaving and that I'd be meeting with Garou at nine o'clock the next morning, I was happy to walk her out.

WHEN I ROUNDED the corner to the house I rented, I was surprised to see a car in the driveway. The forest green Jaguar seemed out of place next to the old brick building, which had been built in the early twentieth century during the Arts and Crafts movement. I always thought it needed a 1920s-era automobile to complete its air of old class. Not that a Jaguar or my BMW were shabby.

"David, what are you doing here?" I asked once I'd parked in the garage and come back out to meet him. He stretched and grabbed his suit jacket out of the car.

"Took you long enough," he said. "I've been here for an hour." His business attire told me he'd been to something important, and my stomach flipped when his sartorial choice clicked into place with the candle smoke and Laura's strange behavior earlier—it was confirmed, the Council had met without me.

"Why? I know I got a head injury yesterday, but I don't recall making an appointment."

"No, but I thought you might like to know what happened in the Council meeting today. You're a smart lad; you'll have figured out we met."

"Ever hear of a phone?" I asked and unlocked the door from the garage into my kitchen. "And we weren't supposed to meet until next week." I kept my tone light to cover my growing sense of dread.

He waved the modern technology off like it was an insistent gnat buzzing around his head. "There's no substitute for face-to-face communication, Gabriel. Electronic gadgets can fail or distort. Morena's always complaining about the battery dying on hers."

"That reminds me..." I put my smartphone on a charger on the kitchen counter. "Would you like a drink?"

"Well, I can't help but notice that open bottle of Oban you've got."

I poured two fingers of the whiskey into a square glass, and he waved off my offer of water or ice to go in it. I grabbed a glass of water and led him into the den, where I sat on the brown and green-striped couch. He took the leather recliner.

"Ah, now this is more like it," he said and leaned back. "Can't complain about this modern invention."

"Right, because back in the day, all you had to sit on were rocks and piles of straw." I took a deep breath, trying to keep my patience, but all I wanted was to take a long run and then a hot bath. Both would help me process the day, but I needed to know what the Council had met about and what it meant for the continuation of the Institute.

"You're getting better," he observed. "I remember a time when you would have snapped at me to spill my news."

"I was very young. I haven't gotten impatient with a Council member since the seventies."

"You're doing better than your father, then. Back in the Victorian days, he was a hothead."

Again, a mention of my father. I wondered if the uniform-clad ghost still followed me, but I didn't feel any cold drafts or other signs of something supernatural, which gave me some small sense of relief. Not that I thought he'd hurt me, but it did cause some discomfort knowing I was being watched and possibly judged.

"Well, I'm not him, although I am starting to grow impatient. You come to my home, drink my whiskey, and drop hints but nothing of substance. What did the Council meet about?"

He set his empty glass on the coffee table and leaned forward. "You."

"What about me?"

"That's what the Council met about: you. That's why you weren't invited."

I raised my eyebrows, my strange meeting with Morena coming to mind. "Are they considering replacing me as Investigator?"

"No, you're coming into your maturity, so they're thinking of promoting you to full Council member."

"About damn time. But why now? I've been mature for decades. I'm close to eighty years old, David."

He nodded slowly. "It's something we don't talk about generally—don't want others to know too much about our inner workings, you see—but that's how it works: the youngest member starts out as Investigator, and if they come into their full power, they get promoted up. If not, they get asked to leave, but that's not happened in recent memory because the Council families are, through careful mate selection for offspring, very strong, and it's rare for one of them to not achieve full lycanthrope power. You were a wild card, though, because of your human mother."

"Wait..." I massaged my temples. "What indicates that something's happening now? As I said, I've been fully grown for several decades."

"Some of it's how you've recently learned to use your werewolf senses while in human form, although you're still developing that talent. You can only use one at a time, after all."

"I thought that was because males don't multitask."

"It's also a sense not unlike what you do with the schoolboys," he continued, ignoring my attempt at humor. "Some things you just know."

"What am I supposed to do? What did the Council decide?"

"We voted four to two to wait it out and see what happens." He drew his brows together. "Some are not convinced that you will achieve full power in spite of the signs, and they're especially cautious because your championed cause—the Institute —seems to be falling apart."

"And you can't tell me who voted against me," I said.

He shook his head. "You can likely guess."

"Probably Cora because of her connection to the Purists and Dimitri, who's been cool to me lately. Why are you helping me, David? You said you had some interest in the Institute, but this is personal, and you could get in serious trouble for telling me as much as you have."

"A very old promise, lad." He drew a yellowed envelope out of his jacket breast pocket. From it, he extracted a letter, its creases darkened and worn like it would fall into pieces at any moment. He held it gingerly and looked at me. "It's from your father."

"To me?" I asked.

"No, about you." He unfolded the letter and squinted at it, although I suspected he'd memorized it by now. "'Lachlan, I hope this greeting finds you well and indeed, better than I am. Our suspicions were correct, and I fear I am in mortal danger. Remember your promise to me, the one you made before I left. Regards, McCord.'"

"What does it mean?" I couldn't help but ask. I struggled to push away the memory of the images of my father's demise, my mother's tear-streaked face and the fear in her eyes.

David re-folded the letter and put it back in its envelope. "He was behind enemy lines, and it's a miracle that letter made it out at all. It's deliberately vague, of course." He looked down at the envelope, his expression one I'd never seen on his face before, of grief and sadness. "Although I didn't want to, I had to keep my distance from you and your mother because you were in grave danger."

"From who?"

He looked around. "Are you sure this place is secure?"

"I believe so. I'm just renting, so I haven't been able to do much to it."

"Then let's go for a run and discuss it somewhere we won't be overheard."

I DIDN'T FEEL David would attack me, but still, since allowing someone to see you change is one of the most intimate things a werewolf can do, David and I split up into different bedrooms to transform into our wolf selves.

If I'm coming into my full powers, why isn't this easier? I thought as I lay on the floor to catch my breath after changing. *Or is this the human half showing through? They always resist change.*

My mind tried to chew on everything David had told me to this point, but I quieted it—there would be enough time for thinking later. We left through a hinged diamond-pane window I'd rigged so I could open it from the inside with my paws. I could get back in from the outside by using my nose to punch in a code on a keypad with extra large keys hidden in the shrubbery.

"Ingenious," David told me telepathically. *"Definitely better than a doggie door. Did you know that's how the vaccine lycanthropes manage?"* He snorted. *"They have no sense of dignity."*

I didn't respond. Lonna told me that was how they did it in the States. "At some point, you just have to get over yourself," she'd said. "Practicality trumps pride."

David led me through the field behind my complex and into a wooded area. The wind whispered through the summer leaves, and woodland creatures skittered out of our way. As a wolf, David was barrel-chested with a little gray showing on his muzzle. In his human form, he outweighed me by a few stone, and while the difference wasn't so drastic in canine form, it was all muscle. It reminded me he'd be a formidable opponent, and I was thankful he was on my side. I also wanted to know what my father's letter meant and grew impatient as he led me through twists and turns, on paths and off them, until we were deep in the woods. He stopped beside a pool in a small grove, and the image I'd gotten from my brief sniff of Selene came to mind.

I'll consider that problem later.

"This will do," David said and stretched out on a flat rock

that was shaded, but I could smell the heat radiating off it in waves of mineral and dry dirt, so I surmised it had been in the sun for most of the day.

I found a soft grassy spot and stretched out. The ground released tangy green smells with notes of damp earth, and I had to fight my wolf side to not close my eyes and take a nap. My human side wanted more information.

David looked like he had the same struggle—his eyelids kept drooping.

"Tell me why my mother and I were in danger after my father died," I said.

He started. *"Right."* He stood and shook himself, then sat on his haunches. *"What do you know of the Order of the Silver Arrow?"*

"Not much," I said. *"I remember hearing something about it in school, but I thought it was dead."*

"It was supposed to have died out long ago, but as with most secret societies, it still survives in some form, but its purpose hasn't changed. If anything, it's become more dangerous."

8

———————

David related the origin of the Order. Back in the eighteenth century, the world was torn apart by war as the British struggled to expand and hold on to their colonies, and the colonies fought to be free of British rule. It was also supposedly the "Age of Enlightenment," but there were those who resisted scientific advancement, and they also succumbed to a sort of xenophobia. The opening of the world frightened the Europeans, and the realization that some people were more than human terrified them.

One of these creatures was a *vargamore*, a half werewolf, half wizard named Sir Dorian Wolfsheim. He had come from Germany and had fought and sailed for the British. He hated his wolf side, feeling it was crass and undesirable with all those messy emotions and urges, and was overly enamored of his wizard abilities. Rumor had it that he started the Wizard Tribunal, not as the governing body it is now, but rather as a punishing body to chastise wizards who were unable to resist their base instincts in the name of science and purity.

Sadly, psychology was still barely a twinkle in the eye of scientific inquiry, so Wolfsheim could not realize his persecution of lycanthropes was an effort to eradicate that side of himself. He went at it with zeal akin to religious persecution with the blessing of the British crown, which had its own bloody history and frustrations with the Scots, who were once again revolting. The clans who fought with Bonnie Prince Charlie had the most lycanthrope blood in their number. Those who fought against the Great Pretender, as he was known in England, were primarily allied with the wizards.

"My family fought on the wrong side," David said. *"And they were part of the packs who failed to show up where they were needed. Something confused and scattered them until it was too late."*

"Wolfsheim," I said. *"As a* vargamore, *he could do that."*

"Aye. And he did. And then he hunted us down systematically until only those of us who could seek refuge on foreign shores or disguise ourselves among those who had not fought for the Pretender were left."

A snapping branch brought both of us into alert stance and sniffing the wind for the scent of a creature big enough to make that much noise. A shiny object flew from the trees and embedded itself in a stump just in front of David's nose. We dashed for cover away from where it must have come from.

"What was it?" asked David.

"I didn't get too close a look at it." I risked a glance behind us. I didn't want to distract him from our flight, but I knew what I'd seen: a silver arrow. That someone could have gotten that close to us told me they had magical help. It seemed we had attracted the attention of a *vargamore*, and someone was in pursuit.

We eventually circled back to my flat, changed back, and dressed.

"How was that possible?" asked David when he walked into the kitchen. "How could someone have just snuck up on us? Someone armed?"

"You know as well as I do," I told him and handed him a

glass with a generous pour of the Oban. "Direction of the breeze and possibly some extra help."

He knocked it back and held out his glass for a refill. I gave him a half pour. He scowled.

"Don't stiff a man who's just had his life threatened."

"Unless you're sleeping over, you need to be able to drive. And that silver arrow was a warning. They could've killed us both if they'd wanted."

He shook his head. "Just fucking great."

"Maybe you need to get better at giving history lessons," I told him. The doorbell rang, and we both startled. "Stay here."

"Insolent pup," he growled, but he didn't move.

I hesitated and grabbed the open Oban bottle before he helped himself again. Not that there wasn't other alcohol in the kitchen, but in spite of his rustic upbringing, David wasn't the type of guest to open something without asking.

His words followed me into the front hall. "If your father wasn't such a good friend..."

I checked through the peephole and saw the last person I expected: Selene.

Protective instincts kicked in. I opened the door and pulled Selene inside. "Are you crazy? You don't know who might be out there."

"What is your problem?" She detached her arm from my grip and narrowed her eyes at the Scotch in my hand. "Are you drinking that straight from the bottle?"

"No, I'm drinking it from a glass like a gentleman," I said and motioned for her to follow me into the kitchen, thinking it would be best to introduce her to David before he surprised us. But when I got in there, I saw he'd left through the side door. His empty glass sat on the counter beside the letter from my father, and the sound of his car's engine started and moved away.

"What's that?" she asked and reached for the letter.

"Official business," I told her and picked it up. It barely had any weight to it, and I handled it carefully.

"From when, nineteen hundred?"

"Nineteen forty-three," I murmured.

Her hand dropped back to her side. "Look, I'm sorry if I'm interrupting something," she said. "I was driving by and..." She squeezed her eyes shut. "That's a lie. I looked you up and found you."

I bit my tongue so I wouldn't ask if she'd consulted her scar-faced concussion-dealing friend before showing up for a visit. "What can I fix you to drink?"

She opened her eyes, and her open face betrayed her surprise. How had she gotten mixed up with that bloke at the pub? She reeked of innocence, but she was no dummy. "To drink?" she asked.

"The rules of hospitality dictate that if a guest shows up at one's residence, one should offer some sort of refreshment. Thus, would you like a drink?"

"Yes, but..." She glanced at the Scotch, then back at me. "Do you have any wine?"

I gestured to my dual zone wine fridge. "Red or white?"

"White, please."

Soon I had her settled with a glass of Chenin Blanc on the opposite end of the sofa. The similarity to David's visit from earlier didn't escape me, but she was nicer to look at.

"So what brings you to Shady Acres?" I asked. "I'm afraid it's not the Scotland in coffee table books."

"It's fine," she said. "It's not so different from home except our historical houses are a couple, not several, hundred years old. As for what brings me..." She looked into her glass. "I wanted to know how the investigation into Otis's death is going."

"I had official business today, so I wasn't able to do any

investigating, but I will give it my full attention tomorrow. I'm hoping Garou will have his reports ready by then."

"Are you going to question us? He already did."

"That depends. Can you add to your statement?"

"Garou implied we were dating," she said. "But we weren't. But still, it's my fault that Otis died."

That drew my attention away from the curve of her neck and the way one button on her blouse seemed to hang on for dear life over her breasts. "Fill me in here. How does Garou's implication cause you to be a murderer?"

She blinked, and two fat tears trailed down her cheeks. "Other people thought we were dating, or at least that we were more than friends. Because we were the same age and American, maybe. Lonna even hinted that it wouldn't be a good idea to cross personal and professional relationships." She snorted. "Like she's not married to her co-director."

"Right. Believe me, we did consider that, but we need both of them. Go on. I'm still not convinced LeConte's death is your fault."

"That morning after staffing, he asked me to walk with him to his office. He said he had something to ask me. I was afraid of what he'd say, he looked so hopeful and afraid all at the same time. I said no, I had things I needed to do before your visit. The next time I saw him, he was dead."

"What do you think he was going to ask you?"

"To go out with him, I guess. I don't know what else it could have been. But don't you see? If I'd gone to his office with him, he might not have been killed or he would have had warning that something wasn't right. You know we hear and smell better than humans do."

"Or they might have gotten you too," I reminded her. "Did you go to his office between his request to you that morning and when we found him?"

"I..." She looked down at her now empty wine glass. "I didn't."

I knew she was lying, but I didn't want to confront her and spook my only link to the murder's witness into running for the States. That she opened up to me even minimally gave me hope she would continue to do so as she came to trust me. "Do you remember anything else unusual about him or his behavior that day?"

"No, only that he was excited about getting the applications. He had a project on the side tracing the family records of known lycanthrope lines, and he was looking forward to putting it all together to see how the subjects' lines intersected with the ones we know about and to isolate another genetic marker to maybe figure out why Chronic Lycanthropy Syndrome fully expresses in some people but not in others." She shrugged. "That's all I can remember."

"I appreciate your coming to visit me today, but was it really necessary?"

"I needed to talk to you outside the Institute. I don't feel comfortable there anymore." She shuddered. "It's like I'm being watched."

I thought about the letter in the kitchen. "I know the feeling."

She stood, and I did as well. "Thank you for the wine," she said and held out her glass to me.

"My pleasure." Our fingertips brushed when she handed the crystal over, and again, I got the image of her as a wolf looking into a pool of water, not unlike where David and I had stopped and been shot at that afternoon.

She looked up at me with a smile she tucked away, and again, I wondered what she'd seen. It was unusual enough for such strong visual images to come through with scent, and for them to do so with touch puzzled me. Was it part of me coming into my full power?

"I should be going," she said.

I followed her to the front door. "Be careful," I told her. "You don't know who or what is out there watching."

With a quick nod, she walked to her car and went to the passenger side before sighing and going to the driver's side. She must not have been in the country that long if she was still trying to drive from the wrong side of the car. I hoped she would remember what side of the road to use.

After she left, I double-checked all my security measures to ensure nothing had been tampered with. All looked secure, and I took a hot shower. When I got out, I saw something scrawled in the mist on the mirror: 204, the number that had been scrawled at the edge of the photograph of my father's mangled corpse.

A chill chased away the heat from the shower, and I hesitated to wipe the fog from the rest of the mirror. Would another face besides my own stare back at me? I licked my lips and tasted salt. Tears?

I wiped the fog from the mirror, but what faced me wasn't my father's or even my face, but a scene from the past. It was the kitchen of my parents' flat in Lycan Village, where a lot of the Council members lived if their own houses were too far away.

"No, I'm not doing this," I said and turned to open the door. The knob stuck. "Dammit, the past is in the past. I have no desire to relive that day."

"Sometimes the past doesn't die." The voice that had spoken to me in the car and in the pub made the skin at the back of my neck tighten.

"No, I'm not going to come down," my seven-year-old voice said. It was the voice of a child simultaneously terrified and holding on to that last shred of hope that if he didn't come

down the stairs, his world wouldn't come crashing down on him, and he wouldn't have to grow up too soon. I closed my eyes and rested my head against the wood of the bathroom door, a lump in my throat.

"You can't avoid the bad things that happen forever." That voice was David Lachlan's, and although the words were harsh, the tone was gentle. I had forgotten he was there when the officer brought news of my father's death. I didn't have to turn around and look to remember the scene. My mother, her hands wrapped in her apron, slumped at the kitchen table with tear streaks on her face and looked into nothingness. David—now my mind filled him in—stood with a hand on her shoulder.

Footsteps came down the stairs, their pace hesitant and defiant, and seven-year-old me stood there, hands on hips, trying to pretend he wasn't crying. The two men looked at him with sympathy and a little admiration, I'd like to think, for his holding on to hope until the very last second. But he couldn't hold on to it forever, and he rushed to his mother, who clasped him to her, the most solid remnant of her lost husband.

The emotions rolled through me then, and I relived the moment when I was that little boy who, in an instant, had had to become a man—the desire for revenge on whoever had done this to my family and anger at the men who had brought the news. And beneath it all, a crushing grief and fear that my father would be disappointed in me and at my reaction.

"I was never disappointed in you. But you can't run from the danger I faced. That was my mistake."

I turned around. The only thing in the mirror that caught my attention was the dark hazel irises of my own frightened, angry eyes. I took a deep, shuddering breath and left the bathroom.

· · ·

I PUT David's letter in my fireproof safe in case he should want it back. It occurred to me I could phone him, but I didn't know what I would say aside from, "I wanted to make sure you didn't crash your car on your way home."

Then I thought about calling Selene, but that didn't seem right, either. First, she was lying to me, but my instincts told me she was in some sort of trouble. I needed to bide my time and get her to trust me before pushing her on it. Second, although female companionship would be welcome, I doubted I would be good company for her. The feelings from earlier had subsided except for a certain restless irritation, and I couldn't sit still enough to decide what to eat for dinner. Nothing sounded good, but I didn't want to go to the pub, come back smelling of smoke, and have to shower again. Finally, I busied myself putting together a meal of steak and greens.

After eating, I flipped through television channels but couldn't find anything interesting. My cell phone ringing, which typically annoyed me, was a welcome distraction.

"Gabriel?" The quaver in Lonna's voice was unusual enough to make me sit upright.

"What is it?"

"Something's wrong with Max."

"I'll be right there."

9

———

I arrived at their house in twenty minutes. The sun lay low on the horizon as a glowing orange ball, putting me in mind of videos showing sunset on the African savannah with the silhouettes of prey animals bounding to avoid predators. In our little world, we no longer knew who was the predator and who was the prey.

Lonna opened the door with Abby on her arm. The baby fussed and whimpered, no doubt picking up her mother's distress.

"What happened?" I asked.

"He came back from the Institute today looking just awful, like he had a fever. I made him lie down, and when I went to check on him, he wasn't breathing." She took a deep shuddering breath. "But he was still alive and talking."

I pushed by her into the house and darted to the stairs. "Why did you call me, not an ambulance?"

She followed me up. "He told me not to call the human doctors, only you."

"When did he tell you? How could he if he wasn't breathing?"

Tears ran down her cheeks, and she gestured to the closed door of one of the bedrooms. "It's the blood magic. I can tell he used it."

When I entered the room, Max sat on the edge of the bed. In the dim light from the bedside lamp, he looked deathly ill. At least he seemed to be breathing.

"What did you do?" I asked and stood what I hoped was a safe distance away. The world of wizards was a mystery to me, but I knew not to get too close to a wounded creature even if he was my friend.

He looked up at me and clutched his stomach. "I didn't do anything. The blood did it to me." He coughed, and a trickle of blood ran down his chin.

"What do you mean, it did it to you?"

"When we found LeConte. I had only worked with small quantities—that was going to be what I used in our method, just a few cc's to guide the reverse vector—but the volume of it there, it pulled something from me."

"That's why you were using the light to look for the murderer's footprints."

He nodded. "I didn't know what his blood did to me, and I felt normal soon after. Only Lonna could tell I was off."

"That was yesterday. Then we found the security guards."

"Yes, and it happened again, but not as much because they'd been bled out and moved. Then this evening, I found where they'd been killed, in the blood storage unit. There was blood everywhere, and it pulled the magic out of me, like a string attached to my gut."

"We need to get you to a healing wizard, or call one."

"No, they'll pull me from the Institute!"

"If you die or turn into whatever the last wizard to use blood magic did, you're not going to be of any help to anyone."

I didn't think he could go more pale, but he did. "Fine."

When I got out to the hallway, I found Lonna standing in

front of a door behind which a very angry Abby vented her feelings about being locked away. "I put her down so I could help you. Is he okay?"

"Do you know any of his wizard friends?" I asked. "A healer would be preferable."

"One step ahead of you," she said. "I called Arnold. He said he'd send someone."

"Arnold?"

She bit her lip. "He's hard to explain. Kind of a wizard investigator, but internationally."

The doorbell rang, and I moved toward the head of the stairs. Lonna tried to follow me, but I motioned her back.

"Calm the baby, I'll get the door and help them attend to Max."

"Thank you. You're a good friend."

I ran down the stairs and to the front hall. All I could see through the peephole was a wreath of mist. When I opened the door, the fog resolved into a mass of blonde curls so light they looked white. They framed a surprisingly young face with wide-set blue eyes.

"So you're the one with the blood magic contamination?" she asked, sounding surprised.

"No, my colleague upstairs is."

She sniffed. "Are you sure?"

"Yes. Please hurry."

She shook her head and sailed past me. The train of her light blue dress undulated over the carpeted floor.

"You wolves are always in a hurry, chasing this or that or the other. Is that what got poor Maxie into trouble?"

"Maxie?" Lonna asked from the top of the stairs. She held Abby again, who cooed when she saw the lady.

The mysterious woman paused for a moment to look at her. "Oh, she's just the image of her daddy, isn't she?"

Lonna raised an eyebrow. "Max is in there." She pointed to the bedroom I'd come out of. "You know him?"

The curls, which were all I could see, nodded. "We were in school together. Took different healing paths. I knew he'd need me someday. Now please wait downstairs. Not you, Wolf-man. I may need your help."

Lonna's face had an understandably skeptical expression, but she moved past her to descend the stairs. "Arnold vouched for you, so I'll believe you," she said over her shoulder. "Just please know, if you harm him, I will not be happy."

"Right." The woman's laugh reminded me of wind chimes. "I've heard you're a fan of evisceration."

"How...?"

"Tut, tut, my dear. Down the stairs you go. I'll answer all your questions after I attend to the patient."

I followed her into the room. Max sat where I'd left him, still doubled over and clutching his stomach.

"Reine," he said. "You still have the same aura."

"Yes, you always said it was hell when you had a hangover." She laughed again, and I relaxed a hair. Whatever she was—I knew she wasn't human—she had that effect. That Arnold guy knew some interesting creatures. She cleared off a space on the dresser and arranged some objects on it. I tried to see, but her billowing hair and dress hid them from me.

"Stand behind the bed, Wolf-man," she said.

"My name is—"

Max held up his hand. "Her kind doesn't need to know names unless it's absolutely necessary," he said through gritted teeth. "I have an exception because we went to school together."

She shook her head, and her curls seemed alive for a moment, like they had small fish darting through them. "You don't ever let me have any fun, and he's a handsome one. Are you ready for a cleansing?"

"What is your price?"

"Max," I said, "money is no object. Whatever it costs, I'll—"

He stopped me with a gesture again. "Shut the fuck up if you know what's good for you."

I shut up. Max was not a fan of cursing.

"Why is he even here?" he asked the woman.

"In case I needed some muscle. As for my price, you have a lovely wife and child. A life for a life?"

Her words spoken in a casual tone chilled me to my core. She spoke of lives as if they were Starbucks gift cards, and it finally got through my thick skull what she was—one of the Fey, possibly a changeling who'd been educated with the wizards and who had gone back to her realm after.

"Absolutely not! Your price is too high." His entire body shivered, and the wheeze in his next breath made my lungs tighten in sympathy.

She ran a hand over his brow. "You don't have much time. There was that opal necklace of your mother's I always admired. It sparkled so with fire and love."

"Fine," he said. "You may have that in exchange for healing me and showing me how to prevent this from happening again."

"Oh, that's two things you want from me." She shook her curls, and this time they seemed to hold a blizzard in them. "Are you sure about the baby? You know I'd bring you a good one in return. And your wife is young and healthy—you'll have plenty more."

"No, you may not have my child. You may have the earrings that go with the necklace."

"All right, but only because I like you," she said. "Now hold him still, Wolf-man."

"How would you like me to do that, Mistress?"

"Grab his wrists and hold them behind him."

"Do what she says," Max told me and placed his hands

behind him. Each small movement obviously pained him, and the cords stood out in his neck, but he remained silent when I grabbed and held his wrists.

With movement too fast for even my eyes, she shoved his head back and stuck a slick-looking black stick down his throat. His throat worked, and he struggled, but he didn't cry out. No doubt he wanted to avoid upsetting Lonna, and jealousy stabbed through my anxiety for him. Not because he had Lonna—we would never have been more than friends—but that he had someone he loved enough he would stifle his basest urges to protect from emotional hurt. My father had been like that with my mother, but that also meant he'd kept secrets from her.

The lady dug around with the stick and finally said, "Aha! Got you, you little nasty." She pulled out a dark blob that glowed with a sickly green light and put it in a leather satchel. Max coughed and fell backwards. I caught him and gently laid him on the bed.

"What was that?" I asked.

"Backlash booger," she said, the concept sounding profane coming from her lips. "Yes, that's what it's called. When you're untutored in powerful magic and you get caught in it, that can happen. It's like a fast-growing tumor."

Max's color crept back, but he still struggled to breathe.

"Now I have to detoxify him from its energy," she told me. "If I left him as he is, another would form. Hold him down and don't let go no matter what you see or feel."

"That sounds ominous."

"All in a day's work."

I helped Max to a sitting position and once again held his hands behind him. She put a hand on his forehead, and—

A torrent of icy glacial water, can't move or breathe or think, just hold hold hold.

I blinked, the after-echo of the water's roar ringing in my

ears, and the reverse image distorting my vision. Surprised not to be soaking wet, I looked down and saw I still held Max's hands. He shivered, but he breathed more easily.

"And that should do it," she said and moved backward. "You can let him go."

"Your grip is like iron," Max said, rubbing his wrists. "Are all of you that strong?"

I flexed my fingers, which felt stiff and cold like I'd been walking around in a blizzard without gloves while holding hands with an ice fairy, maybe Reine's cousin. "I don't know," was the only answer I could manage. "Isn't your wife?"

"She's strong enough," he said, and his half-grin told me he felt better. "As for your hands and anything else you may feel, you'll get your head straight in a few minutes. That kind of magic can throw you if you're not used to it."

I blew on my hands, which stung when the hot air hit them, and I flinched. "Seems like every kind of magic does something nasty."

"Spoken like a true wolf-man," the lady said. "Your kind has never trusted us. Probably for good reason." The look she gave me simultaneously beckoned and warned.

"Thank you," Max said. He stood and stumbled but found his balance back before I could grab him. "When can we start learning the precautions I need to use blood magic?"

"Why didn't you learn them before?" I asked. "It seems stupid not to."

He looked at the floor. "I didn't have access to someone who could teach me, and as I said, I was only using small quantities of it and followed the rules and requirements, such as they are. I didn't know that exposure to a lot of blood would pull the power out of me and corrupt me."

"He speaks the truth," the lady said. "It is a forbidden art for a reason. He knows the rules, but sometimes the spilled life force gets confused and bends or breaks them if the wizard doesn't know the subtleties of the art. It happened to one recently."

"That's why it needs to be studied, not forbidden." Max sat on the bed again. "Who knows how many others have been hurt by experimenting with this type of magic in what they thought were safe amounts?"

"Those politics belong to your kind, not mine." The lady had packed her tools in hidden pockets in her dress. "We can start in a few days when you've recovered. Until then, take it easy, make lots of love to your beautiful wife, and absolutely no magic use."

"That sounds like a reasonable prescription."

"Now the opals?"

I STEPPED out of the room so Max and Reine could complete their exchange and make their arrangements. Lonna sat at the kitchen table with Abby in a high chair beside her and fed her some sort of pureed fruit. My nose told me apricots. When Lonna saw me, she stood.

"Is he...?"

"He's fine, if a little weak. He'll be down in a few minutes. They're finishing up."

She sank to the chair. "Thank goodness."

I sat across the table from her so she wouldn't see my legs shiver. I still had cold flashes, and I hoped they'd subside. "Whatever you do, don't tell that woman your or Abby's names. She's not human."

"I gathered. She puts off some interesting energy. Cold."

"You have no idea."

Footsteps on the stairs told me the strange woman helped Max descend. Lonna stood and hesitated.

"Go on," I said. "I'll keep an eye on Abby."

"Thank you. She shouldn't go anywhere, but you never

know what babies will do if you leave them unattended. Especially that one."

With that vague warning, she left the room, and I took her seat by the high chair. I picked up the spoon, and the baby bounced in her seat.

"Oh, so you want more?" I asked.

She looked at me with big green eyes. She had a couple of smears of orange stuff on her cheek and in her hair, which was reddish blonde like her father's. I thought about feeding her, but had Lonna stopped because she felt the child had eaten enough? Having had no siblings and very little exposure to children, I didn't know what the protocol was for giving food to small people.

A wave of protectiveness for this little family swept over me, and I exhaled slowly to let the pressure out of my chest.

"A wolf needs a pack, my boy," my father said. I couldn't see him, but I knew he was there from the prickling at the back of my neck and the feeling that someone or something watched me over my shoulder.

Abby looked over my shoulder and giggled, reaching one small fist out and opening and closing it. An invisible force pried the spoon from my hand and dipped it in the jar of pureed apricot, then moved it to the baby's mouth, scooping the dribble from her chin and into her smacking lips. The spoon then came to rest in the jar.

"I did that with you once upon a time. You make things too complicated," the voice said, and with a swirl of cold air, the presence disappeared.

"Maximilian wasn't the only one touched by the blood magic," the white-haired lady murmured from the door.

I turned to face her and moved so my body was between her and the baby. "What do you mean, Lady?"

She shook her head. "That's for you to discover in your own time, Wolf-man. As for the babe, do not fret. She is safe from my kind for now. Do watch over this family. They straddle two worlds, which is a dangerous place to be, as you'll come to find out."

With those words, she disappeared. The spoon jumped out of the jar and clattered to the floor, and bright orange mush splattered everywhere.

10

When I woke the next morning, I wasn't sure if Max's illness and the fairy's visit had been a dream. After Reine had disappeared, I'd wiped the floor and left Lonna and Max to their discussion and baby. Max assured me they would be safe, and Lonna already had Wolf-Lonna, her psychic double, on the prowl. I wished I could say I felt more peaceful as I drove home in the late twilight knowing that Max was going to have some training in this dangerous magic he'd use. However, after having seen the toll it could take, I'd lost some confidence in his assurances that he knew exactly what he was doing. Had I pledged my support for the Institute prematurely based on Lonna's and Joanie's word without knowing enough about the lycanthropic reversal process itself? I'd trusted them based on their knowledge and my gut instinct.

Plus, the lady's warning to me to watch over them stuck with me, and I suspected worse was to come. This unease translated into me squinting at every shadow along the side of the road and watching my rearview mirror to make sure I wasn't being followed or stalked by something otherworldly, or that would aim silver arrows at me.

No ghosts visited me that night, and I woke from what I'd perceived to be a dreamless sleep. Detective Luke Garou didn't look nearly as well-rested when I arrived at his office at nine o'clock sharp. His eyes had dark circles under them accentuated by loose folds. "More baggage than a Pan Am flight," we'd say, back when Pan Am was a relevant airline.

I shook my head at that little intrusion from my past, but at least it was from my own past and no one else's. My father's ghost seemed to pull me in that direction. What else did he want me to see? I resisted that train of thought and reached to accept Garou's offered handshake.

"Feeling better, I suppose?" he asked with a barely concealed growl.

I ignored the challenge. "Yes, it's amazing how restorative a good night's sleep or two can be."

He glared at me but didn't respond to my barb. Instead, he said, "And you must then be coherent enough to give a statement as to how you sustained a concussion during your investigation. Lady Morena has cautioned me not to let any detail, however insignificant it seems, slip by me."

"How lovely of her to be so concerned for my welfare," I muttered. The detective was a canny one, I'd give him that. He remembered my excuse for withholding information from him two nights before and threw it back at me.

"I'm ready whenever you are, Investigator," he told me and bared his teeth in an almost smile that was a challenge.

"You do know that with some head injuries, you end up with memory loss," I said. "I'm afraid I can't remember anything that might be helpful to you."

"I'll be the judge of what's helpful." He tapped the eraser end of his pencil against the pad in front of him. "And what's suspicious. Such as your behavior, Investigator."

"Don't challenge me, Garou."

"I'm only doing my job, as you cautioned me to when we met at the Institute. As for why you won't answer my question, could it be that you're protecting someone?"

I stopped myself from changing my breathing pattern, shifting in my seat or doing any of the other nonverbal things that would tell him he'd hit home. "Trust me, I'd like whoever bashed me on the head to be punished for their crime, but I honestly didn't see who did it." There, that was enough of the truth that it would hopefully not come back to bite me later.

"They snuck up behind you? Where?"

"In the alley behind the West Port Inn," I told him. "I didn't realize he was there until he bashed me."

"And you're sure it was a man."

"There aren't many women who can hold me immobile like that."

He raised his eyebrows. "Did he talk to you, say anything?"

"No, he was silent."

"Was anything stolen?"

"Only my pride." It occurred to me that it would have been easier to say my wallet had been, but he would've then asked about me filing a report of a robbery, and I preferred to lie as little as possible. In my experience, lying was more trouble than it was worth and always came back to bite me in the ass.

"Now if you're done with your questioning," I said, "I'm going to resume my role of Investigator and ask about what you've found so far. I read your preliminary report, and you seem to have been adequately thorough with the crime scene."

Garou pinched the bridge of his nose. "It's only been two days. I'm still waiting for the evidence the forensics team gathered at the scene to be processed. Both scenes," he said. "Doctor Fortuna found the closet where the security guards had been butchered last night."

"Excellent," I said, not giving away that I already knew Max had found it and had suffered for it. "I'm sure your people are sorting through it as we speak."

"Don't patronize me, Investigator. You have secrets like anyone else. I know you were at Doctor Fortuna's house last night and that you had a visitor of a supernatural nature."

"And how did you know that?"

"We have someone following the wizard," he told me through gritted teeth. "Not by my orders, but by those of someone above me."

"Interesting." Since he supposedly reported directly to me, anyone above him and me would have to be on the Council.

"Is there some problem with the wizard?" He referred to Max as Reine had talked about Max's family, as more of a curious object than a person.

"He should be fine."

"You didn't answer my question, Investigator." He pointed the pencil at me.

"The wizard Maximilian and all that concerns him is classified Institute business."

"And if you had allowed me more information about the Institute and the controversial nature of its operations from the start, Otis LeConte might not have been murdered. We would have had someone patrolling in and around the grounds." He stood and leaned forward, his palms on the table. "Sometimes secrets can kill, Investigator. I thought you and I were on the same side with trying to expose them for the protection of the Council and all of wolfkind."

"Have a seat, Detective. It's too early for your dramatics."

He sat and rubbed a hand over his face.

"When was the last time you slept?" I asked. The man's behavior at the Institute had seemed odd, especially his inviting Selene to the Solstice ceilidh.

He waved his hand. "The sun is up late, and so am I. I cannot sleep when the sky is light and birds are singing, particularly when something is on my mind like a potentially key witness withholding information."

"They do make blackout curtains and sound-blocking devices."

"I am too sensitive to the sun being out regardless of those things," he said.

I decided to move on. "Summarize what you've got for me so far, and I'll leave you alone."

"As I mentioned, I do not have anything to share about the evidence we collected, but I do have this." He opened a file. "Two groups have come forward to claim the murder."

"Wait, how did they know?"

He pulled a printed article from the Lycan Crier, the lycanthrope news site, detailing the murders.

"This was supposed to have been kept from the press."

He ran a thumb and forefinger over his eyes. "It was. We have a leak, I suspect in the forensics department. It's being looked into."

I kicked myself for being so preoccupied with other Council business and putting out Institute-related fires that I hadn't bothered to look at the news, now delivered to us lycanthropes through encrypted emails with a password. "The groups?"

"Two guesses."

"The Purists and the Young Bloods," I said, thinking of what David Lachlan had told me at the pub. "They were on my list to interview, anyway."

He nodded. "I will take the Young Bloods if you tackle the Purists," Garou said. "You, being a Council member, have easier access to Cora and Bartholomew Campbell."

"Theoretically." I suspected Cora had been one of the votes against me the day before.

He shook his head. "You have a better chance of getting her to talk than I do."

"You could bring her and Bartholomew in for a statement.

The Purists taking credit for the attack warrant their interrogation."

"I would prefer for them not to be hostile when I speak with them. They are more likely to treat the Council Investigator amicably than a humble detective."

The edge of frustration in his voice kept me from arguing, and I understood what he meant. In spite of their supposedly "love yourself no matter who you are" position, Cora and Bartholomew Campbell could out-snob most of the English when it came to social class consciousness, and that was even beyond our lycanthropic tendency to define everyone in terms of where they stood in the hierarchy. I still ranked above Garou when it came to class and old blood, even though I was considered a junior Council member.

"Fine, I'll talk to them, and you can tackle the Young Bloods. Do you know who their leaders are?"

He snorted. "Of course. I have the name of their Facebook page administrator. I will start there and report back to you."

"Of course there's a Facebook page. Idiots."

"We are monitoring it. Don't be concerned—it looks like a typical LARPing organization, except instead of live-action role playing, they engage in live-action complaining about being werewolves. It's rather amusing, actually—they drive the humans crazy."

"Good. I'll let you know if Cora and Bartholomew have anything interesting to say. Oh, and I'm going to talk to Lonna and Max about the applications they'd received for the program today."

"I trust you will share what they tell you if it impacts the investigation," he said, but his tone and the expression on his face conveyed doubt that he could trust me.

"I take my role as Council Investigator seriously, Garou. I would not willingly stand in the way of your job as detective." *At least only to the extent that I'm delaying you going after Selene.*

"It is the unintentional obstruction that concerns me more, Investigator." He stood and held out a hand.

I stood and gave it a hearty shake. "Then you'll just have to trust my judgment."

"Right. Innocent until proven guilty, as the Americans say."

With those words, he walked out of his office and left me to show myself out. I respected his motivation to be thorough, and as I walked out of the small office building that served as the Lycanthrope Police Station—labeled as the Council Offices to throw off the humans—I reminded myself not to be angry with him for doing his job. I also appreciated how he was letting me tackle the Institute contacts in spite of there being a reason for me not to be objective around them, namely the Institute being my pet project, as David had hinted.

That reminded me—he had a story to finish. I called and left him a voicemail that I'd like to meet for lunch, if possible, and headed to the Institute to talk to Lonna. I also called Laura and had her set up something with Cora and Bartholomew Campbell for the afternoon, if she could manage it.

THE YELLOW AND blue-marked police car stood as an obvious reminder in front of the Institute that all was not well. When I'd come on Tuesday, it had been with optimism. On Tuesday night, trepidation. Now on Thursday, it was with resignation that I pulled my car into one of the Visitor parking spots.

The patrolman on duty let me into the empty reception area. I didn't wait long before Lonna appeared behind the window.

"The officer told me you were here," she said. "I'll buzz you through."

She led me through the hallways and up the stairs to Max's office. She unlocked the door, and when we entered, I couldn't help but notice the office resembled that of most physicians, but as I would have expected from Max, the medical textbooks, other references, and papers stood in precision arrangement.

The only messy spot was on the desk, where it looked like Lonna had been sorting through papers. "Garou's men are still processing mine, and since Max is still at home recovering, here I am. Coffee?"

"No, thanks." My interview with Garou had left me sufficiently wound up. We sat, her behind her desk and me in front of it. "How is Max?"

"He's doing well. His friend gave him some interesting instructions as to how he should get well, and I'm..." She blushed, an unusual expression for her.

"You must be exhausted," I said with as straight a face as I could muster. "If only medical doctors prescribed that sort of thing."

"I'm definitely worn out." She bit her lip over her smile and looked around. "Not that I should be discussing this with a proper Scottish gentleman in my husband's office."

I waved away her concern. "I was there when Reine told him, so don't worry about it. Since when do you become nervous about what we talk about? You know you can tell me anything."

"Can I?" Her perfectly arched brows drew together. "Things have changed, Gabriel. What started out as an interesting project and the professional challenge I've been craving has turned into a nightmare, and my husband, the only man I've ever truly loved, is at risk. I try not to be irrational, but you're the one behind us being here and the Institute in general."

"I'm trying to fix it for you, Lonna." I had the image of sitting in front of her with hat in hand—there was that damn imaginary hat again—asking for forgiveness.

"I'm afraid there is no fixing it." She toyed with a pen on the desk, and a tear splashed on the back of her hand. "Three men are dead, another—Max—is injured, and I don't know what poor Selene is going through. I thought she and Otis had some sort of relationship, but now I'm not sure."

I shifted in my seat. Her resigned expression reminded me of the one my mother wore in the weeks after we'd been informed of my father's death. "Then let's start there. If I can't fix this for you, at the very least I have to solve it. Not just for you, but for everyone involved."

She wiped the tears from her eyes. "What do you want to know?"

"Before I continue, I need to warn you that some of this may be shared with Detective Garou, but I promise to be discreet."

"I understand. Do what you have to do. I trust you to balance the secrets necessary for the function of the Institute with the information needed to solve Otis's murder."

"Very well. Tell me about the relationship between him and Selene. Actually, tell me about them in general, and then their relationship."

Lonna leaned back and folded her hands. One index finger moved as she thought. "They were both recruits from Joanie and Iain. Otis was from New York and had impeccable recommendations. He'd worked with Joanie as a graduate student and then did a summer internship with Iain, helping him with the evidence for the Cabal-Hippocrates case, so Iain felt he would be a good fit on the team, particularly since he had an understanding of Chronic Lycanthropy Syndrome from both the inherited perspective and from that of those who were infected."

I took out my notebook and jotted down some information. "So he could have made enemies while he worked with Iain on the case. As I recall, those Cabal-Hippocrates blokes were not to be messed with lightly."

She met my eyes, and I saw the shared memory of being captured and forced through chemical means to change. The echo of those screams lurked at the edges of my dreams, and sometimes I woke from a nightmare of being back there, captive and helpless as I was experimented on. It had happened just after Lonna had changed for the first time, so for her, the memories had been locked away until an incident forced her to remember. I'd never lost them but wished I had.

She shook her head as though to dislodge the recollections and continued, "If Otis did have enemies, Iain didn't mention them. Maybe he didn't know about them."

"He has some family, though. Was he close to them?"

"It's hard to tell. He didn't talk about them much, but a lot of guys don't. I had the impression he'd lived with them while still in the States."

"I'll ask if he'd ever received threats that they knew of. They've been informed, correct?"

"Yes." Lonna looked at her hands. "I can't imagine the horror of finding out your child has been murdered. Iain told them since he'd met them."

"He has his good moments," I said.

"Yes, he has a few."

"And Selene?" I asked before she pursued the Iain line of discussion.

"She's from Georgia. You probably picked up on the Southern accent, although it's faint. She was a CLS recessive until she got the viral vector in a tainted flu vaccine. She was already a psychologist and wanted to use her experience to help others adjust to the major life change that comes with CLS."

It had been a part of my life since early adolescence, so I always had to remind myself what an effect becoming a lycanthrope would have on an established adult existence. "And then help them adjust to not having it anymore?"

"In her interview, she likened it to gastric bypass surgery. People may recognize that letting go of this aspect of themselves would work better for them, but it comes with consequences that may be difficult to adjust to. You and I both know it's a blessing and a curse."

I nodded. "And she has a brother?"

"Yes, and a mother and stepfather. She never said anything about her biological father, but I got the impression he's been out of the picture since she and her brother were children."

"What of the relationship between her and LeConte?"

Lonna bit her lip. "They spent a lot of time together, but I don't know if that's because the four of us were the core team here, and Max and I naturally paired off due to our relationship. They were both Americans in a foreign country, so it made sense. They seemed to enjoy each other's company."

"Did you observe any kind of behavior to indicate that they were more than friendly colleagues?"

"Maybe that they were friends, but that's it. I had a talk with Selene about it just in case, and she denied anything inappropriate."

Lonna's words were consistent with what Selene had told me, but I still felt like I missed something.

"Does Selene have any other friends or acquaintances here that you know of?"

"No, but I try not to be too involved in my employees' personal lives. They aren't allowed to have visitors here at the Institute for confidentiality and security reasons, so I wouldn't know of her social circle. She's an attractive young woman, so it wouldn't surprise me if she's made friends since being here."

With friends like hers... "And how long have she and Otis been here?"

"For a few months." Lonna shook her head. "If I'd known what would happen..."

I covered her hand with mine. "You couldn't have. None of us could."

I sat back just before someone knocked on the door.

"Lonna?" Selene asked. Her eyes widened when she saw

me. "Oh, so that's your car out front. I thought I recognized it from the other day. Did you bring her?"

"Who?" asked Lonna.

"Someone who calls herself Reyna but won't give a last name. She says it's about something Max asked her to do." Her next words made my heart drop. "And Lady Morena is here to see you, Lonna."

11

———

"Don't talk to her without insisting I be present," I said to Lonna. "Damn, her timing couldn't be worse."

"Whose timing, Gabriel?" Morena barged into the office, which suddenly felt like it was half as large. "Thank you, girl," she said to Selene, who stepped back.

"That is Doctor Rial," I said through clenched teeth. "She's a valuable member of the team here."

"Oh." Morena looked her up and down. "Oh! You're Selene Rial. I can see why Gabriel is so taken with you. I could never understand why he was attracted to scientist types. What he needs is a little wife to cook and clean for him, not look through microscopes and work later than he does."

Selene's startled gaze met mine at the same time the heat slammed into my cheeks. "You're speaking without having all the information, Morena, which you always caution those of us on the Council not to do."

"Your schoolboy blush says you doth protest too much." She turned to Selene. "He's right, though. Our Gabriel is a smart one, isn't he? Don't let him get away if you're interested—

most women don't hold his attention long. Okay, you may go. Shoo, shoo."

With one more bemused glance at me, Selene shoo'ed and closed the door after her. Lonna bit her lip, her topaz eyes bright with suppressed laughter, but I didn't find the situation funny. I glowered at my Council head, rank and hierarchy be damned.

"All right, Morena. I've known you a long time. What's with the friendly 'our Gabriel' act?"

Her features snapped back into their typical severe expression, and Lonna narrowed her eyes.

"Yes, Lady Morena, to what do we owe the pleasure of your visit?"

Now Morena did something outside of her usual behavioral repertoire—she pinched the bridge of her nose. "I'm here to personally see how the investigation is progressing. The Council has some doubt that you have the situation under control, Gabriel."

"The Council or two of its members?"

"Make your best guess."

Here was that game again. "Dimitri and Cora?" I asked. "Not that it matters much who it is. Tell them I can't make Garou process the evidence faster, but we do have a couple of leads."

"Yes, yes, I know the Young Bloods and Purists have come forward to claim the murders, but do you think they're responsible?"

I wondered at her strategy—why were we having this conversation in front of Lonna, and what was the true reason for her being here? I chose my words carefully. "I won't know until I talk to them. I have another lead, but I'm still pursuing it," I said, thinking of Selene's "friend" at the pub. The way Selene had talked, he had been at the murder scene. Although I didn't think he'd done it—if he was a killer, he would have finished me off behind the West Port Inn—I knew he must have seen something. The problem was getting to him without spooking Selene or putting her in danger. Maybe Morena's kidding would cause her to let down her guard with me.

"Care to share with the class?" Morena asked. Lonna coughed, probably to hide a laugh.

"It's delicate."

Morena turned to Lonna. "Well, Mrs. Marconi-Fortuna, give me a tour so I can tell the others I've checked things out thoroughly."

"There's not much to see, unfortunately," Lonna said. "It's a typical medical facility with offices, patient rooms, labs, and equipment."

"What about the applications for the first batch of test subjects?" I asked.

Lonna raised her eyebrows at me, and I guessed there was something she needed to tell me, but which Morena didn't need to know. "We're still processing them. There's a lot of information in each of them. Besides, it's confidential medical information."

"Please," Morena scoffed, her tone sarcastic, not pleading. "Remember, this is a special case, and you're outside the normal rules and jurisdiction for protection of health information. I'd like to see them."

"I'm afraid that's not possible."

"Why not?"

"That's proprietary information."

"No, the proprietary information is what you're going to do to cure people of their lycanthropy. The subjects are not."

Lonna fidgeted with the pen again and looked at me imploringly. I understood how she felt—Morena always denied having wizard ancestry, but she was able to put incredible emotional pressure on the people she interrogated.

I decided to intervene. "Let's allow them some more time to

process the charts, and then they can prepare a report." *Because nothing entices a bureaucrat like the promise of a report.*

"Very well, then, you may now show me around Mrs. Marconi-Fortuna."

"If you would give me a moment with Gabriel," Lonna said. "We need to finish our meeting. I'm sure Selene will be happy to show you around."

I had to admire Lonna for standing up to Morena.

"There's something you need to know about the application files," Lonna said after she'd called Selene to come collect Morena and the two of them had left for their tour.

"Is this office warded?" I asked. "We can hear through walls to a certain distance."

"Oh? I wasn't aware of that. Is that only those of you who are born with CLS or all of us?"

"Apparently the development of our abilities isn't as straightforward as I'd thought. We're dealing with a strange mix of science and legend, and I'm still sorting out what's what."

She nodded. "I'd appreciate any information you can give me. If there are different stages to lycanthrope development beyond the initial change and adjustment, it could impact our process."

I hadn't thought of that, but I also doubted any vaccine lycanthropes would be at a stage of development where it would be a problem, all of them having been changed in the last two years or so.

"Right. About those applications."

Lonna bit her lip. "I can show you most of them, but one's missing."

"They're supposed to be electronic."

"I'm aware of that. We got them, and I printed them all out, but the sixth was stolen from my office on Tuesday night."

"And the original uploaded copies?"

"I'm getting to that. When I went to download it again, it

was corrupted. Iain is working on it from his end, as are we, but..." She turned her hands palm-up.

"I see. And there was no scent to suggest who might have been here, killed the security guards, and stolen the file."

"None."

"That suggests someone different from whoever killed LeConte. By the way, may I see his office? Is Garou finished with it?"

"No, he said to leave it alone until they've processed the evidence in case they need to follow up on anything or gather more."

"That's fine, I'll—oh no."

"What?"

I'd just remembered my initial encounter with Selene that morning. "Reine is here to do something Max asked her to do. I bet it has something to do with the blood. I need to find her." I stood. "Do you know where the security guards were killed? She'll either be there or in LeConte's office."

"They were killed downstairs in the blood storage lab before being moved to the CT room." She shuddered. "Somehow all the vials exploded. It looked like something out of a horror movie."

"Whose blood have you gathered?"

"It was a project of Otis's. He asked for us and other lycanthropes to volunteer samples for genetic analysis. He'd even contacted the Council, but I don't know if any of them came through."

I vaguely remembered something about the request, but I was away on assignment in France at the time. "Was any of yours down there?"

The look she gave me called me stupid and some other things lost in translation, but I got the gist. "No, I don't give my blood to anyone, not after what happened at the wizard compound."

I nodded. "I don't blame you, although there shouldn't be anyone practicing blood magic beyond what's happening here."

"As far as we know."

"I need a list of the people he collected samples from."

"The paper copy was in his office, and Garou has his laptop. We haven't been able to determine what's missing from his files since we can't get in there."

The situation got worse with every piece of information, but I could only handle one thing at a time. "I can't do anything about that right now, but I need to get to Reine before she corrupts any possible evidence. I'll check LeConte's office, and you go to the lab. Call my mobile if you find her, and I'll do the same."

"Okay, but it might take a minute for me to get down there, see if she's in the lab, and get back up to the first floor. There's no signal down in the vault."

I HOPED Selene had the good sense to steer Morena away from the crime scenes during their tour. Knowing that some Council members had donated blood for genetic research added a new level of pressure and scrutiny for me to figure out who was behind all this, and if there was more than one culprit. What Lonna had told me about the lab chilled me in particular—it sounded like there was magic involved, which meant a wizard. When wizards went rogue, bad things happened, as Lonna had experienced, and blood could be used to control.

LeConte's office was locked up tight, and I couldn't smell anyone in there, even beyond the overpowering stench of clotted and dried blood. I told my stomach to stop turning, although it wasn't surprising since I had an inner predator, not an inner scavenger. I'd heard tales of were-hyenas but never had the desire to meet one.

Not here, I texted Lonna and headed toward the stairs.

She's down here, the reply said.

The last time I'd approached the basement, it had been from the other set of stairs, so it took me a moment to orient myself to where the CT machine room was. Lonna met me at the vault door.

"This way," she said. "I tried to stop her, but she said she would only talk to you."

"What is she doing?"

"I have no idea."

The scent of blood led me to the blood storage lab, which was about the size of a large walk-in closet. The door stood open, and it looked like a modern art painting with solid reddish-brown splotches in the middle and splashes and spots of it above and below. The light inside came not from the fluorescent fixture on the ceiling, but from Reine herself. She glowed white, and her curls seemed to blow in a breeze only she could feel. A static sensation emanated from her, and all of the small hairs on my body stood on end. I shifted to see if I could stop the distracting tingling sensations on my most private parts.

"Reine, Milady?" I asked quietly.

She un-illuminated, leaving a black shadow in my vision where she'd been. Before she moved, she looked like a photo negative of herself—dark and sinister—and I suspected it was to remind me how powerful she was and that I needed to keep her on my side, like getting the Fey to do anything they didn't want to do was possible or advisable.

"Ah, Wolf-man, you've arrived. I thought it wouldn't take you long. But why did you bring her? I told her I only wanted to deal with you."

The way she said "her" indicated Lonna might be in trouble if she stayed. She got the hint.

"I'll be in my *husband's* office if you need me," Lonna said with a significant look at Reine. Then she strolled off.

I took a deep breath to still the anxiety in my gut. Although Lonna was powerful in her own right with her wizard and werewolf blood, I doubted she'd win a head-to-head contest with Reine. I would have to warn Max that tension brewed between the two women.

"To what do we owe the pleasure of your visit?" I asked once we were alone.

Reine snapped her fingers, and the overhead light came on. Refrigerated cabinets stood along the walls. Most of them held empty metal racks behind intact glass doors. The racks in the cabinets to the left lay at awkward angles, and shards of glass from the shattered doors sparkled under the light. The dried blood made the white doors and metal counter look rusted, and she stood about an inch off the floor so her white slippers wouldn't touch the flaky black mess. Again, my stomach turned, and I told it to still, but the black and white photograph of my father's body blown to bits forced its way into my memory. As a child, my imagination had colored it more vividly than the lurid brightness Technicolor had brought to the movies.

"When you build something to look like a castle, you can expect unpleasant things to happen in the dungeon," Reine said. She floated out of the lab and stood beside me, her feet on the ground. "And the resemblance to Wolfsheim's castle is uncanny. I had no trouble finding my way around."

"Wolfsheim?" I asked. "I've heard that name. Was his castle in Germany or Austria?"

"No," she said. "It was just a few miles from here. The ruins are still out in the countryside."

"Why was there a—you know what, never mind. What is the purpose of your visit?" I knew that her kind would reveal their motives in their own time, but with Morena wandering around—and I had no doubt she would bully Selene into taking her places she didn't need to go—our time was limited.

"Tell me what you notice, and then I'll reveal what I see," she said.

I forced myself to study the scene objectively and not with the sense that the blood inside had belonged to two people who were now dead and possibly to many more who were still alive but likely in danger now.

"The door is interesting because although there are splashes of blood, there are no drips, like they landed there and dried instantly. Also the color. The blood should have darkened by now in this humidity."

"Ah, very good, Wolf-man. What else?"

"It's difficult to tell without the bodies, but it seems the vials to the left exploded with enough force to take the doors with them, but I would need to see the pattern of wounds to confirm the direction the glass shattered. I don't recall seeing scratches or other marks on the guards' skin."

"Good, so you're not assuming the blood in the cabinets exploded, broke the glass, and killed the guards."

"No, although I feel that might be a likely scenario. What could make the blood do that?"

"Magic," she said, as though it was obvious.

"Magic," I repeated. "Tell me what you see."

"Like you, I noticed the lack of drips on the door, like there was something that congealed and preserved the blood right away." She gestured to the cabinets. "The blood is a chorus, each person's sings with its own tone and melody that says where it came from and what it is."

"It sounds like you're hearing the DNA."

"Whatever you want to call it. The blood from the two guards—a double bass line, boringly human, but faint like it was stifled before it was spilled. As for what's in the cabinets, it is theirs as well." She looked at me. "There are no others. Once your detective Garou does his analysis, he will find that the blood exploded outward from the guards in a directed manner, destroying the empty vials in the cabinet."

"What can make a man's body explode, especially in only one direction from the throat?"

She looked up at me with an expression of pity. "There are more things in Heaven and on Earth, Horatio..."

"A Fey who quotes Shakespeare. Be still my heart."

She laughed her wind-chime laugh. "It's more interesting than saying you don't want to know."

"But I do want to know."

She gestured to the mess. "Max could have told you. Blood magic has many forms. Some can use it to control. Others to destroy. And as for the quote, William was a dear."

"So you're older than you look."

"As are you. And we both have our secrets. You just don't know as many of yours. Now leave me. I will seal the blood so that it won't hurt poor Maximilian again, and I'll do the same upstairs."

"Could you wait until our detective finishes what he needs to do?"

"No, it is necessary now. Sealing the blood will allow it to rest, which will allow the spirits attached to it to be at peace if nothing else stands in their way. Plus, I need to remove the contamination from Max's wards around the building and land —his using blood magic, even in small amounts, damaged the spells and allowed the intruders to get in. Nothing I do will interfere with the detective's work."

"I trust you," I said, realizing I did.

"Oh, do you?" She flashed me a wicked grin, and before I realized her intention, she pulled my head to hers and kissed me on the lips. She tasted of honeysuckle and sweet wine, and the passion she ignited flowed through me in golden waves. The static came back, and I pulled her to me to quell the tingling that became a burning need.

I barely heard Selene's "Gabriel, oh!" before Reine pushed me away with a mischievous laugh.

"That'll teach you," she said. "Remember, my kind is never to be trusted. Nor are most others." With a chuckle that lingered in the air, she disappeared, and I turned to face Selene.

12

"*Don't be a coward, Son,*" a ghostly voice said.

"I'm not," I replied through clenched teeth. It was embarrassing enough to have been caught by Selene, who stood at the end of the hallway, her mouth open, one hand over it. Her blue eyes were so wide I could see the whites clearly. But that the specter who was likely my father had also found me with my hand in the Fey cookie jar burned any fear I might have had of him away.

"What. The hell. Is that?" Selene asked and pointed a trembling finger over my left shoulder.

I turned but couldn't see anything other than the blood-splotched door.

"Tell me what you see," I said. I clenched a fist to give my frustration somewhere to go—why could I only hear and not see him?

She backed up one shaky step. "It's a man. A bloody man. In uniform, maybe second World War."

"I'm going to come toward you slowly. Tell me if he follows."

"No, no Gabriel, please stay there. It obviously wants you, not me."

"What if I told you he's not dangerous? He's..." I took a deep breath. "He's my father, and I'm trying to find out what happened to him. You're right about the uniform—he died in World War Two."

A chill breeze stirred my hair and turned my cheeks cold. Then the relative warmth of the basement hallway returned.

"He's gone," she said and sagged against the wall.

Remembering her tendency to faint, I hurried toward her, but she waved me away. I stopped a few feet from her.

"Don't worry about me," she said. "I'm fine, just fine. It's not like I can get my blood warmed by a white-gold fairy, and I don't have any ghostly parents following me around."

I rubbed the back of my neck to release the tension from my jaw clenching, a stress habit I'd never managed to break. "I was hoping you hadn't seen that."

"The woman practically glows, Gabriel. Actually, she does glow. How was I going to miss it?" Then she stopped and studied me. "But why would you care if I saw it or not? It's not like you and I have a relationship where it would matter."

Damn these Americans and their directness. But this was a side of her I hadn't seen, and I stepped closer, fascinated by the emotion sparkling in her eyes. *Could she be jealous?* My mind ticked through the potential ramifications and how I could use them to my advantage to find her scar-faced friend.

"We obviously have some things to discuss," I said and tucked a copper strand behind her ear.

She stepped back and narrowed her eyes. "Yes, we do, but not like you think."

"Then perhaps you would allow me to take you to dinner?" I turned up the Scottish charm again. "We could clarify the nature of whatever this is between us and share what we know about LeConte's death."

"I've already told you everything."

Again, I decided the less I gave away, the better. Might as

well make her wonder. "I have a few more questions to ask you, but I'd prefer not to do it here. These walls have ears."

A shudder accompanied the frightened glance she darted over my shoulder. "And god knows what else."

"Right. Dinner tonight?"

"Tomorrow," she said. "I've got plans tonight."

"Tomorrow is the Solstice. You told the detective you had plans."

"They fell through. I was thinking you could take me to the ceilidh."

"Being in that crowd will make it difficult to talk," I said, "especially about our unusual situation."

"I'll feel safer with people around. Let's see how the evening goes, and we can decide from there."

"Fair enough. I'll pick you up at six?"

"Fine. My address is in the file you no doubt have."

She turned and stalked down the hall. I didn't bother to stop the grin that broke out on my face—*she was jealous!* I'd have to thank Reine the next time I saw her, which hopefully wouldn't be soon. She'd reminded me all too clearly that fairies were trouble with a capital T.

When I reached the first floor, my phone buzzed with several messages and reminders—Laura had come through for me, as always, and it was time to go meet Cora Campbell, fellow Council member and the wife of the Lycanthrope Purist cult leader.

"I took the liberty of having the cook prepare a light lunch for us," Cora told me when I arrived at her estate and her butler took my raincoat. We skipped the cheek sniff—neither of us enjoyed the other's company, so we minimized contact. She maintained that having a lot of property due to her own wealth and not from organization funds kept them from being a real cult, but I didn't buy it. Her charismatic husband didn't mind the label, and indeed, he flaunted his ability to be a thorn in the Council's side through his wife's influence.

"Where is your husband?" I asked once it became apparent Bartholomew Campbell was nowhere in sight.

"He got called into Headquarters for a meeting, but he said you're welcome to stop by after we talk."

Cora Campbell looked late middle-aged, which meant she was at least ninety, perhaps older. She wore a dark blue dress that clung to her ample curves, and her dark hair didn't show any gray, although she had some laugh lines at the corners of her eyes and mouth.

"Dreadful business at the Institute," she said once we were seated and warmed our hands with delicate china cups of tea.

"You do cut right to the chase," I told her. "And of course you know why I'm here. The Lycan Crier got a letter from someone in your organization claiming responsibility for the murder of Otis LeConte."

She shook her head and placed her teacup on the saucer. "I can't say who sent the letter—how would I know?—but I can assure you, no Purist would do something as messy as murder a human in cold blood. We take our gift as predators seriously, but we do not act like common animals. There are other ways to eliminate problems."

"Oh?"

Lunch arrived on covered silver trays, which uniformed staff removed with a flourish. Rare tuna sat on a bed of greens, and a side plate held lemon, but no dressing. *Great...* Cora was on a diet again, which likely meant the first part of the next Council meeting would be spent listening to her extolling it and trying to get everyone else to join her in doing it. I bit my tongue before I asked if she intended to remove me by starving me to death.

"Politics, Gabriel. Words are much more effective in

removing rivals than is violence. You do lack a certain subtleness, you know. I've often said so to Morena."

"And what has she said in return?"

"You're still young and have a lot to learn. Although we're not so far apart in age, you and I. And you have a pretty face to go with your nice body."

The look she gave me dialed the atmosphere up from moderately awkward to severely so. Mindful that she might be playing the game she'd just described, I chose the course of avoidance and moved on with my questioning.

"Tell me your whereabouts on Tuesday morning."

She nodded. "I was here getting ready to host a Purists Ladies' Luncheon. You can ask any of the staff."

"Right, I'm sure they'll all vouch for your alibi. And your husband?"

"He was at the headquarters. I'll refer you to his staff. Surely you don't think one of us would have done such a foul deed?"

"Of course not." But I could get a warrant to look at telephone records and search emails. "However, as the leader of an organization claiming responsibility—"

"Which we are not. Claiming responsibility, that is. As I said, I cannot fathom why anyone from the Purists would do that. Murdering humans goes against our core philosophy of treating our lycanthropy as a gift and using it responsibly to show our kind that they need not be afraid of the urges, which can be channeled into more productive means."

"Like hunting on lands that aren't yours," I couldn't resist saying. A case had come before the Council the previous year.

She dismissed my challenge with the same airiness she'd exhibited when she'd paid the trespassing fine. "The forest was wild long before humans came around with their petty sense of ownership."

I doubted she'd take so kindly to someone hunting her game on her property, but I didn't want to antagonize her.

"Is there anyone within the Purists who might be holding a grudge, someone who would want to make you look bad?"

She tapped the tines of her fork against her lips. "None that come immediately to mind. We're blessed with loyal organization members and staff for the most part. You'll have to ask Bartholomew if he's gotten any complaints from the Headquarters employees."

"I'll do that."

"As for anyone outside the organization, we do have many enemies. Again, you'll have to get it from Bartholomew, but we've compiled a list of those who have threatened or otherwise been unpleasant to us."

"Thank you," I said. I didn't expect that list to be useful—the Purists weren't very popular outside their own little circles—but maybe it would have some overlap with someone else.

"And now for some sparkling water with lime to help cleanse us of impurities." Cora signaled to the butler, who served us tall glasses. My stomach growled when I smelled the lime he squeezed into the water.

"Ah, Gabriel, you men do have all the luck with metabolism," Cora told me.

NOT HAVING HEARD BACK from David about lunch, I stopped at a pastry shop in the little town between Cora's estate and the Purist Headquarters for a meat pie. As much as the cult might want to embrace their animal sides, Cora might find it unpleasant when they rebelled in hunger, at least if that was how they were all eating these days. Not that I had a problem with fish, but I needed more than scraps not to feel hungry. Yes, if past patterns held, we were going to get a diet lecture at the next Lycanthrope Council meeting. If the Council was a family, Cora was the crazy aunt who insisted everyone listen to her latest fad.

In spite of our long lives with points of connection, Bartholomew Campbell and I had rarely met, and I couldn't remember what the man looked like in person aside from slick and untrustworthy. I pulled up pictures from his appearances at public events on my phone as I ate my snack to try to jog my memory. Finally, I found a good one with enough resolution it wouldn't pixilate when I zoomed in. It showed Bartholomew and Cora at a charity event the year before. She wore a black dress and a somber expression, but he was all big teeth and confidence. Like her, he had wavy dark hair that he allowed to grow thick and full as a sign of virility. Unlike her, he'd not aged much, looking about forty or so to her late forties/early fifties appearance. I couldn't remember the year they married, a date that would likely be adjusted for the press so as not to give away their long life spans. That he had allowed himself to be photographed so much indicated the extent of his ego. In spite of the human world being aware of Chronic Lycanthropy Syndrome as a psychological disorder of impulsivity, they weren't aware of us as werewolves. And that was how we tried to keep it.

When I arrived at PHQ, the headquarters for the Purist business/cult, I was surprised to see the parking lot almost empty. Was it a holiday?

"Most of the company has Solstice week off," the pretty young secretary explained to me when I remarked on how quiet it was. She tucked her dark brown curls behind her ears, which sparkled with diamond stud earrings. "We have a retreat center in the Hebrides that they go to for learning and reflection on this sacred time."

In other words, it was "get the culties away from society and use the energy of the pagan feast of enlightenment to further confuse them" time, but I only nodded politely and said, "I see."

"But Mister Campbell is here and said he'd see you when you arrive. I'll just let him know you're here."

"So you don't get the week off?" I asked after she'd informed him via intercom, but he'd asked me to wait until he finished a phone call.

"No," she said with a pout. "Mister Campbell says he just can't do without me. I'll be going next week with him and his wife."

"That's too bad you couldn't go with the rest of the company, but I'm sure your services are indispensable." *As your hastily and crookedly buttoned blouse shows.* I guessed my arrival had interrupted them since there were no other signs of hanky panky, most notably the odor one would expect. I said a prayer of thanks to whatever gods might be listening. Sometimes a sharp sense of smell wasn't an advantage.

"Mister Campbell will see you now."

I walked into a corner office with a view of the town, hills, and forests that surrounded the office park. It was high up enough that to see the peasants parked in the lot below would require an intentional look downward. Bartholomew Campbell sat behind a large modern metal and glass desk and looked not at all flustered in his tailored suit. Perhaps he really had been on a phone call and not doing other things. He didn't stand when I entered.

"Ah, McCord, is it?"

"Yes, thank you for seeing me today, Mister Campbell. I hope I didn't come at a bad time."

"Not at all, nothing that can't wait 'til a bit later." His handshake was firm, friendly, and I hoped, clean. It was the kind of handshake that welcomes you to the club, wink wink, nudge nudge. Everything from his wavy product-laden hair to his shiny black shoes solidified my dislike of him, and I wanted to grab the little secretary and bring her into the real world, show her there was something better out there and not all men were predatory creeps like her boss. Not that kidnapping women was something I typically did.

"So how's the little woman?" he asked.

"I'm not married."

"Oh, a handsome guy like you, unattached? And one of us too. You know women are drawn to our power especially once we embrace it as we should."

"And how is that?" I asked and then mentally kicked myself for playing right into his spiel.

He stood, and the bulge in his pants was unmistakable, being at eye level to my sitting self. I averted my gaze and groaned inwardly—flexing his power by trying to convert me was going to be foreplay for Bartholomew Campbell.

"I know you're familiar with our organization, Mister McCord." He gestured out of the window. "You're familiar with our holdings and properties, so you know our influence. Yet you've never come to any of our celebrations or accepted Cora's and my invitation for dinner."

"I just accepted Cora's invitation for lunch, for which you were too busy." Although I resisted the temptation to put "busy" in air quotes, I allowed my skepticism to come through in my tone. "I'm not interested in joining your organization or in playing political games. I only socialize with people whose company I feel I would enjoy, and this isn't a social visit."

He shook his head. "Cora has spoken highly of you," he said and sat. "But she's said you're stubborn." He shifted his weight, and I hoped something pinched him in an uncomfortable spot.

The skin under my nails itched like I wanted to change and challenge him, but I forced my hands to be still and took a couple of deep breaths to deactivate the fight-or-flight, but mostly fight, system.

"I would say you're in a strange position, Mister Campbell." He narrowed his eyes at me, and his lip twitched. Would he dare bare his teeth? I leaned forward—*bring it*—but I kept my tone polite. "As I said, I'm not here for a social call. I'm wondering what you know about the letter that was sent from someone in your organization to the Lycan Crier claiming responsibility for the murder of Otis LeConte."

He dismissed it with a wave of his hand much like his wife had done. It occurred to me they had practiced the reaction together to perfect their synchronized condescension.

"We have many enemies, Investigator."

The use of my title made me sit up straighter—could he be acknowledging my Council authority? I let him keep talking.

"Yes, I'm fully aware of why you're here. The question is why you're bothering us instead of trying to catch the real criminal."

"Well, if you'd tell me who that is, I'd be happy to go chase him or her. Meanwhile, if you can't tell me who did it, then I'd appreciate knowing where you were on Tuesday morning."

"I was out of town at our retreat center getting it ready for the Solstice gathering. I believe my secretary told you about our annual company retreat?"

"And would she or anyone else be able to verify you were there? When did you return?"

"I just got back yesterday. And yes, several of my staff people were there with me. Not my secretary, though."

"Interesting." Especially considering the nature of their relationship. "I would need someone not directly involved with your organization to provide an alibi. A shop girl, perhaps? Or a chips girl?"

"And what are you implying?"

"Nothing." I leaned forward. "But keep in mind, I am the Council Investigator, and some things are very obvious."

He scribbled a name on a piece of paper and slid it across his desk. "Here. This person will be able to verify I was in Oban on Monday night."

The paper had a woman's name on it. "Not Tuesday morning?"

The smug arch to his eyebrows indicated he'd been welcome to stay over.

"As you mentioned, you have money, holdings and property. Those talk. I need a copy of the itinerary for your trip including where you stayed and ate."

"Are you implying I'd bribe someone to give me an alibi?"

"You said it, not me."

He pushed himself up on his hands and towered over me. Something stirred in the pit of my stomach and drove me to my feet, my hands clenched in fists. He bared his teeth, and I returned the expression. Instead of attacking, he nodded like I'd confirmed something for him and turned his back on me. I was dismissed.

"Power, McCord," he said over his shoulder when I reached for the doorknob. "Remember, women love it."

The feral expression on his face made me feel sorry for the poor secretary.

13

The secretary stood when I exited and pulled down the front edges of her blouse, which was now buttoned properly. It was probably a size too small and strained across her small breasts. I smelled her perfume—less delicate than I expected for her build—and when she looked up at me, her lips parted, and her eyes glazed over.

"What can I do for you, Mister McCord?" she asked and licked her lips.

The cortisol and other chemicals associated with the change coursed through me. Good gods, what had that monster trained the poor girl to do, to respond to? I deliberately recalled the feeling I'd gotten when Reine cleansed Max, torrents of icy waters pouring through me. "I need a copy of your boss's itinerary for his recent trip to the Inner Hebrides and the list he's compiled of his enemies. His wife mentioned it to me."

"I'll be happy to get those for you." She moved like she was in a dream, and whatever it was rising up in me wanted to growl at her to move faster, but I calmed it with another deep breath that she must have taken to be an impatient sigh because she sped up.

"Jade, get in here!" Bartholomew's shout made us both jump, and she shook her head, her cheeks warmed by a blush. I glanced at Bartholomew's door, which stood cracked open.

"This is all I can give you," she said and handed me a stapled stack of papers.

"Thank you," I said.

"You're welcome." Her big brown eyes glanced worriedly toward the door, and the sunlight highlighted the flecks of gold in them. My sensitive ears picked up the impatient breathing behind it, and it occurred to me she wasn't looking forward to the upcoming encounter with Campbell.

"Do you want to go grab a cuppa?" I asked. "It's about time for tea."

The sad smile she gave me twisted my heart and made her look older than her years. "Not today, but perhaps soon." She looked pointedly at the documents she'd handed me. "You'd better go."

A wave of anger rose from the center of my gut, and I had to leave before I rescued her from Campbell.

"Fuck it," I said and turned at the door. "Jade, come with me."

She hesitated from where she'd emerged from behind the desk and shook her head. "Maybe later," was all she said, and then she practically ran into Campbell's office.

"Laura," I barked into the phone once I got into the elevator bay. "Open a Council Investigation on Bartholomew Campbell for sexual harassment immediately."

"Will do, Boss. Do you have solid proof?"

"Not yet," I said, but I'd just found the scrawled phone number at the bottom of page three. "But I will soon."

THE ELEVATOR that picked me up was the only one that went all the way to the basement. I wouldn't have remarked on it, but the smell of kerosene and pipe smoke—the same odor I'd picked up in the forest behind the Institute on the day LeConte was murdered—hung faintly inside. I doubted a human would have picked it up, and perhaps not even a weaker lycanthrope. Campbell hadn't smelled of it, so who did? I pushed B for the lower level.

The doors opened into a white-painted corridor that ended in a metal door. I followed the smell down the long hallway to the end and to a set of stairs. No light illuminated the stairwell, so I felt my way down two flights to a locked door. I took out a handkerchief—thankful I'd kept that remnant of my earlier life when men carried them all the time and before the ubiquitous paper tissue had made an appearance—and felt around the door through it so I wouldn't leave any fingerprints.

The rough surface of the wall stopped at a cool, smooth edge, and below it, squares—a keypad. I listened to make sure no one else was down there, took out my phone, and used the torch app. The metal keys didn't show any wear, and I wished I had my fingerprint kit with me so I could see what numbers had been pushed most frequently and make a guess at the code. Perhaps Jade could enlighten me. I'd call her that evening right after I phoned Selene to confirm our date for the following night.

IT WAS after five by the time I made it back to Lycan Village, and I stopped into Marley's for a pint. David Lachlan waved me to an empty stool beside him.

I joined him and ordered one of the local brews, which I knew to not be too bitter.

He held up the small glass of whiskey he was already halfway through. "It's amazing, lad, how this witches' brew and the fizzy stuff you're about to drink are made from the same basic ingredients, but it's what's done with them that matters."

My beer arrived, and I clinked it to David's glass. He tossed it back, thunked the glass on the bar, and gestured for another.

"That's your fifth, Lachlan," Troy, the regular evening barkeep said. "D'you have a way home?"

"I'll take him," I said. "But maybe you should give him a water first."

"Aye."

"Since when do you care about the state of my mornings?" David asked.

"If you're going to wake up with something ugly in your bed, it needs to have looked pretty the night before. That's not going to apply to you, my friend, unless you've got a magic mirror."

"Ha!" He clapped me on the back so hard I saved my beer by an act of grace and possibly a small miracle of the suspension of gravity.

I wiped the spilled beer off my hand. "Watch it—you're wasting those good grains."

"And malts and hops and god knows whatever else they've got in there." He squinted bleary eyes at the amber-colored liquid. "It's all in what you do with it, isn't it? What you do with what you've been given."

Troy slid a glass of water, no ice, in front of David, who scowled at it. "Nothing good in that lot. Just hydrogen and oxygen. Nothing that'll wet a man's throat."

"Drink your water, Lachlan, and I'll give you another whiskey." Troy rotated his massive shoulders in a seeming stretch, but the action flexed his biceps.

David nodded. "Fine, fine, I got it. I'll drink the blasted water, but you better make that last one a double."

"Sure, I'll pour it from the tenth instead of the fifth and size it accordingly," Troy said with a grin, and I laughed.

David, obviously too drunk to understand fraction-related humor, just said, "That'd be grand."

Troy made sure David killed off the water before he gave him another whiskey.

"Now I'll be pissing all night," David grumbled. "Haven't broken the seal yet."

"Here's to a werewolf-strength bladder," I said, and we toasted to our good fortune.

"Aye, that's one of the *good* things about what we are. There's plenty of bad too."

He lapsed into gloomy silence, and I sipped my beer and let the events of the day run through my head. I'll admit to lingering on the kiss from Reine and the conversation with Selene and skipping over the unpleasant encounters with the Campbells. Cora had to know what her husband was up to. We didn't have highly developed senses of smell for nothing, and detecting relationship infidelity was easier for us. On the other hand, if she was going to treat him as a true alpha, he could mate with as many females as he wanted.

No, I wasn't going to embrace my wolf side to that extent. I was fine straddling the line between animal and human. Wolves never drank alcohol, after all, and that was what sometimes made life bearable.

I shook my head. My thoughts had become morose like David's. "What's with you, anyway?" I asked him.

"What do you mean?" He looked at me sideways.

"You're testing your lycanthrope tolerance and bladder strength, and you've made some comments indicating you're not happy with something. There's nothing worse than a werewolf in a philosophical mood."

His shoulders heaved, and I couldn't tell whether it was a shrug or a sigh. "I've been thinking about the letter, Lad. I shouldn't have given it to you. I've just put you in more danger."

"Danger comes from lack of knowledge, not too much." Max's complaints about how blood magic would be less dangerous if they could study it came to mind.

David shook his head, and it seemed to get heavier with each swing, but he continued, "You weren't getting shot at with silver arrows before I gave you the letter. I told your Da I'd take care of you if something happened to him, and I can't fail now."

This was news to me, and it unlocked something. The flood of memories kept me from saying anything. I recalled David as having been a peripheral presence in my life during my short childhood and what felt like an even shorter adolescence before my first change at age thirteen. My mother, a human, had long suspected and feared I'd end up like my Da.

At that point, I'd gone to the Council School—it hadn't been a disciplinary academy then—and found out about my kind and the special kind of responsibility we had to keep our hormones under control when we had the power of an apex predator. I graduated and went on to Oxford at age seventeen and was made Council Investigator at age twenty-two, no other family members being available to fill the appointment. David had been the one to orient me to the Council and my role on it, but I hadn't thought there was anything odd or significant about it.

"Let's not talk here," I said. "I'll grab some food and take you back to your place. Troy, two roast beef sandwiches, take-away."

"Good move," Troy said. "Bread'll help. Chips with those?"

"Yes, the more absorbent material, the better."

In ten minutes, we were on our way in my car. David slumped in the passenger seat, his eyes closed. The late sunlight gilded the sides of the trees we passed, and I felt the thrum of energy that comes with twilight in old forests. Today it was stronger than usual, and I kept one eye out for Reine's ilk and/or ghosts, friendly or otherwise. As if on cue, I heard the voice from the backseat.

"Poor fool couldn't hold his whiskey when something was bothering him. He's a better celebratory drinker."

"I don't have time to deal with you now," I said as quietly as I could through clenched teeth.

"Sorry," David said. "Then why did you offer to take me home?"

I cursed our preternatural sense of hearing. "Not you, you daft fool, you must be hearing things."

"Or you are," he said.

"Right. Either way, just focus on not throwing up in my car."

"Don't worry, I'll tell you if I need you to pull over."

We arrived at Laird Hall without incident, and David waved away my offer to help him.

"I was drinking whiskey before you were even thought of, pup," he told me and almost careened into the door. He righted himself.

"Then you've had time to learn to pace yourself better."

"The nightmares, my boy. The nightmares."

At least yours aren't ambushing you in the bathroom. I took the key that kept missing the lock from his unsteady grip and let us in. In spite of our long association, this was the first time I'd seen Laird Hall. The castle had been built back in the Victorian era once history had afforded enough distance from the Battle of Culloden for the families who'd been on the wrong side of the war to come out of hiding and reestablish themselves. However, the family constructed it on the original site of their medieval fortress, and some of the old stone had been incorporated into the new castle. It gave the place a patchwork old and new atmosphere, and David had continued the tradition, sometimes to a ludicrous degree, as I saw in the den, where a suit of armor stood by a large flat-screen television.

"Is it standing guard?" I asked, pointing to the armor.

"Old Gareth there provided a great reception boost when we were still dependent on aerials. Drink?" He held up a crystal decanter and a glass.

"No thanks. One of us needs to have his wits about him."

"We both do." He poured a glass of water from another fancy-looking pitcher and sat in a large leather armchair. I took the one beside it, opened the bag with the sandwiches, and passed him his dinner. The combination of the savory gravy-meat aroma with the old castle smells brought to mind the feasts that must have occurred here and in the original Laird Hall. I felt like I straddled several points in history and blinked to clear the dizziness and bring myself back to the present and the warm, heavy sandwich in its paper in my hands. We ate in silence for a few minutes.

"Do you have the letter?" David asked.

"No, it's at home in my safe, but I wish I'd brought it back to you." I tried to keep the irritation out of my voice but must have failed.

"Nightmares get you too?"

"No, worse. I must be going nuts because things got strange after you left. It's just not possible for what happened to be real."

He barked a laugh. "Right, because it makes perfect sense that we should turn into large predators at the full moon."

"Touché, but I don't appreciate it invading my home."

"What's haunting you?"

"Not sure yet." I didn't want to tell him who it was. If he felt that badly about having failed my father, then who knew what he'd do if he knew the ghost was hanging around? Especially considering David's drunken state, although he seemed to be returning to lucidity quickly.

He nodded. "It'll let you know somehow what it wants. Damn ghosts are nothing if not persistent."

"Very true. By the way, just how closely involved were you in my life? I remember you being there, but it's all foggy."

He snorted. "That's because you couldn't bother to sit still long enough to see what was right in front of you, and I couldn't get too close."

My male suspicion kicked in immediately. "Did you and my mother...?"

He almost choked on a bite of roast beef and coughed until he cleared it. "No, Mary was a beautiful girl, but she wasn't for me. Plus, she never stopped mourning your father. The day the telegram came was the day the lass started to die."

The look in her eyes, reinforced by the bathroom vision, came back to me. Or maybe it had never left, and I knew he spoke the truth. She'd never been the same, and when she'd gotten cancer at age forty-three, she hadn't fought it, just slipped away.

"I can't imagine my father would have wanted that for her."

"Nor do I, but that was her decision. I did my best to watch over the two of you and convince her to take care of herself, but I had to do it without putting the two of you in more danger. I'd gone to the Continent for a couple of years, and that's when she got sick. By the time I returned, it was too late."

"For what?"

"I could have convinced her to seek treatment, such as it was back then, if I had been able to talk to her about it sooner. Of course she never mentioned it when I called. When I returned and saw how sick she was, the disease had already spread to her bones."

I nodded. "And she died soon after."

"Leaving you without both parents. It was another way I failed your Da."

The way he looked at the swords hanging on the wall concerned me. "You're particularly morose tonight. What does all of this have to do with the letter? What kind of danger were you afraid of putting us in, besides getting shot at with silver arrows?"

He balled up the sandwich wrapper and threw it into the bag. "There's something I need to show you, but it will have to wait for another time. I need to look for it in my archives, and I

had to build up some liquid courage to go into the dungeon."
He shook his head. "Talk about ghosts."

I checked my watch. It was getting late, and I needed to call
Selene to confirm our date the next night and Jade to set up a
meeting. Plus, David blinked sleepily at the candles in their
sconces. Perhaps he had managed to pickle himself into
oblivion and now, with a full stomach on top of it, found sleep
difficult to fight.

"I'll leave you, then."

"Aye, and be careful of what lurks in the forest."

14

___

Once I returned to my house, I left Selene a voicemail confirming I'd pick her up the next day at six o'clock and the address, which Laura had sent me. I wondered what Selene's plans for the evening could be, but it was none of my business unless she was hanging out with the scar-faced assailant, in which case she wouldn't invite me along, anyway.

My next call was to the number Jade had given me on the third page of the itinerary printout. She picked up on the second ring, and it sounded like she was in a club somewhere.

"Oh, right, I remember you!" she shouted over the music, and I had to hold the telephone away from my ear.

"Can we meet tomorrow?" I asked.

"Can't. Campbell pushed the trip up so the whole happy fucking family can be together." Her level of sarcasm indicated she was either pissed drunk or pissed angry, maybe both. "Meet me out tonight."

"Where?" I asked.

She rattled off the name of a bar in Inverness, which was

about forty kilometers away. I told her I'd be there as soon as I could.

"Don't rush, love," she said. "I'm supposed to be out recruiting other young lovelies like myself for Bartholomew's harem so we can pretend he's the big bad wolf and let him chase us all over the islands. Might as well let me find a few stupid ones so I can say I've done my job." She rang off and left me looking at my phone with a mix of disgust and confusion.

"What does a seventy-something-year-old who looks like a thirty-year-old wear for clubbing?" I asked myself and looked in my closet. The weather forecast said the temperature would drop, so I chose a green shirt, khaki pants, and white sweater I hoped wouldn't get spilled on. Not that it mattered overmuch—I'd learned long ago not to become too attached to clothing. Nothing ruined garments like changing into a wolf without getting undressed first, but sometimes it couldn't be helped.

The bar Jade had specified was near the others in Inverness's city center. I lucked out and found street parking not too far away in an alley. I walked a block and found the place called Raven's on a narrow street that had been closed to automobile traffic. It sat at the bottom of a tan stone building, and blue light spilled through its windows and onto the cobblestone sidewalk. Again, the juxtaposition of old and new disoriented me, but a tug on my sweater brought me back to the present. I looked down to see Alexander, the little clairvoyant from the school, grinning up at me.

"Mister Gabriel?" he asked.

"Hello, Alexander," I said. "Where are your parents?"

"Da and his girlfriend are over there." He gestured over his shoulder, where a man and a woman stood with tolerant but uncomfortable expressions on their thin faces. She had a take-away bag in her right hand from one of the restaurants I'd passed. I raised my hand, and they reluctantly waved back.

"What is it?" I asked as I walked toward them to introduce

myself, but Alexander held me back with another tug to my sweater.

"They know who you are from the Council," he said. "Father recognizes you from the pub. I have a message."

"What is it?"

"Don't go into the blue place. It's not safe for you."

"Who told you that?"

"I didn't ask who she was. You said not to strain myself, but she had fishes in her hair."

Reine. "Thanks, Alexander. You have a good evening."

He looked up at me with those serious brown eyes. "You're going in there, aren't you?"

I didn't feel like getting into a conversation about the trustworthiness of the Fey. If the pub wasn't safe for me, I needed to find out why since it could potentially impact Council dealings. If everything did turn out fine, it would be one more reason not to trust the white-blonde fairy the next time she appeared.

"It's complicated," I told the boy.

The "bullshit" look he gave me seemed out of place on his small face. "That's what grown-ups say when they don't want to explain something. Don't say I didn't warn you." He turned and walked back to the adults. His father waved, and I recognized him as one of the other lycanthropes I occasionally encountered at Marley's. I made a mental note to talk to him chap-to-chap one night about his strategy of "toughening Alexander up" by sending him to the Council School. Meanwhile, I had a mysterious woman to meet.

"IDENTIFICATION?" the brawny lad at the door asked me, so I showed him my ID – which the council had updated with a realistic birthdate every ten years or so – and he let me in. I found Jade at a table in the back with a couple of other young women.

"Oh, is he the kind of man you get to be with in your club?" asked one of them. She batted her eyelashes at me.

"I'm not with her organization," I said. "I prefer to think for myself."

"Oh, that's too bad." They stood. "Maybe catch you next time, Jade."

She watched them leave, her expression exasperated. "Thanks. Now I'm going to have to stay out all night to catch more."

I sat beside her. "Or you could just quit the cult. You seem to have a pretty good idea what it's all about without having bought into the brainwashing. Except for the affair you're having with Bartholomew."

"Oh, but it's not just an affair. You see, he loves me. He's going to leave Cora for me." She didn't sound like a lovestruck young woman but rather like someone who was enacting a battle strategy.

Even so, I figured I'd put my two cents in. I'd heard similar words from other women, and it never worked out for them. I told her as much and finished with, "And they usually find happiness with someone else soon after." I couldn't help but think of Joanie and Leo.

"Like you?" she asked. "You're like Bartholomew. You've got power."

I stopped myself from recoiling at the comparison. "I wouldn't say I've got his kind of power. I don't use women like he does. You must have some doubts about him if you invited me out tonight."

She stirred the dark red concoction in her glass with a cocktail straw and took a sip. "You need a drink," she said and signaled to the waiter. He leaned over, and she whispered in his ear.

"Table service? What is this place?"

She looked around with a proprietary expression, a female

predator in her hunting grounds. "It's a little classier than most of the pubs here, and the patrons often have more money. Bartholomew likes that."

I recognized her for what she was—a beta but also a hunter. "He's recruiting humans? That's in violation of Council policies."

"It only goes against policy if he's luring them in to change them. He keeps them on the edge of the organization in perpetual 'development classes' while draining away their money and resources."

"That's illegal in their world and in ours."

She sipped her drink. "They're looking for something more than ordinary life. Is it really illegal if we're giving it to them, even if it's only in a peripheral sense?"

"What do they think they're signing up for?"

"Worship in an ancient Celtic rite."

The server brought me a cocktail before I could order.

"What is it?" I asked, but the whiskey, bitters, and orange smells told me. "An old-fashioned?"

"Like you," she said. "A hero at heart. They just don't make guys like you anymore." She stirred her drink again.

Meanwhile, the one she'd ordered for me had more of a kick than I expected, and I put it down after two small sips. "That's enough for me. I need to drive back to Lycan Village."

"Stay for a bit." She put her hand on my arm and looked up at me with her big, brown eyes. "I have some friends coming to meet me here."

"What kind of friends? Other Purists?"

She shook her head. "No, you'll see. Oh, there they are now." She waved one skinny arm to signal a tall couple dressed in leather and denim. The woman's long blonde hair flowed out from beneath a leather top hat, and the guy had a lush blond beard. At first glance, they seemed annoyed to see me, and then they smiled, showing their teeth.

They're lycanthropes.

With the odds now three to one that I would get out of here unscathed, my mind reviewed the exit strategies it had formulated upon walking into the place.

"Alice and Rob," Jade introduced them. "This is Gabriel. He's the Council Investigator."

They nodded. "We've been wanting to meet you," Alice said and sat in the chair Rob held out for her. "We're very interested in the work the Institute is doing."

"And how would you know about that?" I asked.

"Well, there was the article in the paper," Rob told me, taking the other empty chair and sitting too close for comfort but far enough for politeness. "But you know it's hard to keep a secret among our kind for long. We'll sniff it out, if you'll pardon the pun."

What had Garou said? Alice and Robert MacLemore, the leaders of the Young Bloods, liked to hide in plain sight, and here they were with a representative of a rival organization. "Speaking of keeping secrets," I said, "you know you're risking exposing all of us with your social media presence. I should shut your page down."

Alice laughed, but her smile didn't rise above her beautifully high cheekbones. "As if you could. We'd only pop up elsewhere, and we don't recognize the authority of the Council. We're humans with a health problem we'd like access to curing, not werewolves."

"And where will I find you two nights from now when the moon is full and singing in your blood?"

She gazed at me for so long with her big blue eyes that Rob tensed. "At home, tranquilized with anxiety medication and antipsychotic drugs that will leave me hung over for two days and make it harder for me to work on Monday. It's hell, Investigator. I've already lost two jobs due to weekday absences." Her eyes sparkled, but it wasn't with moonlight. I wondered if they might be crocodile tears, but her distress seemed genuine enough. "The moon won't cooperate with her timing, so we need your help."

I glanced at Jade, who turned her glass between her palms. "Strange company you're keeping considering who you work for."

She lifted her thin shoulders. "I work for myself, not Bartholomew Campbell and his group of crazies. There's a reason I'm the worst recruiter beyond the fact that most of us can't be found in the cities anymore because it's too difficult to be what we are in an urban environment."

"So why do you work for him?"

She looked at me like I was dense. "So someone can watch what he's doing. Luckily he's gotten so inflated with his alpha wolf thing that he wouldn't even consider I'd betray him, not his cute little secretary."

Her statement didn't ring true. Spies didn't necessarily sleep with the object of their observation. It occurred to me she was either unsure of what she was doing or, more likely, wasn't being honest with me.

"Inflated, perhaps even tumescent," Rob interjected.

I snorted, but Jade didn't find it funny.

"Just because I'm willing to use unorthodox methods to stay close to the leadership doesn't mean you have any space to judge."

"Your methods aren't unorthodox," Rob said and put an arm around Alice's shoulders. "They're the oldest methods in the world: to get to the king, you get to the queen or get in his bed, sometimes both."

"I doubt Cora is into that," Alice said. "Leave Jade alone, Rob. She's the one who got the letter off from their headquarters claiming responsibility for the murder."

I took another swig of my drink. Some of the ice had

melted, making it less strong. "And I can guess where the other one came from and just how not responsible you are."

"We needed to get your attention and that of the Council," Alice told me. "But we're not murderers." The waiter put a pink drink in a martini glass in front of her, and she sipped at the edge.

"You have it," I said. The girl just got more stunningly beautiful the more I talked to her, and... *Oh no.* I looked at my drink. What had they mixed in there? A glance around the bar revealed several of the young people looked my way, and now I was aware of it, I felt their gazes land on me too frequently. Jade watched me intently as Alice and Rob bantered. At some point, Alice's hand found its way onto my knee.

"I should be going," I said and tried to stand, but my legs wouldn't work, and I flopped back into the chair.

"You shouldn't be driving." Alice threw some money on the table. "We'll take you home. Jade, will that cover it?"

"Yep, we should be all set." Her small mouth curled into a feral smile like a wolf about to snag a rabbit.

"I'm fine," I said. "Just need some water." But when I blinked, the pub tilted, and my stomach churned. I kept myself from throwing up through sheer will and throat muscles of steel.

"You're not okay, mate," Rob said. "We'll take care of you."

"I'm sure you will." I commanded my legs to move, but they refused. I looked around for some sort of friendly face, but most of the ones there only had mocking expressions. I'd stumbled into a den of Young Bloods, and I suspected I'd be carried out if something didn't change soon. But what did they want to do to me? Hold me hostage until they got access to the Institute?

"Drugging and kidnapping me isn't going to make me sympathetic to your cause," I said to Alice.

"No one said anything about kidnapping. We're just going to bring you back to our flat to sleep it off."

A dark figure made its way into the pub, its hat pulled low over its brow to shade its face. It wore a large jacket and tan pants. No one looked directly at it, but all got out of its way. When it paused at our table, Jade didn't look at it, but she stirred her drink with such speed an ice cube flopped over the side of the glass, and Rob pulled his collar up around his neck.

"Did it get cold in here?" he asked.

Alice looked around. "It's just another pub ghost. You're too sensitive."

"You say you want a sensitive bloke you can talk to, but I'm too sensitive." He spoke rapidly and rubbed his neck.

A blast of cold air down the back of my shirt made me jump to my feet, and this time my legs worked.

"Thank you for your hospitality and the drink," I said, "but I need to get going."

I followed the ghost out of the pub, and it vanished once we stepped into the cool night air. I walked a block and leaned against the wall of another bar, listening for sounds of pursuit. The staccato click of Alice's boots came to my ears, and I ducked into a doorway that was deep enough to keep me hidden.

"What the fuck was that?" she asked someone, presumably Rob. "How did you let him get away?"

"Didn't you feel it?"

They continued to argue as they passed me, and I slumped against the door, wishing I hadn't worn a white sweater. They didn't see me, however, and passed on. Something like static thrummed in my chest, and I recognized they probably felt the same tension. Encounters with a ghost could do that to you, and I wished I'd seen my savior's face. Perhaps it had been my father, but he had never produced such a feeling when he appeared to me before. Could it be whatever they'd laced my drink with?

Speaking of which, I needed to move on, but now that the crisis had mostly passed, my adrenaline reduced. Although my brain worked and ticked through my strategy, my knees went soft, and I couldn't feel my tongue. I feared someone would find me passed out in a doorway like a common drunk, and what would that do to my hope of becoming a full Council member? Our politics were not so different than humans' after all, except that we excused less bad behavior since an out-of-control lycanthrope could cause more damage.

The door opened behind me, and I fell backwards, landing on my arse with a disgusting splat.

"Gabriel?" Selene asked and looked down on me with wide eyes. Whether they shone with fear or surprise, I couldn't tell, because that was when I blacked out.

15

———

The smell of strong coffee woke me, and I opened my eyes to an unfamiliar ceiling of draped cloth. I found myself in a canopy bed that was, in a word, girly, and it brought to mind an incident from my childhood when I'd slept over at a friend's house and woke to find myself the victim of his sister and friends' cosmetic attention. A hand over my face revealed I wore no makeup, but I also had no clothing on other than my underwear.

"Your outer garments were filthy," a female voice said. "You landed in a puddle of vomit when you fell. You're lucky it didn't soak through, although your white sweater might never be the same."

I raised myself on one elbow and saw a dark-haired beauty wearing a silk kimono-style robe sitting at the dressing table. She didn't hold any of the cosmetics, just looked at them wistfully, from what I could tell from her reflection in the mirror. The bedroom was old-fashioned with wardrobe, dresser, and the bed and dressing table. Although the furniture was likely antique, the clothing strewn about was modern, but not on a scale large enough to fit the voluptuous woman who spoke to me.

"Who are you?" I asked. "And where am I?"

"That redheaded girl brought you home. She lives here. As for me, I'm only a shadow of what's gone before. Someone wanted me to check on you, so now that I have, I can be off. Good luck, young man. You've gotten yourself into a real mess, and not just your clothing." With a wink to me in the mirror, she disappeared.

"Lovely," I said and covered my face with my hands. "More ghosts."

"More what?" asked Selene as she opened the door. She carried a tray with an American-style breakfast of bacon, eggs and biscuits. My nose also picked up coffee, and I scooted up to a sitting position.

"Ghosts," I said. "Did you realize you had one?"

The color drained from Selene's face, and she looked around. "Not that I've ever seen, thank goodness. I heard this place was haunted. It's how I was able to get it so inexpensively. You'd think you Scots with your haunted as hell country would be used to them. I never will be, though."

"You're babbling. Don't worry, she's gone."

A lovely shell pink flush came to her cheeks when she saw my tented boxers, and I pulled the sheets over my lap. Surely she wasn't so innocent she didn't realize what happened to men first thing in the morning? Not that I could blame my body's current state solely on morning wood. The collar of her cream-colored shirt draped low and caressed the tops of her breasts before the folds of fabric gave way to a fitted center and then a skirt that hugged her curves and long legs. She placed the tray on my lap gently.

"Is that, uh, comfortable?" she asked and wouldn't meet my eyes.

"I'm fine physically but a bit uncomfortable mentally. How did I get here? Where are my clothes?"

She sat on the bed and exhaled, obviously relieved for the change of subject. "They said dry clean only, so I had to send them out. Trust me, you didn't want to wear them in that nice car of yours."

I picked up a piece of bacon and took a nibble. When my stomach didn't object, I assembled a bacon-egg biscuit. "And the means of my arrival?"

"I was out with some friends last night. They helped me bring you here."

"What friends?" Not a gentleman friend, who would likely have objected to me sleeping in her bed and not on the couch. The idea relieved me. Dammit, I did not need to become attached to this woman even if her damsel-in-distress demeanor activated every single one of my rescue tendencies, both man and canine.

"No one you would know. They're fellow Americans. Why were you in the club door? It's supposedly a secret speakeasy."

I chewed a big bite of biscuit and considered how I should answer her. The truth seemed paranoid in the light of morning, especially since I didn't seem to have any adverse effects from the night before. If anything, I felt like I'd slept solidly, but not drugged.

"What time is it?" I asked, hoping to put her off her question.

"About one in the afternoon."

I dropped the biscuit. So much for no adverse effects. I reassembled what was left of it and tried to piece together the night while I chewed. "Why did you let me sleep so long?"

"I tried to wake you several times, but you were solidly out." A door opened and slammed shut somewhere outside the room, and she stood, her expression dismayed. "Oh, no. Not now."

"What?" I shoved the tray aside, and coffee sloshed over the side of the mug and pooled on the white napkin beside it in a spreading stain.

"Get dressed," she whispered. "Here." She pulled a man's checked shirt, T-shirt, and jeans out of the closet and handed the garments to me along with a ball cap.

"I would never have picked you for a cross dresser," I said.

"They're my brother's. Luckily he likes his clothing big, so it should fit you. Go in the bathroom and pretend you're messing around under the sink like a plumber."

"All right."

"Oh, and no matter what happens, don't come out. You have no idea what's at risk by you being here."

With those cryptic words, she walked out of the bedroom, and I got dressed in the borrowed clothing, which were snug but fit adequately aside from the jeans making my underwear crawl up my arse. I wondered if I should pull them down to show some crack, but the T-shirt and over shirt were too long to milk that effect. I knelt in front of the sink and opened the cabinet doors underneath.

Why did she bring me here if it was too dangerous? She knows where I live.

With eyes closed, I activated my lycanthrope hearing.

"Did you think you wouldn't be followed? Watched? Where is he?"

My skin prickled. It was the scar-faced Englishman. I wondered if he had his big friend with him.

"He'd obviously had too much to drink," Selene said. "I couldn't just leave him passed out there. Besides, helping him might get me brownie points with the Council. That's what you want me to do, isn't it?"

"Not if it pisses off the boss. He doesn't want another man in your bed."

In a second, I was on my feet, but Selene's words kept me from doing anything. "What does he mean, 'another'?"

"Don't forget what's at stake here."

"Curtis wouldn't want to put me in danger, and he certainly wouldn't want me to whore myself out to a monster." Her voice broke on monster, and my heart cracked along with it and her quiet sobbing.

"One misstep, Selene. That's all it will take for you to lose everything." The door opened and shut, and I dashed into the living room. She stood with her back to me, and both hands were middle finger up toward the door.

"Watch this, you bastard," she said through her tears.

"Good girl," I said. "I haven't a clue who he was or why he upset you, but good for you."

She turned, and her tear-streaked face compelled me to cross the room in two big strides and take her into my arms. She buried her face on my shoulder, and every sob pressed her closer to me.

"There, there," I said and stroked her hair while mentally kicking myself. What sort of thing was that to say? I sounded like someone's nanny, and the woman in my arms was definitely not a child. She was in some sort of trouble, yet she'd risked her good will, if that was what it could be called, with the scarfaced gentleman's leader and then lied for me. The question was, why? I doubted she wanted "brownie points" with the Council, as she called them, or that wasn't all she wanted.

As for our current situation, my own plumbing had certainly taken notice of Selene's soft curves pressed against me, and I feared she would notice.

"What's wrong?" I asked when she seemed to quiet down. "Who was that guy?"

She sniffled and pulled back. "Someone who appears when I least want him to." She walked to the love seat and lowered herself to one side of it, her hands clasped in her lap. I sat on the other cushion close enough to put an arm around her shoulder, so I did. She didn't pull away.

"That's not really an answer. You're in some sort of trouble. How can I help?"

"No one can help me," she said. "I need to figure this out on my own. Besides, you have enough on your plate with Otis's and the security guards' murders."

"You never know how things are connected," I told her. "As for Otis and the security guards, you've been keeping something from me."

She looked out of the window. "I've been keeping lots of somethings from you, Gabriel, as much as I don't want to."

I scooted closer and leaned toward her. "Like what?" I murmured in her ear.

She turned, which brought her lips mere centimeters away from mine. "Like how this is dangerous for both of us, but I want it."

This boldness was so in contrast to the innocent and guileless Selene I knew that I had to stop myself, but millimeter by millimeter our lips grew closer. She closed her eyes, and I saw the dark mascara at the tips of her copper-colored lashes, more makeup than I'd seen her wear at the Institute, and it was early to be ready for our date.

The cosmetics and clothing clicked into place—she had laid her own trap for me, and it occurred to me that her confrontation with the scarfaced gentleman had been staged. I placed a hand on her chest and stopped her.

Her eyes fluttered open with surprise, and I wanted to think her mouth formed an O of disappointment partially because of the missed kiss, but I knew better.

"Let's save it for our date tonight," I said. "I can't do this while wearing your brother's clothes."

She wrinkled her nose. "Good point. That would be weird. I'll take you to your car."

WE PARTED with an agreement that I'd pick her up at six as we'd originally planned, and my clothing would be back from the cleaners by then, so I could get that as well. I grabbed a cup of tea at a shop and headed home to shower and catch a quick nap. Whatever they had given me at the pub the night before hadn't quite worn off yet in spite of my long nap, and the effects came over me in intermittent waves.

My cell phone battery had died sometime during the night, which was odd since it had a full charge when I left to meet Jade. When I put it on the charger in the car, it buzzed with several missed calls and voicemails. The first was from Garou asking how my conversations with the Campbells had gone and offering to update me on his attempts to reach the leaders of the Young Bloods, who had so far not returned his calls. Then Lonna had called with "a question, but nothing urgent" about Selene. Finally, Laura from the office had left a frantic message asking where I was and why hadn't I come in today because she'd typed up my notes and Morena wanted to talk to me, and she'd tried my house several times, and why wasn't I picking up? When I scrolled through my missed calls, the ones from my office were by far the most numerous. She wasn't usually one to be flustered. My phone wasn't charged enough for a call, so instead of going straight home, I headed toward Lycan Castle, where I'd see what was going on and switch my phone out in case the dead battery meant someone had done something to mine.

"What the hell are you wearing?" asked David when I ran into him in the entrance hall. I'd forgotten about my borrowed clothing in my rush. The last time I'd appeared that grubbily at Lycan Castle was in the middle of the eighties when a water pipe had burst in the middle of the night and we all had to scramble to save documents and records. That had also been one of the few times I'd seen Morena out of her normal prim and proper state. Her slightly less gray hair had stuck out at all angles from her head. I still brought that mental picture to mind sometimes when I needed to remind myself she had a human side. David had been on the Continent, but his office hadn't seen any damage.

"And is that a baseball cap in your hand?"

"Yes, I suppose I must have grabbed it in the car." I put it on my head. At least now if I wanted to remove a hat, I could.

"What does the A stand for?" David asked. "And were you undercover?"

"You can say I was." Or at least under the covers. It was a pity nothing interesting had happened, but at least I'd learned I needed to be extra cautious around Selene and her friends. Part of me still wanted to protect her, but I told my chivalry to shove it. She was an adult and could make her own decisions, and if she'd gotten involved in sketchy company, I couldn't do anything about it except try to have her removed from the Institute before she did any damage.

David followed me up to my office, and in spite of his girth, he didn't get winded on the stairs. I supposed he had his own kind of disguise, particularly in this version of modern society where people attached more and more judgments to body size.

"Do you need something?" I asked when we were alone on the twisting tower stairs.

"No, I just thought I'd follow you to see Laura's reaction."

I turned to see him grinning. "You need to get out more."

"Hey, it takes a lot to shock her. It'll be fun to see her flustered. She's pretty when she blushes."

I knew Laura was one of us, but David's behavior made me wonder if they'd shared something in the past or if he wanted to in the future. Not that it was a good idea to sleep with staff, your own or a colleague's.

He wasn't disappointed when I walked into the office with him close behind, and Laura looked up, squinted, and then let out a little shriek.

"Gabriel? You look like a plumber."

"His arse isn't voluptuous enough for that," David said with a snicker, and Laura blushed.

"As he is my boss, I don't want to consider his rear end. Stop being one," she snapped at him, but the look in her eyes wasn't angry.

Another thing to think about, albeit a minor one. "What did you need me for?" I asked. "You called me ten times and left me a frantic voicemail."

"You were supposed to meet with Morena at ten this morning so you could talk about what she found during her visit yesterday. She waited for an hour."

"Oh, you're in trouble, lad." David grinned. "I might have to wait around for this one. Knowing Morena, she'll be on you as soon as she finds out you're back. She has a sixth sense for when someone she's mad at appears at the Castle."

"Her 'sixth sense' is more likely a network of staff people who tattle," I grumbled. I rubbed my temple, where a slight throb threatened to bloom into a full migraine headache. Thank goodness Selene had fed me a decent breakfast so my stomach didn't react.

The phone rang, and all three of us looked at it.

"Investigator's office," Laura answered. "Oh, hello, Morena."

I waved my arms to tell her to put Morena off, but it didn't work.

"Yes, he's here. I'll tell him you're on your way."

"I can't meet with her looking like this," I said and tossed the baseball cap into the corner. "I'm going to shower and change, and then I'll beard the dragon. David, there's no reason for you to be here."

Like Laura, he refused to take the hint. "I've got nothing better to do right this moment. Besides, you need someone to stall her so she doesn't invade your shower."

"Good point, and horrifying thought." I walked into my office and slammed the door. Fifteen minutes later, I was ready. As soon as I exited the bathroom, I heard Morena's voice.

16

———

"I don't care if he was undercover, over cover, or between covers, he needs to see me immediately."

"He's not decent, Lady Morena," Laura told her, her tone soothing.

"Damn right, he isn't." But she sounded somewhat mollified. I debated waiting in my office to hear the fun, but then I remembered they'd be able to tell, either through scent or the sound of my breathing, that I was done. I opened the door.

Morena stood in the center of the room with feet planted and fists curled. The image of a two-year-old fireplug getting warmed up for a tantrum came to mind, which mixed so many metaphors it made my brain hurt. The shower had helped my headache somewhat, likely due to the warm water loosening up my neck tension, but when her gray eyes met my hazel ones, my temple throbbed again.

"What's the rush, Morena?" I asked as she stalked past me.

David caught my eye and pantomimed that he'd texted me something. I nodded to show I understood and followed the irate Council leader into my office.

"To what do I owe the pleasure of your visit, Morena?" I

asked. She stood with her back to me and looked at the fireplace. From her stance, I would guess she glared at it. I took the opportunity to check the text on my now charged mobile: *She's angry bc worried. Go easy on her.* That made me pause and back down from whatever I was going to challenge her with.

"This." She spoke in a low voice and held out a piece of paper, a printed email:

We have your Investigator. If you want to see him alive again, release the Institute formula for lycanthropic reversal. Anything experimental is fine. You're not moving fast enough on it, so we will.

What followed were instructions for how and when to transfer the information to them and a timeline.

"Well, this would have never worked," I said. "I doubt the process would move that quickly, and where are they going to find a wizard who'll do blood magic? It's a good thing they were bluffing."

She turned, and her red-rimmed eyes surprised me. Had she been crying?

"You can joke all you want, Gabriel," she told me in that low, even tone that disturbed me even more than her ranting. "I thought it must be a bluff too, but when you didn't show up to our meeting today..." Her chest heaved with her breath. "And then we couldn't reach you, and they sent this." She pulled a folded photograph out of her pocket, a printout of me sitting at a table with a group of people who all faced or turned away from the camera. I stood out in my white sweater and could pick out who was who because I'd been there, but no one else's face showed up clearly.

"Still not conclusive evidence that they had me. I was out last night in Inverness. Anyone could have taken that picture."

"So where were you this morning?"

Another wave of fatigue overtook me and knocked my knees from under me. I plopped into my desk chair. "Drugged up at a hot woman's apartment."

Her eyebrows shot up her forehead. "Gabriel, you ass. I can't lose another..." She shook her head. "What happened?"

"It wasn't recreational drugs that laid me out. I escaped from the group that was going to kidnap me, but they'd already slipped the substance to me in a drink. I was passed out until one o'clock this afternoon."

She lowered herself into a chair on the other side of the desk. "How could you be so stupid?" she snapped. "You should know better than to put yourself in that kind of position."

The return of the old Morena dispelled the awkwardness of her concern. I knew better than to smile, though. "It was part of the investigation, and I didn't think a drink served to me in a bar by a waiter would be contaminated." I rubbed my eyes. "Obviously I thought wrong, and my thinking has been screwed up since. I need to tell Garou who I was with. I suppose you've told him to try and trace the email?"

"He's been working on it, but it's been routed through too many servers and hacked addresses, so there isn't a clear trail."

"I don't suppose you had anyone looking for me?"

"David was supposed to have done that."

"Well, he found me," I said with a shake of my head. "The old dog didn't give me any indication something was amiss, either."

"That's him."

"Right." I leaned back. "Tell me about your visit to the Institute yesterday." Had it really been only yesterday? It felt like a week had passed.

"It's a beautiful facility if you ignore the murders and the fact it now reeks of spilled blood. Oh, and your little friend Doctor Rial is lying about something. Or at the very least hiding something."

"I agree, but I can't determine what." I decided to trust Morena since she had been mostly honest with me. "She's keeping some odd company, an English bloke with a scar on one cheek. Dark hair, squinty eyes."

Morena smirked. "Does he really have squinty eyes or is that your impression since the young lady is spending time with him, and you'd rather be the one on her calendar? And is this the one who gave you the concussion?"

"You've been talking to Garou."

"Of course I've been talking to him. He's the chief of our police, and he didn't believe you when you said you couldn't remember who attacked you."

"It's the truth. I didn't see whoever bonked me on the head, but it happened after I'd followed Scarface into the alley behind the West Port Inn after he met with Selene."

Morena tapped her fingertips together. "Something is teasing my memory, but it's not coming out. I'll think about it."

"I'd rather you keep this between us," I told her. "I'm telling you because you're our leader, and the situation becomes more dangerous by the day, so if something happens to me, you and David will have to carry on without me. I don't trust any of the others."

"Don't be a sentimental fool, Gabriel, and aside from that ninny Cora—how her father talked me into letting her assume his position on the Council once he died is still beyond me—the Council is trustworthy."

"Is she a full member?" I asked. "Has she come into her identity? She's not that much older than I am."

"It's different for females. We mature faster. As for you, I can tell it's happening, which is a relief. You never know what will occur with a human-lycanthrope mix."

"You've mentioned that." I recalled the strange wave of something that had tried to take over at Campbell's office. "What will it feel like? How do I know it's happening?"

"It's unique to everyone, but you will know when the process is complete. You should feel stronger and have more abilities. Now, getting back to your job as Council Investigator, you need to let me or David know whenever you go somewhere so we can follow up if you disappear again."

"That's ridiculous." The words came out before I could stop them. "I'm not a child or a teenager with a curfew."

"Right, but someone is after you, and I doubt they'll stop now that you've managed to escape. The alternative would be to take you off the case."

"Fine." I felt like a bloody adolescent. "Then I'll let you know I'm going to the Solstice ceilidh tonight with Selene. I'm hoping she'll slip and reveal some information that will be helpful. I agree with you she's involved somehow."

"I never said that, only that she's hiding something." With a smug grin, she stood, and I got to my feet. "I'll have Laura make you some extra strong tea. Then you best go get ready for your date. You can report to me tomorrow."

When she left, I sat and rubbed my temple. Whatever had tried to possess me at Bartholomew Campbell's office stirred from my toes to my groin, but it didn't make it beyond my middle. I was just too damn tired. Still, it felt like a trap tightened around me, and I wasn't sure who was behind it, the Young Bloods, the Council, or someone else pulling the strings.

With a sigh, I grabbed my spare phone and my keys and left. David wasn't in the office anymore, and I guessed he'd left with Morena. For the first time in years, I felt like I had parents. Laura looked up from the electric kettle.

"Are you heading out already?" she asked.

"Yes, I have something to do this evening."

"Be careful," she told me, and with a very un-Laura like trembling lip, she put her hand on my arm. "We were all worried about you this morning."

A sense of foreboding followed me all the way down the stairs and out to my car. Their concern was touching, but it seemed extreme for the circumstances. What did they know that I didn't?

WHEN I GOT HOME, I cleared the messages from my machine including one from Jade that she was headed to the coast with the Campbells but wanted to make sure I was okay. I bared my teeth at the sound of the deceitful little bitch's voice, surprising myself with the depth of my anger. The final one was from Selene, who'd called while I was at Lycan Castle. She said she had errands to run and would just meet me in the village at Marley's at six-thirty. I texted her that I would be fine with that, and with the extra half hour, I decided to take a nap and try to sleep off the remnants of whatever they'd given me.

I woke to my telephone ringing at five-thirty, having slept through the alarm I'd set for five.

"Gabriel?" asked Lonna after I answered. "Did you get my message earlier?"

"Yours and everyone else's."

"Oh, did something happen?"

"Yes and no. What do you need? I'm running late." I took a deep breath. "Sorry, don't mean to be snappish."

"Don't worry, I'll make this quick. Has Selene mentioned anything to you about her brother?"

That woke me fully. "Not really. Why?"

"I don't want to say over the phone, but it would be great if we could meet soon. Are you free for lunch tomorrow? I know it's a Saturday."

The uncertainty in her tone convinced me more than her words that something was amiss. We agreed on a time and place for me to meet her and Max for lunch.

I got ready and headed toward Lycan Village. The Summer Solstice Ceilidh drew people from around the village as well as tourists, so I had to park on the outskirts of town and walk, bringing me to Marley's at six forty-five.

Selene waited for me at the bar with a tall cocktail in front of her. It was clear and bubbled slightly.

"Not a beer drinker?" I asked.

She stood and kissed me on the cheek. "Not really, and their wine list isn't great. Would you believe I'm nervous?"

"Perhaps." I gestured for her to resume her seat. "I'll stand since I was either sitting or lying most of the day. Thank you for caring for me last night."

"You're welcome. I don't know you very well, but I could tell something was very wrong."

I refrained from saying I felt the same. No need to spook her. Troy the bartender passed me a pint of my favorite brew, and I sipped it, thankful that here, at least, I could trust the staff not to slip something to me.

"Is this your first ceilidh?" I asked.

She shook her head. "I've been to ones associated with the Highland Games in Stone Mountain and Culloden, Georgia, but it's been a while. I'm sure they're better here."

"Is your family of Scottish heritage?"

"Yes, and Irish."

We chitchatted about her family, about which she was deliberately vague.

"What about your brother?" I asked. "You had some of his clothes, so is he here?"

"He's doing a year abroad here, well, in Stirling, and keeps some stuff at my place for when he visits so he doesn't have to pack too much. He's kind of a last-minute guy."

"I'll be sure to wash the clothes before I give them back to you."

She looked down and stirred her cocktail, which she'd hardly touched. "There's no rush. I don't expect to see him for a while. So what are you drinking?"

I got the hint that her brother was a sore subject, and I guessed he was probably too engaged in his college life to visit his sister very much, which hurt her feelings. Still, Lonna's question came to mind, and I made a note to ask her about him again after she'd imbibed and relaxed more.

We agreed to have dinner there since everywhere else would be just as crowded, and she'd already put our name on the list for a table. Soon they seated us in a booth, and we had some privacy, although I was aware the other lycanthropes could listen to us if they desired.

"What are you doing with the Institute being closed?" I asked. "That must be boring."

"We had today off, so I caught up with house stuff. And woke up with a handsome man in my bed."

"Ah, yes, it's a pity he wasn't more functional for you."

That blush the color of the inside of seashells came to her cheeks again. "That's fine. It was nice to have someone to make breakfast for. It's been a long time."

If anyone was listening, they were probably very confused or intrigued, so I decided to steer the conversation in another direction. "You're from Atlanta? You don't have as much of an accent as I would expect."

"A lot of us from there don't. It's a pretty diverse place with people from all over. Have you ever been?"

"Only through the airport. How did you meet Iain?"

She looked down at the water the server had set in front of her. "I sought him out after the Cabal-Hippocrates case made the news. Of course I was familiar with CLS as a psychological diagnosis, but the more I dug around, the more I came to suspect they weren't just talking about a disorder of impulsivity."

"This was after you'd been infected?" I blocked out the surrounding noise so I could hear her low words.

She rolled the straw wrapper into a little cylinder. "Yes. I'd started experiencing symptoms, and I wanted to know if anyone was working on a cure. It was really disruptive." She met my eyes. "It's hard, you know, having these limitations, especially for those of us who weren't raised in a community that could give us support and help with dealing with them."

"So you didn't know any others like us?" I kept my words deliberately vague as she had. "Did anyone else in your family have symptoms or signs to indicate you had the genes?"

She looked up at the server, who had just approached with another round of drinks, and the expression on her face said relief. We ordered our food—fish and chips for her, braised brisket sandwich and chips for me—and she excused herself to go to the restroom. I mentally sorted through our conversation and made a note to talk to Iain about both her and LeConte. There had to be a reason why those two had made the cut to work at the Institute.

By the time she got back, the live music had started, so we had to yell to hear each other or text. We ate with minimal conversation, and after I paid, we walked into the night air toward the old part of town with its square. When our feet met cobblestones, I couldn't help but become more alert to every shadow and dark space, particularly as we passed the West Port Inn. I caught her looking at the alley as well.

17

"Is everything all right?" I asked.

She looked up at me. "I guess. You know, that green shirt makes your eyes look more hazel than brown. It's a good color on you."

"You're good at changing the subject. What's going on?"

"I don't know." She rubbed her arms in spite of the air being warm. "I guess it's Solstice energy plus the full moon being tomorrow night. It all makes my hair stand on end. Don't you feel it?"

I suspected her discomfort came from being constantly watched by Scarface and his crew, and I resisted the urge to bare my teeth at every shadow to show I protected her. The most convincing lies had an element of truth, and she seemed to need information, so I went with her little deception. "I've been dealing with it for so long I'm aware of it about as much as a sailor notices the rocking of the deck under his feet. If I think about it, yes, I cannot help but feel it. Generally I note it and move on. How long have you had CLS?"

"About two years. I had just gotten infected when the Cabal-Hippocrates story broke."

"So you've had a few seasons."

"Yes, but it all feels very raw still. What about you? How long have you been living with it? Lonna said you have the hereditary version of CLS, so you must have grown up with it."

"Our symptoms manifest around adolescence."

"That's a tough time. And your parents helped you through it?"

Her curiosity seemed genuine, and anyone who knew me had the information, so I didn't see the harm in sharing. "My father had died by then, and my mother was human. I was lucky to have the support of the community, especially the Council, to help me adjust to it."

"Right, because untutored male adolescent lycanthropes can be very destructive to themselves and their families." There was no mistaking the bitterness in her tone.

"You've met one?" I asked.

She didn't answer for a few seconds. Then she said, "I'm sorry, I was thinking about something else. Tell me about the square. It all seems very old."

"You're making me remember my history. I haven't been in school for a long time. Most of the Scottish towns that started in the Middle Ages have a Market Square like this one, where farmers and artisans from the surrounding areas would bring their goods to sell on Market Day."

"What's that stone thing in the middle?"

The square was so packed with people I could barely make out the Market Cross, a six foot high cylindrical structure in the center. Lycan Village had a particularly nice one carved with wolves and lambs together, like a stone prayer for peace between the two halves of our nature.

"It's called a Market Cross. It marked the square, and it's where the town crier would stand to make announcements. We don't know much about the village since little was written down, and a fire destroyed that in the eighteenth century. We do know that lycanthropes have been here as long as anyone could remember."

This time when she shook her head, it was the slow undulation of disbelief. "And the humans... They were okay with it? Or did they even know?"

"We're good at keeping our secrets." I glanced sideways at her. "As you've found. If you need to hide something about yourself to survive, you do it, no matter what else the cost. Wizards, us... The ones who didn't succeed were burned at the stake or worse."

"That's fascinating." She ran a finger over the weathered stone of the building we stood beside. "If these stones could talk..."

"They probably wouldn't have the patience for us," I finished for her. "They'd tell us to leave them in peace, we have no idea of the passage of time and how all fades away, so what does it matter?"

She rewarded me with her quick smile, and for the first time all evening, it illuminated her entire face. "True. Rocks wouldn't make great therapists, would they?"

We wandered into the square and picked up a couple of beers from a vendor. The aromas of a festival swirled around us —people, fried and sugary food, spilled beer, and the indefinable scent that comes with a summer day that's been neither too hot nor too cold.

"So a ceilidh is a festival?" Selene asked.

"Not exactly. They just have the pre-ceilidh gathering here. It's more of a big party where people get up and share their talents, whether it's music or storytelling, with each other."

"Oh, right. There were always optional ones to go to with the Games in the States, but I never knew exactly what they were. And there's always booze."

I toasted her beer cup with my own. "Always."

She took a big swig, and I wondered at her alcohol

consumption—she made good time through that big beer, and that after two cocktails, which I knew Troy didn't mix with a light hand. Did she always drink like this? Granted, I'd never seen her in a social setting. I hoped I wouldn't end up with a passed out redhead on my hands. If she were to end up in my bed, I wanted her to be fully aware and wanting to. On the other hand, she was under a lot of pressure, and I had no doubt Scarface and his ilk hid among the crowd and watched us. The thought made me want to put my arm over her shoulders, but I held back. There was no point in antagonizing them until I got more information.

"You and your brother never attended a ceilidh here?" I asked.

"We haven't been here that long," she said. "Curtis only started at Stirling in the Spring. I guess there was maybe one at the university for Burns Night at the end of January." She sounded like she was trying to figure it out herself. "We've been so busy setting up the Institute and getting things ready we haven't had a lot of time for recreational or cultural activities."

Yet she'd met a group of fellow ex-pats to go clubbing with. Not that I knew how long they'd been going or how frequently. She seemed mostly relaxed, likely due to the alcohol, but I felt myself treading the line between friendly "getting to know you" inquiry and interrogation, and I had to bite my tongue over most of the follow-up questions that came to mind.

My entire body tingled, and I saw a familiar curly white-blonde head of hair moving toward me. The awkward moment when Selene had caught me kissing Reine—or Reine kissing me, rather—came to mind, and I steered her away from the possible confrontation. The sensation of a drop of cold water trickling from the base of my skull down my back and into the crack of my buttocks made me clench my teeth against a shiver, and the Fey's bell-like laughter wove under and around the crowd noise. So she'd spotted me, but I hoped she wouldn't pursue, particularly as she'd warned me not to trust her or anyone.

Selene seemed not to notice, and we paused in front of the dance stage, where a group of little girls did the traditional arm-up hopping dance while judges with clipboards looked on.

"Did you dance as a child?" I asked.

Her smile slipped, but she held on to a grim grin. "No, I didn't have the opportunity. Money was tight and went to other things."

She moved on toward the Market Cross, and I followed her.

"Oh, that's beautiful," Selene said. "I never really looked at it before."

She took out her phone to snap a picture of one well-preserved lamb and wolf pair toward the top where the stone flowed up and flattened out to make a podium-like structure for the town crier. When she held it up, a blur snatched it from her hand.

"Thief!" she yelled. "My phone!"

I took off after him. He was fast, but obviously human. It had been too long since I'd been on a real hunt, and I had to quell the urge to change and go after him as a wolf. He ducked and wove through the crowd, me right behind him, until we reached the edge of the square, and he darted into an alley. I followed him and saw Selene's phone on a crate but no thief. My heart hadn't sped up during the chase, but now it thudded in my chest. Why would anyone steal the phone except to...

...to separate me from Selene. I grabbed the phone, and a piece of paper fluttered to the ground.

We warned you to stay out of our business. Now you and the young lady will pay for your mistake. At the bottom was a crudely drawn arrow.

I rushed back to where I'd left her by the Market Cross, but she was gone.

"Did you see where the young woman who got her phone stolen went?" I asked a teenager I thought I'd seen there before.

"Yeah, she talked to a policeman, or I guess that's who he was, and went off with him."

"Was he in uniform?"

"Nah, but they're always undercover here. Had a nasty scar on one cheek. Don't think I've seen him before."

"Thanks." I wandered around and hoped to catch her scent, but it was elusive with all the other ones, and I couldn't exactly close my eyes and activate my wolf senses while walking. I'd probably get taken in for public intoxication. I found a spot at the edge of the crowd and leaned against the stone of the building we'd commented on earlier. Her scent floated around me, but I couldn't tell if it was because she'd been here earlier with me or again.

"Trouble, Romeo?"

I straightened up. Even in jeans and a stylish ice blue canvas jacket over a white T-shirt, Reine looked otherworldly.

"I don't suppose you saw where my friend went?"

"Perhaps I did or didn't, Wolf-man." She leaned against the wall beside me with crossed arms that pushed up her breasts and showed she didn't wear a bra under her shirt.

I directed my gaze to her eyes. "If you did, I'd appreciate you sharing any information. I feel she's in danger."

"Oh, you have no idea the extent of trouble that girl is in. Her brother too."

I had to stop myself from taking that informational bait. I didn't have time for a tale. "Do you know where she went?"

"You know the rules, Wolf-man. I demand a price for my help." She leaned closer so our lips almost touched, and every little hair on my body reached toward her in spite of my best efforts not to respond to her enchantment. "Giving it away for free isn't fun for anyone."

"What do you want? My firstborn is out of the question."

"Ah, a pity since you'll make beautiful babies once you get around to it. No, I want something different from you, Wolfman. I want your name."

Her words trickled over me like a bucket of cold water, and I stepped back. "It's pretty widely known and available to anyone who wants to look for it."

"Right, but it gives me more power if you give it to me."

"What do you want it for?"

She studied her nails. "You never know when I might have need of an Investigator, and I want to be able to call you."

"I'll give you my phone number."

"Not like that." She gave me a stern look. "Do you want my help or not?"

"How do I know I can trust you, especially if I give you my name? You've warned me and gotten me in trouble before."

"You do learn!" She clapped her hands. "Good doggie. Now go back to the West Port Inn and follow your nose from there. This is your last freebie."

She tapped me on the nose, and the shock went to my core and spread out in the urge to change. I staggered along the sidewalk and willed myself to remain human, at least until I could get away from the square and to somewhere private.

"Gabriel?" David Lachlan put a hand on my arm. He took one look at my face, nodded once, and tugged me into an open doorway.

The sharp smell of lemon-based cleaner and cool scent of Freon from a window air conditioner anchored me in my skin, and I blinked in the dim light.

"Just breathe through it, boy. The alpha in you wants to get out. What happened?"

I gasped out the story of Selene's phone and her getting kidnapped, although it sounded like she'd gone with the guy willingly. What did he hold over her? And then Reine's interference.

"That one wants you to grow into who you are quickly," he said. "Otherwise she wouldn't bother so much with you."

"Why? And what about this?" I pulled the paper I'd found under Selene's phone out of my pocket, and he squinted at it.

"I should've known they'd be involved," he said. "Go ahead and change, see if you can find her. I need to go into my family archives and do some research. But when you do find her, don't let her out of your sight."

"Right. What is this place, by the way?"

"An old chapel converted to an office. But I remember it as it was, and the owners let me have a key since I'm good at getting their doors unstuck and helping with other old building problems." He turned away. "Now do what you need to."

Before I could ask who owned the offices and why he helped them, the spiritual pressure rose from where my feet met the ground, through my legs to my stomach and torso and down my limbs. My head snapped back, my neck shortening, vertebrae shrinking, and I fell to all fours. Whereas before, I'd felt like external hands molded and shaped me, now it happened from the inside and more gently so I could observe with curiosity as my body rearranged itself. When my mind changed from man to wolf mode, the confusion only lasted for a second.

"It does get easier for some," David murmured. "One of the benefits if you're lucky enough to come fully into your power. It shouldn't be taking you so long, though."

I shook myself to unlock any remaining tense muscles and align bones and ligaments. *"Maybe it was whatever they gave me at the pub last night."*

"That's a story for another time. Go find your female."

He opened the door for me, and I slipped into the shadows. Although werewolf legends abounded in our little corner of Scotland—for obvious reasons—I didn't want anyone to get enough of a look at me to identify me as more than a strangely large wolf-like dog. Without feeling like I'd just been through a meat grinder, my senses sharpened faster, and I found myself catching intriguing whiffs as I followed my and Selene's trail from earlier back toward the West Port Inn. My scent weakened while hers strengthened, so I knew the fairy had steered me correctly, although I still didn't know why. Selene's companion's, however, wasn't what I expected. I'd hoped he would smell of pipe smoke and kerosene like whoever had murdered LeConte, but forest and earth predominated—like Reine's was of snow and honeysuckle.

The reason for her involvement seemed clearer—she was interested in the scarfaced man.

18

———————

It didn't take me long to find Selene. She walked toward me out of the alley where I'd been attacked. Her expression seemed dazed, and she nearly tripped over me when I stopped in front of her. She dropped her gaze to my face and blinked.

"Oh, Gabriel," she said. "Why are you like that?" She looked around. "Someone could see you," she whispered. "Where did you change?"

"A friend helped me out. Where did you go? What happened?"

Our questions crossed in the mental space between us, and she knelt down, put her arms around me, and buried her face in my fur.

"Let's go somewhere," she said. "I can't handle any more people."

"All right. Let's go to my place."

"Mine is closer," she said. "And I have your clothes there. I forgot to bring them with me tonight."

"Won't they be following you?"

She pressed her lips together and shook her head. "No, they've made their point. They don't need to."

I wanted to snarl at the idea that something had been done to her, but I didn't want to scare her. She drove her car since my keys were in my clothes, which David now had. If she had a tracking device on her vehicle or we were being followed, I couldn't tell. Nothing smelled out of the ordinary, and no one automobile or moped stayed behind us for long. As much as Morena wanted Max to be followed so the wizards wouldn't spirit him away—and good luck with that if they really wanted him—I reminded myself to ask to have Selene followed. That I had to request something like that reminded me how powerless my position truly was.

Selene pulled all the way into the drive. "So no one will see you from the street," she said and opened the door for me. "I'm not supposed to have pets."

I followed her inside, and she went into her bedroom so I could change back to human form in the living room. This time, I uncurled from the inside out, again without the pain that normally accompanied my transformations. When I stretched to encourage the last few parts to pop back into place, I saw her watching me from the door. The expression on her face revealed puzzlement and something else—fear?

"Why are you glowing?" she asked.

"What do you mean?" I looked at my hands. Nothing.

"You have—had, it's gone now—a white-blue outline." She looked down and then to the side. "I'm sorry. I thought you were done. It was about ten minutes. It usually takes me five or six."

"You have my clothes?"

She nodded. "In the bedroom. Go ahead and get dressed if you like. Do you need undergarments? I put out a pair of boxers I'd gotten for Curtis for when he stays here, but they've never been worn."

"Thank you." I had to squeeze by her to go through the

door, and our bodies brushed together. She put her hands to my cheeks.

"You're freezing!"

"I don't feel cold on the inside."

She moved her hands to my chest, her nails trailing through my chest hair. "All your skin is cold. Get in the bed."

"Selene, you know what happens to us after we change. It would be...hard...for me to be in your bed."

She looked up at me, and her hungry gaze met mine. Her hands slipped around my sides to my lower back, and she pressed herself into me. "You're already hard."

I recalled our interlude from earlier and how I suspected she'd tried to seduce me. "What is your game, Selene? What happened to you in the square?"

"Strip poker," she replied and gave me a wicked grin. "I always won in graduate school. Poor boys never kept their clothing."

"It seems that you should be the one with the handicap in this situation, not me."

"Get dressed, then, and we'll both have a chance to get what we want."

I found my clothes in a dry-cleaning bag and put on the boxers, my T-shirt, my shirt and sweater, and my pants, which fit a little too snugly over that part of me that wondered why we weren't doing anything useful and taking her up on her very obvious offer.

Settle down, I told it. *I need to think with my brain, not you. We need answers.*

When I walked into the living room, I saw her sitting at the kitchen table with a bottle of wine, two glasses, and a deck of cards.

"I didn't have any playing cards, only the Tarot deck I picked up in town when I first got here. I took out the Major Arcana cards, so they should work like a regular deck."

"I recognize these," I said and flipped through them. "They're by a local artist."

"You can deal. Five card draw okay?"

I gave her a look. "Why do I feel like I'm about to get card sharked?"

"You want answers. I want to see you naked again. Whoever loses the hand takes something off."

"Or gives an answer," I told her.

"Fine."

The cards smelled vaguely of their plastic coating and resisted my attempts to bend and shuffle them, but I did it passably and dealt out five cards to each of us. She looked at her hand and gave me one to exchange, which I did from the top of the deck.

I looked at my cards: Ace of Cups, Seven of Cups, Eight of Pentacles, Nine of Swords and Ten of Wands. "I'll keep these."

"Okay," she said. "Show me."

I laid my cards on the table. "Straight with Ace high."

She studied my cards. "That's an interesting combination. I've got two pair." She laid them out. Sure enough she had two sevens and two nines, so I won the hand.

"Fine, I get an answer," I said.

She pouted. "Are you sure you wouldn't rather have me to take something off?"

"I would, but that's not what I need most." Heat crept up my neck. "That's not what I meant, but I do need to know who your scarfaced friend is and why he's stalking you. Also what is his involvement with the Order of the Silver Arrow?"

She slumped back in her chair. "That's three questions. I'll answer the first." She took a sip of white wine. "His name is Rhys Cromwell. He works in town as a carpenter and occasional bodyguard. He's from England but has been here for several years. And he is neither a boyfriend nor a friend, so he's no threat to you."

"I would beg to differ. That tells me a few things about him, but not the important ones."

She grinned. "That was all the information I have to answer your first question. Deal again."

I did, and this time, she exchanged three cards. I did the same. She won that round, so I took off my sweater. The next game was mine with a full house.

"So why is Rhys never far away?"

She rubbed her temples and then drained her glass of wine. "That's a more complicated answer, but it boils down to the fact that his boss has something of mine that means a lot to me, and I have to do something in exchange for getting it back."

"His carpenter boss or his bodyguard boss?"

She shot me a "don't play with me" look. "Neither."

"That's not fair," I said. "You withheld important information when you answered the question of who he is."

"Fine, I'll take off my shirt." She pulled her v-neck shirt over her head. Her breasts filled out her lace bra nicely, and I almost forgot my question. "Deal again."

By that time, the bottle of wine had been drained to half empty, but I hadn't had any. She had bright red spots on her cheeks, and her eyes took on a glazed look. The more we played, and the more she told me, the more I smelled her fear. Our game was no game, but rather an act of desperation. She needed my help but couldn't ask for it directly or... Or what? She'd risk losing whatever Rhys's employer held?

She won the next hand with two pairs to my nothing. "All righ'. Take off your shirt."

I did as she commanded, and we faced each other topless, although she still wore her bra. Somehow the sight of all the skin seemed more intimate than when we'd been wolves in the woods, although we'd technically been completely naked at the time. Without taking her eyes off my chest, she said, "Deal."

I pulled the bottle of wine to my side of the table but didn't pour. "I think you've had enough wine and poker. You obviously want me to ask you something, but you don't want to tell me outright. That's fine. I understand the power of words. But I can't help you if you're going to harm yourself in the process."

"The only harm I'll come to from this is some embarrassment and likely a nasty hangover," she told me, her words clearer than I expected. "You see me as an innocent victim, and perhaps I am." She took a deep breath, and her breasts caught my attention.

I dragged my eyes to her face. "But...?"

"But I'm responsible for the trouble I've gotten myself into, and I have to deal with it. I appreciate your trying to help me, but it's not necessary." She stood, but her foot caught on the chair rung, and she stumbled. I stood and grabbed her before she fell.

"You're right about the wine." She held on to my arms and pulled into me, possibly to stabilize herself, but I became very aware of her soft skin and the scratchiness of the lace bra against my chest. "I don't know what I was thinking."

This behavior and her earlier disorientation only further convinced me that someone had messed with her head. But who and why?

"Go get cleaned up," I said. "You'll feel better after a shower."

"Will you come with me?" she asked with a coy look. "Wash my back?"

"I'll tuck you in after your shower, but that's all I'm going to do. We can talk more tomorrow when you're not intoxicated." *Or otherwise influenced.*

I waited until I heard the bathroom door close and the water start, and I pulled on my shirt and sweater. The room had gotten cold when she pulled away, but not ghostly cold—I hoped—just chilly summer night in Scotland cold. Yes, I would have loved to have warmed her up, but it had to be her choice with her mind unclouded by alcohol or whatever else had happened to her between when her mobile was stolen and when I found her.

I grabbed the wine bottle and her glass, and when I turned to put the glass in the sink, I noticed she'd put the Major Arcana cards on the counter. The artist who had designed the deck was a friend of mine, and I always appreciated her drawings, so I looked through them after putting everything else away.

The Moon card almost made me drop all of them. An image of Reine smiled up from under her cloud of white-gold curls as she poured out the stars from a silver pitcher against a royal blue background.

The next card also took my breath away—Rhys without his cheek scar as the Devil.

Yes, I would have to visit Veronica, the artist, the next day.

The shower water stopped, and the noises of Selene getting dressed came from the bedroom. She walked into the living room wearing a large T-shirt, soft pajama shorts, and a very embarrassed expression under a full-force redheaded blush. She sat beside me on the couch.

"I made my shower a cold one," she said. "And as the water washed over me, I realized what a fool I've been acting tonight. I don't know what got into me." She slumped back and pulled a pillow over her stomach. "I'm sorry."

"What happened after that kid snatched your phone? Where did you go with Rhys?"

"That's the strange part. I don't remember. Or I do remember, but it makes no sense." She closed her eyes. "It was a small chapel just off the square. It looked like an office building from the outside. I saw...something. Like a person, but more like a skeleton, and it told me I needed to seduce you. I resisted, but then I felt a sharp pain in my thigh." She rolled up her pants to show me a bruise. "And suddenly it made perfect sense." She frowned. "Why? What good would my seducing you do for him?"

"That's a very good question." I hadn't moved my hands, and my fingers itched to stroke the soft freckled skin of her left thigh. The energy of the Solstice poured into the room with the light caramel rays of the setting sun, but I resisted giving in to my temptation. Someone else wanted it too badly, which put both her and me in danger.

"I should go," I said and heaved myself off her low couch. She stood beside me.

"I understand. And thank you for not taking advantage of me."

I turned toward the door, but then looked back at her. "Do you have someone to change and run with for tomorrow night's full moon?"

"No. I was just going to go to the Institute and run around there. Garou has men there, and Max should've strengthened his wards around the property, so it should be safe enough."

"I'll join you."

"Thank you. And Gabriel?" She touched my shoulder.

I turned to face her. "Yes?"

She stood on tiptoe and kissed my cheek. "I enjoy your company, and I think I'm starting to care for you. I wanted you even before they tried to make me seduce you. I just wish I knew how much were my feelings and how much was their manipulation."

I drew her into my arms. "I care for and want you too, Selene. Let me know when you figure it out." I leaned down to kiss the top of her head, but she looked up, and our lips met. She tasted of mint and sweetness and moonlight, and I saw her as a wolf running free through a forest with trees I'd only seen in the American southeast. The places where our bodies met heated, and I growled and pulled her closer to me, but then I remembered—this is what Rhys's boss wanted, and until I knew more, I couldn't put her at risk.

Is this my punishment—uncertainty about what's going on between us?

I pulled away, and she stepped back, but her hands lingered a moment longer than they needed to.

"Right, tomorrow night, then?" she asked.

"Tomorrow night. See you at the Institute at sundown."

MY CAR WAS STILL at the pub, and my car keys and cell phone with David, so I headed back that way to see if he was there. If not, Troy would let me call him or crash in the little apartment above the bar.

The long walk through the stretching shadows of sunset that faded into the dusky gloom of twilight gave me time to clear my head and sort through what Selene had told me and what I'd seen.

Rhys, and by extension Selene, were involved with the Order of the Silver Arrow, which held something Selene desperately wanted back. My instincts and common sense told me that seducing me wasn't their endgame for her, but what was? Probably something having to do with the Institute. I'd learned the night before that others wanted to know how to use the reversal process, so could that be it?

Reine kept popping up, but what was her connection to Rhys? It couldn't be a coincidence that there were pictures of both of them in the Tarot deck. I'd visit Veronica Chalice before my lunch with Lonna and ask her. As a seer, she knew my secrets but had always been happy to keep them. I hoped she'd be willing to share a few of hers.

An even bigger crowd stuffed the pub, and it took me a moment to sort out the sounds and smells. The live music continued, this time with a different, louder band. Sunscreen and sweat predominated the smells along with the golden brown scents of an obscene amount of fried fish and potatoes. My stomach growled, and the man in front of me stepped aside with a startled, almost frightened expression.

"Sorry, mate," I said. "Long day."

He put his arm around a dark-haired woman, and pushed through the crowd away from me. The pub mirrors were too far away for me to check my reflection, but something felt...off. I pushed through the crowd to the bar, and as luck would have it, David sat there with a pint in front of him.

19

———

"Go on, then," David said to the woman next to him. "My friend's here. I'll call you tomorrow."

I raised my eyebrows and watched her sashay off through the masses, which was impressive considering there wasn't room enough between people to sashay.

"New friend?" I asked and slid onto her just-vacated stool.

"I couldn't just wait here forever without company," he told me with a wink.

Troy placed a pint of something dark in front of me. I gave him a skeptical look. "You know I don't do stouts," I told him.

"Try it. It's a dark brown someone brought me from the States. Called Drafty Kilt."

I sniffed it and took a sip—malty, yes, but with a nice sweet/bitter balance. "Okay, not bad."

With a satisfied grunt, he walked to the other side to take someone's order.

"Find her?" asked David. He spoke in a low voice so only I could hear him, and I had to really narrow my auditory focus to pick out his words.

"I did, and I got a few more answers, but not much. Also,

did you know our Fey girl is the moon in one of Veronica's Tarot decks?"

He coughed. "Doesn't surprise me. Veronica gets most of her stuff from dreams, she told me. The silver one has been hanging around long enough it would be hard for her to avoid being spotted by someone like V. Where did you see the card?"

"At Selene's."

He smirked. "Ah, the old Tarot reading to get them into bed trick. Nicely played, lad."

"What? No, nothing like that happened. Well, maybe a little something like that, but Selene's virtue is intact, at least where I'm concerned."

"A good woman needs to be cultivated." He nodded at his beer, which he sipped more slowly than the previous night. "Like the ingredients for good ale."

"Are you going to wax philosophical again? If so, I might go get in a run and meet you back here to pick up my car keys and clothes."

"I have them in my vehicle. If you really need to run, come to my place. The grounds are secure. It'll do you good."

I put down my beer, which had tasted good until we started talking about running. Now I wanted refreshment of a different sort. David signaled to Troy that we were ready to pay, but the brawny bartender waved us off.

"The system that runs the till is down. I'll get it from you lads next time."

"That's not good for them," I said to David once we got outside the press of sound and bodies. I took my first full breath in what felt like ages. "No one carries cash anymore."

"Hopefully the tourists do."

I followed him in my car to his place, and he showed me to an upstairs bedroom to change. Although the sun had set, its reflection on the almost full moon carried its Solstice energy of light and hope tempered with the sense of the turning of the year and the days getting darker from here. Life and death, death and rebirth...

And through it all, we stand guard over those whose lives are shorter than ours, saving them from themselves and dangers they can't even imagine. The Lycanthrope Creed, an ancient document only known to the Council members and which is read at the Winter Solstice meeting, hinted at such dangers. I supposed there might be a different piece of paper or parchment that full but not junior Council members had access to.

I trotted down the hall, my claws clicking on the wooden floors. David showed me how to get out through the kitchen and where to ring to come back in. He didn't reveal his own private exit and entrance to the castle, and I hadn't expected him to. Although we were becoming friendlier, we respected each other's secrets.

"While you're gallivanting about, I'll go to my Archives and find those documents I mentioned to you."

A breeze stirred the grass on the lawn and the leaves of the trees beyond into a beckoning whisper, and I followed it. A hint of chill rode the wind, promising that winter and snow and ice never lurked too far away in this part of the world. I wondered if Selene had ever had a white Christmas and if I could convince her to stay here in Scotland for the holidays.

Don't be an idiot. The girl's secrets make her dangerous, not cuddly. But she'd looked so sweet and confused after her shower, although her kiss hadn't conveyed innocence. Her complexity, how she simultaneously asserted her independence but obviously needed help, intrigued me. I'd told her I cared for her, which was true. I feared I was falling beyond "caring" to something deeper, and it frightened me.

My head will be clearer after a run.

David's property had once been a hunting estate, and the forest had remained mostly untouched. Spicy, earthy smells emerged from the ground as I ran over it, and large rocks radiated the heat of the day. Once I looked at their silver-edged shape, I noticed the boulders seemed of regular dimensions and appeared to have been laid out in a sort of line, although too few of them remained to tell what their purpose had originally been. An old Roman road, perhaps? A wall?

Intrigued, I followed them. Nocturnal creatures beckoned me to hunt them with their scurryings and squeaks followed by freezing or darting when I drew near, but the human part of me had found a mystery, and I wanted to solve at least one today.

The forest gave way to grass and shrubs, an old sheep pasture judging from the smell. David's wards ended, but I was too intrigued to stop. The rocks continued their march across the landscape, soldiers frozen in time. Wisps of fog wreathed through the long grass and curled around the scrubby bushes, and the thick silence that accompanies power descended on the field.

I stood, ears swiveling to catch some sound, any little noise to indicate danger. The unnatural silence blanketed everything like thick snow, and moonlight made the fog glow, furthering the illusion of a winter field. The whiteness highlighted the dark stones, and I discerned a pattern to them. What had seemed random scattering now filled in as the remains of walls and corners, perhaps the decrepit ruins of a castle of some sort. Why the stone hadn't been plundered for other things, I could only guess—the sense of foreboding and Stay Away they emanated. Who could put a spell that powerful on them that it would last even when the castle crumbled? The only wizard I'd heard of who was that powerful in the area had been Wolf-sheim, but he was dead, wasn't he?

The creature that had put the spell on Selene, the one that had confused her into pursuing me—and who's to say that wasn't the aim all along?—had been powerful. Only a few wizards could manipulate intention like that. How had she described him? *Like a person, but more like a skeleton.* And Wolfsheim had been the leader of the Order of the Silver Arrow. Perhaps he still was.

Now what few hairs hadn't been standing up did, and I bared my teeth toward the center of the field—*"Whoever or whatever you are, I will figure you out, and you will not take that girl away from me."*

A weak threat, to be sure, but I suspected he hadn't been challenged in recent memory. A cloud covered the moon, the fog disappeared, and the noises of the night returned. Whether the illusion had been a warning or a revelation on this the shortest night of the year remained to be seen. Reine's words popped into my head, and I promised myself I would return when I could stand on two legs with my human judge of perspective and see if this could be the ruins of Wolfsheim's castle. Reine had mentioned it had the same layout as the Institute, so I could use that as my guide.

I backed out of the field, turned, and loped through the forest back to David's manor.

ONCE I HAD CHANGED and showered, I met David in his dining room. He handed me a glass of Scotch.

"Trust me, you'll need it," he said.

David opened a small trunk that looked like it had spent some time underground judging from the dirt and damp stains on it. When he lifted the latch on the front, my ears felt stuffed and then cleared like they had when Reine had disappeared earlier.

"What was that?" I asked. "Did you just release some sort of spell?"

"Not something the Council Investigator needs to know." He grinned at me over his shoulder. "In spite of commerce between wizards and lycanthropes being forbidden for hundreds of years, it might have happened a few times, probably more than the Council would be comfortable with. They sometimes needed our protection; we occasionally needed their spells."

"You had to do something before security systems were invented, I suppose." I looked around the room and smoothed the hairs that stood on the back of my neck. "There's more than one in this house, isn't there? That explains how your lands are warded."

"There might be a general sort of compulsion ward to make sure no one but me wants to stay down in the dungeon looking through the Archives too long."

"You have friends in low places."

"And you've been to too many pubs where they play American music. Aha!" He pulled a folder from a stack of them.

"Is there something that keeps the documents from rotting?" I asked.

"Yes, it's called acid-free storage folders. Try not to touch the pages too much when you read them."

"Right."

I reminded myself that David was over two hundred years older than I was and likely had more secrets than I would ever know. The knowledge made me happy he was on my side.

He had me wash my hands and put on cotton gloves before we opened the envelope. While I cleaned up, he placed a cloth over half his dining room table and, with gloves on, spread out the faded letters, some of which had obviously traveled quite a distance judging from the stains on them. Other splotches made me wonder if they'd been removed from corpses after battles, but I squashed that queasy train of thought.

"Where did you get these?" I felt compelled to speak in hushed tones out of respect for the history in front of me.

"Some were passed down to me. Some were given to me. The rest I hunted down or found." He said the words like a prayer of gratitude. "Like this one." He pointed to one on the bottom right of the table. "It's from a soldier who died at Cullo-den. Not many of the lads could read or write, but this one had sailed abroad and had learned along the way. He sent it to the village priest with instruction to read it to his wife."

The narrow black scrawls flowed into the wrinkles of the letter, and I could barely make out the words.

"He's warning of a demon he saw in the night?" I asked after squinting at it for what felt like hours, making out the uneven lettering. Perhaps the soldier had been using a rock or some other non-flat surface as his makeshift desk.

"Yes." David nodded at me like I was the student and had just said something clever. "Read what else it says."

I got back to work and leaned in, but not so close I would damage the fragile paper with a stray breath. As I read, I trans-lated the old, stilted phrasing into modern language. "Tell me if I'm getting this right. *When the demon appears, madness grips the men, and they lose the ability to think for themselves. I fear that should the Hanoverians not kill us, the demon will cause us to lose our minds. Hide yourselves, my dear ones. Darkness falls upon the land if man has commerce with such creatures, and all hope may already be lost.*"

"Very good."

A chill breeze passed through the room, and the lights flick-ered. "Tell me you don't have ghosts," I said, but then a familiar shadow of a man in a helmet and a long jacket faded in against the fireplace. My jaw clenched. *Of all the times for the stupid thing to appear.*

"I don't, but it appears you do," David said. He backed toward the door, his eyes wide and face pale.

"As far as I can tell, he's mostly harmless."

"It's the mostly that concerns me, lad."

The ghost shadow lifted an arm such that the dark column of his sleeve grew across the floor, table, and letters until a finger pointed at one of the newer-looking ones.

"That one's from your father," David whispered. "Quick, read it."

I didn't want to take my eyes off the shadow, and I resisted the urge to back away toward David. "It looks like a fairytale. *'Once upon a time two boys ran toward the woods to hunt wild boar. One stayed behind to guard the entrance to the path, and the other proceeded with much caution but with haste because he knew he would become the hunted in the blink of an eye and the wink of a tear. Once in the forest, he came upon a grotto with a beautiful waterfall...'"*

The shadow lengthened to the last paragraph, so I skipped to it.

"*'Why do you hunt me?' The boar king's voice held the cries of the children he had devoured, and the boy trembled, his arms and legs tied to his body by fear and something else he could not name. The demon towered over the child and looked at him with flaming red eyes and gnashing pointed teeth that dripped with the black blood of those he had eaten.'"* The words stopped there, and I picked up the paper to look on the back, but there was nothing.

I looked up at the shadow, and a childhood memory floated to the surface of us in our flat before the war started. I sat on his knee and smelled his pipe smoke in his sweater even though he wasn't smoking at the time. Pipe smoke and wool, that was his smell, and after he'd died, I would go in the closet and lie down among his clothes because just smelling them would make me forget he was gone for a little while. But that night, I'd asked for a scary story, and he'd told it to me, and then again on the following night and every night after that. It seemed he felt it was as important for me to know it as it was for me to hear him tell it. He stopped after I developed nightmares of being chased and my mother scolded him that I wasn't old enough for such dark tales.

I continued with the story from memory. "So then the boy looks at the boar king and tells him that he doesn't feel appetizing, and please could he just send the boy on his way? He would never eat pig again, not even a little slice of bacon. But the creature only laughs at him and tells him he doesn't let his food go for free, he has to pay a price, and perhaps he would allow the king to eat his friend and his sister instead, two lives for one."

It reminded me of Reine bargaining for Max's life with his wife's and daughter's. Damn fairy folk.

"The boy, of course, refuses. The boar king tears him to pieces and finds him so delicious he vows to hunt the rest of his family down, but while he's eating him, the friend sneaks up and beheads the boar king. His blood mingles with that of the slain boy and brings him back to life, and his family is happy to have him back even though he's never the same again. Because—"

"You cannot be touched by the boar king whose name is Death and return to your family the way you were." The ghostly voice filled the room.

"Simon?" David stood up straight from where he'd been leaning against the doorframe. "Simon McCord? Is that you, lad? I'd know that voice anywhere."

20

———

The shadow disappeared, and the letters scattered in a blast of chill wind. We gathered them back up without saying anything. The delicate process of moving the ancient paper only aggravated my already foul mood.

"Why not just tell me what they say? Why show them to me?" I asked once we had them arranged again.

"Why not tell me the ghost was your father?" David countered.

"It's not exactly a comfortable thing to say, 'Oh, by the way, I think my father and your best friend is haunting me. He says hello and might pop by later.'"

David shook his head, but he smiled. "Words have power, Gabriel. You were named for the messenger archangel—that's significant."

I had always wondered. My name had always made me stand out among the Anguses and Ferguses and Charlies of my school. "What happened to my father, David? Was he torn apart by the boar king or the demon the Culloden soldier mentioned or some other kind of supernatural creature? My mother always told me a German shell had gotten him, and he hadn't felt anything."

"You've seen the pictures." It wasn't a question. He stacked the letters in preparation for putting them away. One caught my eye.

"Yes, I've seen the bloody, awful pictures of what was left of him. Stop—what is that one?"

He paused, and I picked up the paper by the corner and held it to the light. This one looked like it had been crumpled, thrown away, and then fished out of the dustbin. In penciled letters so faint as to almost fade into the wrinkles, I read a single word. "Wolfsheim? The *vargamore* who started the Order?"

"Yes, Wolfsheim. That one was retrieved during the first Great War from a street urchin who had lifted it off a gentleman I'd been following."

"Who was the gentleman?"

"Someone I never had the fortune of knowing. He turned up dead. All these letters are pieces of a puzzle, and when put together, they show how the Order of the Silver Arrow never died but rather continued to play a part in the misunderstandings that occur between the human world and ours."

"I heard the name 'Wolfsheim' again. Ah, right, from Reine."

"Yes, she shows up every so often. Not sure how she fits in with all this, but she does seem to appear whenever the Order gets active."

"She's the one who mentioned it. She said the Institute was built along the same plan as Wolfsheim Castle, so she easily found her way around."

"Call me a conspiracy theorist, but I don't believe that's coincidental." David sat on one of the formal dining room chairs and grunted. I lowered myself onto another one.

"We can always talk to the architect. He's one of us, and

local. But first, tell me about the Order and what you think it had to do with my father's death."

"Your father was no ordinary soldier, Gabriel. Simon McCord was a spy, but not for the Crown. He of course answered to the Council and was to gather information on both sides, but especially on the activities of the Order on the continent because we suspected they were involved somehow."

"Right, particularly with the Nazi concentration camps. It sounds like their agenda."

"Aye, if Wolfsheim could have found a way to do that to us, he would have."

I had always been proud of my father for serving the Crown, but now a new feeling swelled in my chest – curiosity – enhanced by the bitter edge of the desire for revenge. The author of my father's death had stepped from the gloom of history. "How old would Wolfsheim be now? You said he got started in the eighteenth century, and no one knew how old he was then."

"Right, and even then he appeared as an older gentleman, so one would think he had a few hundred years on him already." He glanced at the sideboard. "This conversation requires a drink. Whiskey?"

"Please. And damn. He'd be five hundred years old by now at least. If he's still alive, which is highly unlikely, even for us."

David rose and poured drinks for us. I wondered if he had an alcohol station in each room of the house.

"It's unlikely but not impossible," he told me and handed me a drink.

I took the heavy cut glass tumbler from his hand and looked at the volume of liquid in it. "I hope you don't mind a houseguest if you expect me to finish all this. My liver doesn't have as much practice as yours."

"Just drink up. I have plenty of room."

This stuff had more peaty flavors to it than the first whiskey he'd given me, and I suspected he didn't drink it as often as the other. It burned going down and left a smoky scent at the back of my palate and sinuses.

"Okay, what did you need to lubricate me to tell me?" I asked once I finished half the glass and set it on the table. The smoke in my throat led to the sensation of fire in my belly.

David finished his glass, and his eyes had gotten red-rimmed and teary. "Your father had no business being near the battlefield where they found him. None. He was supposed to have been in Antwerp with the Belgian resistance."

"Brugge isn't that far from Antwerp," I said. "But what was he doing there?"

"He was either lured or tricked into going there." David looked into the fire. "I wish he could tell us."

"I'll ask him the next time he appears."

David snorted. "That's the problem with ghosts. Considering he died violently and is here rather than there, he's likely lost a lot of his memory with the transfer. I suspect if he could, he would've told us by now. When did he start visiting you?"

In spite of my intention not to, I took another swig of the Scotch. "The day of the murders at the Institute. I swear I hadn't seen him before."

"That speaks of a connection, now, doesn't it? The demon on the battlefield and the one in our midst."

"But why?" I swirled the drop of amber liquid at the bottom of my glass. "I can see how they would be interested in the reversal process, but how could that be related to a trap and murder in the Second World War?"

"If you figure that out, you may solve both mysteries."

Now that Selene was opening up to me, I hoped she'd tell me why the scarred Englishman had been at the murder scene and arrange for us to meet peacefully. I needed to know what he'd seen and why he was spying on us. My instincts told me he hadn't been the murderer but might have if given the opportunity.

Yes, Selene was in more danger than she realized if this was all connected. Luckily I didn't mind keeping an eye on her.

THAT NIGHT, no ghosts or visions bothered me, and I made it to Lycan Village in time to visit the crystal and magic store where Selene had gotten the tarot cards. Veronica Chalice's shop smelled of herbs and incense and other fruity and earthy scents. I never claimed to be a sensitive, but whenever I walked in there, I felt tingles along my spine, at the base of my skull, and along my fingers.

Veronica herself greeted me and caught me flexing my hands and rubbing my thumbs over my fingertips to dispel the feeling that they were waking up after I accidentally slept on and numbed them.

"I just got some new fluorite in," she said. "It's itching to be picked up and held. Maybe it's calling to you?"

She plucked a round green and purple stone the size of a large marble off a stand and handed it to me. Its coolness dispelled the tingles.

"It likes you," she said, and her smile lit her entire face like she'd made a royal match. "It's been a while, Investigator McCord. What brings you in today? Surely the fluorite didn't call to you all the way out in Shady Acres."

"No," I said and handed it back to her. She placed it on its stand among some other brightly colored stones of various shapes. "I'm here as part of a case, I think."

"You think?" She raised iron-gray brows the same color as her long, flowing hair. Today she wore a dress the color of storm clouds, and her hair and clothing blended together to give an impression of rain and sorrow.

"Do you recall selling one of your local tarot decks to a

young woman with red hair?" I asked. "I know it's a lot to ask you to remember one customer considering how busy you are during the tourist season." Indeed, it surprised me how quiet her shop was, but I imagined a lot of the tourists were sleeping off their Solstice ceilidh hangovers.

She picked up a clear round ball. I raised my eyebrows.

"Clear quartz. It helps me think," she said before I could ask.

"Oh, you don't gaze into it and get the answers?"

She grinned. "That's not one of my talents, I'm afraid. Now hush if you want me to remember your redhead."

"It's actually not the redhead I'm so much interested in." I coughed when she gave me a skeptical look. "Okay, maybe I am interested in her, but the deck intrigues me the most."

"Oh, I remember her now. An American, right? Poor girl seemed troubled, more so than my average patron."

"That's probably her, then. Big blue eyes?"

"Yes, and a delicate face. Unique for one like you." She didn't say lycanthrope or werewolf out loud; most of us didn't since few knew about us, and I appreciated her discretion.

"Oh, we don't tend toward 'delicate'?" I couldn't resist teasing her. "What are we, then?" I shook my head. Something about the shop made it hard for me to concentrate, but it was also that since Veronica knew who and what I was but didn't have any kind of agenda with me, I could relax around her.

"You're sharp, clever, tough. Your bones tend to be thick and strong, your jaws square and your shoulders broad. Even the women. Lady Morena? She could stop a lorry."

I coughed to hide my laugh at the image her words prompted. "Why is that, do you think?"

"I'm a psychic, not a doctor. Perhaps it's all the running over uneven ground. It builds up your bone thickness and density. Or that your bones have to be strong the way they're reshaped and molded. Otherwise, they'll break."

"Do you think the redheaded American is in danger of breaking?"

She looked at the quartz in her hand, and a little line appeared between her eyebrows when she pondered. "No, but she carries a great burden she's had for a long time, and recent events have only made it worse. Coming here was a last resort for her. Her type—and by that I mean scientists—don't seek out magical solutions."

"What else did you give her?" I asked. "Or sell her."

Veronica flashed a quick smile. "You know I'm a fair saleswoman, Inspector. I wouldn't have sold her anything that wouldn't help her."

"What do you know about these?" I asked and pulled out the two Major Arcana cards I'd "borrowed" from Selene the other night. She took them from me.

"They're from the deck I designed," she said. "What else do you want to know?"

"Well, what inspired you to draw these particular people?"

She handed them back to me. "Some of my paintings come to me in dreams, some in visions. I walk through the fields a lot. Perhaps something inspired me out there."

"You're lying to me, Veronica," I said. "If you're frightened of these two, I understand why, but it's important for me to know who they are, or at least who they are to you."

She turned her back on me and grabbed a soft cloth, which she polished the round quartz with. She then placed it on a plastic holder on a brightly lit shelf and stepped back and gazed at it.

"Veronica," I pressed, "I'm serious. People have been killed, and the man is the one who is connected to whatever is keeping Selene's lost object."

"I cannot tell you much about him," she said, "only that he is not like me or even like you or the others you have been associating with. He is more like the Moon." Again, I admired her ability to avoid saying names or anything else that could summon one of them.

"So why is he the devil in the pack?"

"He once was good, but bitterness and the desire for revenge have turned him against others. If you've seen him, you noticed the scar on his cheek. That was made by an iron weapon wielded by one of your kind at Culloden. His imperfection prevents him from accessing his full power or returning to his home, and so he has sworn revenge and has proven to be an eager mercenary for those who seek to harm you."

She turned to me, and I saw the tears in her eyes.

"I didn't mean to upset you," I said.

"You place me and every one of your kind in danger by pursuing this line of investigation." She shook the cloth at me. "And I fear I have made a grave mistake by using his image, even without the scar, if someone has been able to recognize him on the cards."

"You knew the risk when you painted him."

She bowed her head. "It was a compelling dream, and I had to."

"What of her?" I asked and pointed to the moon card. "I can't decide if she's harmful or not."

"The moon reflects the light from the sun, and while it may give clarity, it also paints with confusion because you know better than I that objects seen by moonlight do not give away all their secrets."

"True," I said. "But that doesn't really answer my question."

"I don't have an answer, Investigator, only that while she brings confusion, she can also give enlightenment by helping you see things in a different way."

"That makes sense from our interactions so far, but I fear she is going to try and exact some sort of price from me."

"Her kind will always seek some sort of advantage. Don't let her, if you can."

"And did you see her in a vision as well?"

"No," Veronica told me. She plucked the fluorite off its holder and held it out to me. "She commanded that I paint her and include her in my deck, and I couldn't refuse. That you're here tells me that she already has some power over you, so please take this in the hope it will help you keep your clarity."

"Thank you, but why this and not the quartz?"

"It likes you. I suspect you'll need more than just that before this is all over. Take this ribbon and crystal holder and keep it on you always, even when changed."

I didn't relish the idea of a stone marble bouncing against my chest, but I didn't tell her that. I pulled out my wallet to pay her, but she stopped me.

"Consider it a gift," she said. "One given without conditions."

"Is there such thing?"

"I suppose you'll find out."

21

———

When I exited Veronica's shop, my phone pinged with a text from Lonna suggesting I come to her place for lunch since Abby was fussy, and she had only just been able to get her down for a nap. I texted back, offering to pick up something for us, and we arranged that I'd grab something from the cafe we were to have met at and bring it with me.

I arrived at her house with salads and salmon quiche, and Max met me at the door before I could knock.

"Thanks," he said and took the bag. He looked markedly better from the last time I'd seen him, but the tension around his eyes and smudges under them indicated some rough nights. "I'm afraid none of us are sleeping well these days."

"How so?" I asked and followed him inside.

"Abby's having night terrors, I'm having nightmares, and Lonna's not getting much rest between the two of us. We just got Abby down for a nap, but she probably won't be asleep for long."

Indeed, Lonna's beautiful light green eyes seemed even

lighter with the dark shadows she sported under them, but she smiled when she saw me and gave me a hug.

"Have you thought about moving out for a while?" I asked. "Maybe there's something left in the house from the Fey's work or the blood magic contamination."

Max sighed. "I've tried everything I know to cleanse the place and put up extra wards. No, I'm likely the cause of it."

Morena's warning that the Wizard Tribunal wanted to pull Max from the Institute came to mind. "Have you heard at all from the wizard leadership? Could they be involved?"

Max and Lonna exchanged glances.

"Might as well tell him," she said.

"The Tribunal wants me to appear at the European head-quarters next week. I fear the worst."

"Which is…?" I imagined wizard jail as a place where their wands would be locked up and their hands tied behind their backs.

"They're going to want to decontaminate me from the blood magic use, and their process is even worse than Reine's because they lack her precision and power."

"Wait… I thought they sent her to you."

"No," Lonna said. "Arnold, who's a representative to the Tribunal did with the hope that if she came, no one would find out, and that would be that. But someone ratted us out."

"No wonder you're having trouble sleeping." I handed the take-away cartons around. "What are you going to do?"

"I can go on the run with Lonna and Abby, but I fear that will not be a viable plan considering our daughter is already displaying magical talent," Max said. "Someone will notice something."

I nodded, remembering the strange behavior of the spoon when I was watching her.

"He could go without me and Abby," Lonna pointed out, "but then we'd have to go into hiding separately because they might try to use us to get to him." She reached her hand to Max, and he took it.

"I'd never let anything happen to you," he said. "I'd die first."

"I know, and that's what frightens me."

I stuck my fork in the quiche so it stood straight up. "Or you could put yourself under the protection of the Lycanthrope Council and seek asylum with us. Lonna and Abby are part wolf, so it could work."

"And it would endanger the already tenuous peace we have been working on between wizard and werewolf kind," Max said.

He had a point, dammit. "What would change their mind?" I asked. "How can I defend you?"

Lonna's tired sigh told me it would be something huge and impossible. "We need to prove that use of blood magic, specifically Max's use of it, is for the greater good. If we could get the Institute reopened and start our reversal process studies, they might hold off. The first test subjects are only awaiting the go-ahead before they come over."

"Right," Max said. "Nothing motivates the wizards like curiosity. They consider themselves to be a group of scientists above all."

"I wonder who reported the incident." I took a bite of salmon quiche and thought through the possibilities. "Garou has a man following you, so it could be anyone connected to the Council. My guess would be one of the Campbells because they're most invested in stopping our project."

"Right." Lonna agreed. "Didn't someone from their organization take credit for LeConte's murder?"

I nodded. "They did, but without Bartholomew and Cora's knowledge, and I doubt it was either of them. I've talked to the person responsible for the letter, and I know she didn't kill

LeConte—it was just a political stunt. The Purists aren't as cohesive as they'd like to seem."

"How close are you to finding the killer?" Max asked.

Now it was my turn to sigh. "My one witness is difficult to pin down and likely isn't even human."

"There was a witness?" Lonna asked. "That's fantastic! They can identify the killer."

"Not so fast," I told her. "As I said, he's not human and has given me a compelling warning to stay away from him and his business." I told them about Scarface's friend bashing me on the head.

"Oh, so that's how you got the concussion," Max said. "How is it doing, by the way?"

I felt along the back of my head. "Not even a bump, and I haven't had any symptoms since that night."

Lonna, who had disassembled most of her quiche after a couple of bites, toyed with a piece of fish on her plate. "That reminds me. I know you've been seeing Selene. Has she said anything about her brother?"

"Not really other than that he's a student at Stirling and she doesn't see much of him."

"She told us the same. I'll be right back." Lonna left the room and returned with a leather satchel. She pulled out a manila envelope festooned with postage. "Iain gave up and mailed this to me when we couldn't get the last application to transfer electronically."

"That tells me another energy wizard is involved," Max noted. "I'm looking in to who it could be, but my resources are limited at the moment."

"What about that Arnold guy?" I asked. "He seems to have some mysterious connections."

"Not reachable. It seems like everyone wants to play the 'sabotage the Institute' game," Lonna said and pulled out a stapled stack of papers. "This is the missing application."

"How did you get it so quickly?" I asked and took it.

"Iain has connections," Max said.

I read through the materials for a young man Corey Richardson who had gotten Chronic Lycanthropy Syndrome from a tainted flu vaccine. Everything seemed in order. "What am I looking for?" I asked.

"Look at the copy of the ID," Lonna said. "I thought something looked odd about it, but it wasn't until I looked more closely that I saw it."

The driver's license had been copied in color. Underneath it was a note that said, "Passport pending." I looked over the license and noticed that it had just been issued a few months before.

"So he just renewed his driver's license?" I asked. "That's not suspicious. It's odd he didn't have a passport, though it looks like he's about to get one."

"Right, and now look at the picture." Lonna handed me a magnifying glass.

It showed me a young man with dark hair and blue eyes. The eyes looked familiar, but lots of people have eyes that color. Something didn't match. "The hair looks dyed."

"Very good," Lonna told me. "Max suggested we do a background check—which we're doing on everyone from now on—and this came up."

She gave me another piece of paper. One Curtis Southerlin Rial had applied and been granted a legal name change to Corey Stuart Richardson.

"The sixth application was for Selene's brother," I said, and the air in the room became stale and stagnant as her lies and evasions and half-truths piled up around me.

"There's no Corey Richardson or Curtis Rial enrolled at Stirling," Lonna told me. "Iain's still on faculty there, and he checked. Wherever Selene's brother is, he's not there."

"Selene said Scarface and his friends had something of

hers, and it was obviously important enough to be able to manipulate her. I wonder if they have Curtis. But why would he change his name to apply for the reversal process other than the obvious that his sister works at the Institute, and that would be an ethical conflict for her?" I tapped the papers. "There's something else going on here. Whatever it is, we need to ask Selene, but it needs to be somewhere Scarface and his buddies won't be following her."

"Will you be seeing her again soon?" Lonna asked with a sideways glance from under her lashes.

I knew that look, a female on the hunt for gossip. "We're going to change and run together for the full moon tonight. We were going to do so on the Institute grounds, but I'd rather be somewhere safer. David Lachlan has warded grounds. Perhaps he would let us borrow his estate."

"That sounds like a good idea," Max said. "That way you have backup if you need it. He's a canny old wolf. I've not talked to him much personally, but he does seem to see and hear a lot."

I nodded. I would also ask him if he knew anything about the Order's activities in the States.

My phone rang when I reached my car after having left Lonna and Max's place. Selene.

"I can't do tonight," she said, her tone breathless.

"Where will you run, then?"

"I don't know. I just... I just can't."

I closed my eyes, shut off my own mixed feelings, and analyzed the layers of emotion in her tone. There was fear...and anger. Mostly anger. And impatience.

"What's pissed you off?" I asked.

A sharp inhale, and then an exhale heavy with frustration. "If you must know, that thing I've lost, they're close to returning it to me, but I must meet them tonight after midnight."

"Oh, then we'll have a couple of hours so you can get your change and run out of your system and meet them with a clear head. And I can go with you, make sure they're not going to pull a fast one on you or give you something other than what you're expecting."

She chuckled. "That would be very difficult. My...thing...is very unique. There's only one of it." A deep breath. "Okay, we can meet up, but I need it to be closer to the Eastern Pond, and you're not coming with me after."

That's what you think. The connections between my experiences wove together into a map, the ruins I'd discovered in the center. I bet that was where the *vargamore* was hiding.

"David Lachlan's estate is in that area. I'm sure he won't mind," I said, sure to keep my tone nonchalant. "I'll email directions to you."

"I'll likely be followed all evening, as usual, and I don't want to endanger either of you. I'll run to his place—they won't expect that. Can you have clothing waiting for me?"

"I'll drop by to pick some up now." *And I don't care if they see me. They need to know you're under my protection whether you like it or not.*

SELENE MET me at the door. I ignored the bag she held out to me and stepped past her into the apartment. I don't know what I was looking for, only that I wanted some evidence she hadn't been keeping such a big secret from me, that she had some valid reason for not asking me to help her.

"I'll draw you a map so you know where to meet me," I said. I opened my mouth to say more, but she held her hand up.

"I'm pretty sure I can find you on the Institute grounds," she said.

"The place I'm thinking of is easier to explain with landmarks."

She dropped her bag by the front door and nodded. "That makes sense. I can memorize it before tonight. My paper and pen are in the office."

She left me standing by the couch, and I studied the pictures on the end table while feeling in my pocket for the fluorite Veronica had given me. Not that I knew if it would indicate anything interesting like if the apartment was bugged through electronic or magical means. Obviously something had changed since the previous night, when she'd felt free to be open with me. I looked around to see if I could spot anything suspicious.

The photos were just of Selene and a young man I recognized from the information Lonna had given me, no parents or friends, in different settings and at different ages. Someone must have taken the pictures, I reasoned, since they were snapped from too far away to have been "selfies". Curtis grinned, but in a few of the photos, Selene gazed off camera, her expression pensive. The Tarot deck sat on the table as well, and I slipped the two cards I'd borrowed back into it before she returned.

She stood at my shoulder as I drew a rough outline of the area with Lycan Village and Laird Hall marked. I wrote on the map, *Can we talk freely here?*

She shook her head.

How did you get away to call me earlier? was my next written question.

Ran to Veronica's shop, she answered on the page. *Tell you more later.*

I nodded and drew the directions out for her.

"Great," she said, "I'll see you tonight." She put her arms around me and leaned into me, her head on my shoulder. I wanted to believe it was a gesture of trust and desire, but there were other agendas at play, and I couldn't be sure.

What the hell? I thought. I put my arms around her, held her close, and rested my chin on top of her head. Her shampoo smelled of lemon and some sort of herb, maybe rosemary. It was a strong scent for someone who seemed so delicate and buffered by different forces, but it reminded me that she'd kept her secret from Lonna and Max, who were two of the smartest people I knew. What chance did a guy like me who'd been out of school longer than she'd been alive and who didn't have any kind of scientific training have to outsmart her? All I could do was hang with her and hope for the best. As I'd learned, smart people tended to get themselves in the worst trouble because there are some things you just can't think your way out of.

She pulled away but didn't let go, and I gazed at her face. She didn't say anything, but her eyes told the story—she needed something solid to hold on to, and she was scared, so scared of what was going to happen to her and her brother. For the hundredth time, I wondered what she'd gotten herself into, but this time it was followed by the realization that perhaps her brother had been the culprit all along, perhaps even since childhood. I commanded my plumbing to stand down, we didn't need to get distracted by a pretty face and a nice set of—

She stood on tiptoe and pressed her lips to mine. It didn't take much nonverbal persuasion on her part to get my mouth to open for her, and I tangled my fingers in her hair, releasing another wave of scent that mingled with that of our desire. Although it was only afternoon, the full moon sang in my blood, wanting me to make her mine.

In front of whoever was watching or listening to us. That reminder crashed through me like the cold water of Reine's intervention with Max, and I put my hands on Selene's shoulders and stepped away.

"We'll continue this tonight," I rested my forehead on hers. "I don't feel like putting on a show," I whispered in her ear.

"Understood, and thank you," she replied with a nod. She walked me to her front door and handed the bag of clothes to me. "See you tonight."

22

———

"What do you see in the lass?" David asked. "She's pretty enough, but she's trouble. And she's a scientist. That's almost akin to being a wizard."

We stood in his kitchen, where I cooked dinner for him and Selene. She hadn't arrived yet, so we were able to discuss her freely. Correction—he felt free to question me about her.

I sliced tomatoes for atop the rocket salad with a vinaigrette and pondered his question. "I suppose it's because she's beautiful, yes, but also there's a sadness like she hasn't ever been able to let go and enjoy herself fully. She has the same look in her eye as I remember my mother having after my father died—she's hanging on for someone else, not for her."

"You can't save your mother through this girl," David said and sipped his Scotch. "You're only going to disappoint yourself and her by chasing that ghost."

We both paused, but my father's ghost didn't make an appearance. He'd been strangely silent and absent lately after delivering his warning about the battlefield demon and the Boar King, neither of which made sense to me in my current context. I wondered if that was who or what had Selene's brother, especially now I knew a dark Fey was mixed up in it. Every so often I looked out the window at the back lawn that stretched to the woods in hopes of seeing a small red wolf coming our way. I had her clothes in an upstairs bedroom waiting for her.

That reminded me of our encounter the previous night. "I can't figure her out. She's so vulnerable, but she keeps insisting she can handle her own problems. Yet she's caught up in something big, and I know it has something to do with our Institute."

"Do you trust her?"

I paused. "I would like to, but I don't know yet."

For before our run, I'd planned a dinner of venison with bramble sauce, salad, and berry tart, but as the time for Selene to arrive came and went, and the shadows from the woods lengthened to dusk, I had David eat and finally decided to go look for her.

"Be careful out there," he warned. "My lands are warded, but the properties around me aren't, and who knows what lurks in the woods?"

I went into an upstairs bedroom to change. It faced the east, and light from the rising moon spilled through the windows. The sensation that I'd felt in Bartholomew's office, that of some force rising from my toes through my legs and torso and spreading outward from my solar plexus, overtook me, and I barely got my clothes off before I had to curl into a ball, contracting and then expanding into my new shape. My palms and fingers, feet and toes met the floor as paws and claws, and the warmth of fur enveloped me like a velvet blanket inside my skin. Although I felt shrunk and pushed and pulled, this transformation was still not as bad as it previously had been, and I was grateful for it.

Instead of having to catch my breath, I yawned with my

wide jaws and tasted the scents of the bedroom—the cleaning products and the lemon-rosemary scent of Selene's things. I stuck my head in her bag and sniffed them, anchoring her unique scent in my memory so I could track her.

"You look less winded than usual," David commented when I met him downstairs. "You must be getting better at it."

"Right. It's another manifestation of my lycanthrope power, isn't it?"

"Quite likely. That's good—you're going to need it at Monday's Council meeting."

"What do you mean?"

"Later. Go find your girl."

THE MOONLIGHT, warm in spite of its cool color, caressed my fur, and I had to remind myself to focus on the task at hand rather than the desire to howl and play with the moonbeams. The silvery light had never felt like anything externally before, just a desire in the blood to run with my pack. Now whatever had prompted me to change also propelled me to find Selene and protect her, who would be the first in my own little pack.

A breeze brought her scent to me, and I followed it through the woods over and under fallen trees, silvered branches and bushes. I may have found a thorn with my foot, but I shook it out and licked the rusty blood away. The single-minded purpose of finding she who I wanted to protect and make my own drove me forward. I vaulted over chasms I would not have dared to leap otherwise and ignored distractions—a badger hissing at me from its nest and one of those strange stones I'd discovered on my previous jaunt.

She stood waiting for me on a rock over a pool, and I panted, looking at her with relief and some irritation that she'd stood me and David up for dinner.

"Where were you? I was worried."

"I couldn't make it. They called and wanted me to come sooner, so I had to. I've only just now gotten here, and I couldn't remember which way to go."

I leapt to join her, and she pressed her body to mine. She shivered in spite of her fur.

"Lie down. I'll keep you warm."

She did as I said, and I curled up with her until she stopped shaking. Then I asked as gently as I could, *"What happened?"*

She sniffled, a surprisingly human sound for her current form. *"They brought me to what I'd lost, and it was there, but it wasn't the same as I remembered it or wanted it to be."*

"Tell me what it was. Or let me guess—your brother?"

She looked at me sharply, and the expression in her eyes told me I'd guessed right. *"How did you know?"*

I stood and paced. *"You didn't think we'd figure it out eventually, that the sixth file that wouldn't upload was your brother's application? Your friends, or whoever they are, didn't realize that by trying to block it, they were calling attention to it."*

She regarded me with a bemused expression on her canine face. *"Congratulations, Sherlock. It seemed a pretty good plan at the time, but you don't have the whole story."*

"What is the whole story, Selene?"

"It's the oldest story in the world, Gabriel." She shook her head and put it on her paws. *"And I didn't see it. I'm so stupid."* The bitterness and despair in her tone drew forth my desire to protect her from whatever trouble she'd gotten herself into, but I needed more. I needed her to be honest with me.

"Tell me everything from the beginning."

"Can we go back to David's house? He needs to hear some of this, too. It reaches all the way up to the Council."

· · ·

Typically after I run at the full moon, I feel sated like I've consumed rich food and alcohol with my spirit, not my body, although sometimes I do hunt. The venison we'd had for dinner was meat from an animal I'd caught and killed at Lycan Castle. Tonight, lured on by the promise of discovering Selene's secrets—and I'll admit to wanting to finish what we'd started with the stolen embrace at her apartment—I kept my alertness. That was how I knew something was terribly wrong when we arrived at Laird Hall.

On the surface, the castle looked the same, but something moved in the shadows, and it wasn't David. The shape of my father's ghost stepped forth, his hands up, and I slowed to a trot. I saw him just before the aroma of pipe smoke and kerosene wafted to me, and my hackles stood alert—it was the same scent I'd found at the Institute, but this time it was stronger. The perpetrator was still there, and this time he wouldn't escape.

A hiss and spark made me skid to a halt and dart to the side as quickly as I could. Selene did likewise, and the warmth of an explosion bloomed at our backs. It knocked us off our feet, and every bit of my fur was flattened by the pressure wave. I curled around Selene so my back took the brunt of the heat, and the smell of singed hair embittered the sweet scent of the summer night.

"Are you okay?" Selene asked.

"I think so. My backside is likely bald, but I don't feel any burns or severe injury, at least not yet. Are you all right?"

"Yes. What was that?"

"Some sort of explosive. Someone doesn't want us getting into the house."

"It's the same person who killed Otis. I remember that smell."

We kept to the shadows of the woods and circled the house. My back felt stiff, and I wondered if I could be more hurt than I thought. Thankfully the incendiary device hadn't thrown any shrapnel, at least not in our direction. Without David to let us in, I didn't know how we would get into the house, but I also knew he would have some way to do so. He'd spoken of secret passages, and I tried to mentally map out the dungeon as it would be beneath our feet. Not that I'd been in it, but I'd visited other houses of that age and knew the general layout.

"What are you looking for?" Selene's mental voice still held an edge of panic.

"The way in he'd use when he's running by himself. Keep watching the house and lawn and tell me if you see anything interesting."

"Right."

Finally I found a grate that opened with a hard press of a lever, and we descended a steep tunnel into the gloom. The grate clicked closed behind us. Even with my wolf eyes and their superior ability to make out objects in the dark, I couldn't see very far in front of us, and at points, the space was so narrow we had to crawl. An occasional whimper escaped my lips when my back touched the top of the passage and pain stabbed through me. The tunnel opened up into the lower hall I remembered, but another grate blocked us in and wouldn't give when I pushed against it.

"Dammit," I couldn't help but say. *"We're stuck."*

"Is there a similar catch on the other side?" Selene asked. *"If so, maybe you can get a paw around."*

I tried and found one, but the angle was wrong for me to get enough pressure on it to open it. Selene tried as well, her paws being smaller, but it was no good.

"I'm going to change," I said. *"Maybe I can get it with my human hands."*

"I'll give you space."

She backed up, and I hesitated. David had asked me if I trusted her. Transforming back, especially hurt as I was, would put me in a very vulnerable position, especially at that final moment of disorientation before my brain changed from lycanthrope to human mode.

Screw it, I do trust her. I have to.

I changed back into a human. The process bumped me against the sides of the tunnel, and I became all too aware of my injuries as muscles and skin rearranged themselves.

"*You're burned,*" was Selene's assessment. "*We need to get you medical attention.*"

"First we need to get un-stuck." I tried to reach my hand through the holes in the grate, but it wouldn't fit. "Damn, I'm too big. Your hand might work, though."

"*I'll try it, but I need room to change. It's too narrow back here.*"

I scrunched against the wall and hissed at the searing pain along my lower and middle back.

"*I'm sorry,*" she said. "*I'll try to make this quick.*"

She took a deep breath, curled up as tightly as she could, and unfolded into a lovely, naked, sweaty female body. If my back hadn't been throbbing, I would've enjoyed the view better. I also felt a pang of guilt that she hadn't hesitated like I had.

"Sorry," I said.

"For what?" She wiggled to try to lie on her stomach, and I hissed when she bumped me. "I'm sorry," she said. "God, we sound like a couple of Canadians. You're going to have to lie on top of me so I can get my hand through at the right angle."

"Are you sure? I might crush you."

"Support yourself with your arms."

We rearranged, and in order to keep from bumping my back into the roof of the tunnel, I had to keep myself pressed to her backside. Her breasts ended up pillowed on the backs of my hands. *I'll enjoy remembering this later. In the meantime, hurry.*

"I've almost got it," she said. "How are you doing up there?"

"Truth be told, I'm no longer as aware of my back."

She shook with her chuckle. "Happy to be of service. Glad you're keeping your sense of humor."

The catch gave way, and the door opened...inward.

"Argh," she said. "Can you scoot back or change again? I think I can squeeze past."

"Change, right. Maybe not. Not enough room with both of us being human. Can you?"

"I don't think so. I don't have it in me. Okay, scoot back, then."

I did, and she ended up with her ass in my face as she swung the door inward.

"Now let's find David," I said.

"Can you change back into a wolf? We're pretty vulnerable here."

I shrugged, and pain shot along my shoulders and down to my butt. "I dare not until I can get treated for these burns."

We crept along the walls and stuck to the shadows as much as possible. No ghosts, friendly or otherwise, came to bother or help us. Selene, stuck in her human form due to physical and emotional exhaustion, was only slightly less vulnerable than I because of my injuries.

"Take my hand and lead me," I said. "I'm going to turn on my werewolf hearing and smell so we'll have that, at least, but I need to close my eyes."

"Okay, but I don't know where I'm going."

"Straight down the hall. There's a door with a staircase on the other side."

She took my hand, and I closed my eyes and activated my lycanthropic senses. The hallway sprang to relief with its mélange of musty, dusty, and cool smells. There was also a hint of pipe smoke and kerosene, which had perhaps been cleaned out by the fresh air from the ventilation shaft. And, of course, our sweat and human smells, which yelled our presence to any creature that may be near. Luckily it seemed that whoever had been down here had already left. And blood—more than there should be for it to be mine.

Then I turned on my wolf ears. The hall came alive with the scratchings and skitterings of small many-legged creatures in the walls and along the floor. I opted not to tell Selene about the animal life of the dungeon, although being from the Southeastern United States, she'd probably taken care of her share of them. Something about her, possibly the way she'd handled Morena or how she carried herself, told me she wasn't the type to yell for daddy to come kill the bug. She led me with some hesitation, being limited by her human vision and having to feel along the walls.

"What's down here?" she asked. Her voice sounded loud in comparison to the other noises I'd been concentrating on. "Is it a real dungeon? Do you hear or smell anything?"

"Nothing human or lycanthrope. As for where we are, David has a special room where he keeps his documents, and otherwise he uses the cells for furniture storage."

She didn't speak further until she came to the end of the hall. "I think I've found the stairs."

I opened my eyes, and the noise- and smell-scape of the dungeon retreated. I ignored the urge to pop my ears to clear them, knowing it wouldn't do me any good. A sigh bubbled up, and my back throbbed in time to the inhale and exhale.

Selene opened the door slowly and stopped when it squeaked like it wanted to let forth a mighty haunted house creak.

"Can you squeeze through?" she asked.

"Yes." I sucked my stomach in and slid through sideways, only barely grazing my injury, which still burned, although not as badly as I'd suspected. My previous head injury came to mind and the speed at which I'd healed from it, so I wondered if the same might be happening to my back. That made me even more eager for Selene to clean it up—I didn't want the skin and muscle to heal over bits of rock and dirt that could cause infection, scar tissue and other problems.

Selene followed me, and in the dim light from the open door at the top of the stairs—suspicious in itself—all I could see was her delectable female outline and shape. The kerosene-pipe smell lingered more strongly here, as did the blood, and I gestured for her to get behind me in case someone waited at the top of the stairs for us. We ascended into a scene of horror.

23

———

The scent of blood was neither subtle nor hidden, and I easily followed its trail to the dining room, where David—or what was left of him—sat tied to one of his chairs. Either he'd decided to look back through his documentation on Wolfsheim or the intruders had found it because the now familiar papers sat scattered over the top of the table. Splotches of blood punctuated the statements and pictures in a fine spray. More blood coated the floor and windows. David sat with his head back, his throat a gaping testament to the powerful, violent magic that had been wrought upon him, similar to the security guards at the Institute. It was only later that my mind would remember his lips curled in a smile.

Selene's horrified gasp reminded me I wasn't alone.

"Oh, god, it's just like Otis," she said and covered her face.

I pulled her to me and bent my head to hers, but the image remained even when I closed my eyes. Nausea warred with a howl that rose up from my gut, and Selene pulled away when the tremors started under my skin. She backed up, one hand over her mouth and the other arm across her stomach, and she fell to her knees. The same force that had come over me in Bartholomew Campbell's office and after exploded outward. I changed quicker than ever before into an animal larger and fiercer than my previous manifestation. I did throw my head back then and howled with rage and despair at the last link to my father's past being gone and the budding friendship lost.

"Calm yourself, son." It was my father's voice, or what was left of him. The memories I craved had died with David. The ghost stood there, and with my wolf eyes, I saw the red glow around him. His face, illuminated by some inner light and no longer hidden under the brim of his hat, appeared clear to me, and his eyes regarded me with compassion. Now the pressure tried to turn into a sob, difficult in my wolf form, and it came out as a whine.

"David's dead, and my only link to the killer is..." I looked at Selene.

"I can't." She shook her head. "If I do, they'll kill Curtis."

Now disappointment stabbed through me, and I growled. *"Can't you see that they'll kill him eventually regardless of what you do? And now that you know their secrets, you're in danger too. We all are."*

"No one comes from an encounter with Death unchanged," my father's ghost intoned and disappeared.

Selene stood and ran from the room. I followed her upstairs to a bedroom, but she locked the door before I could get in. I looked down the stairs, and the flickering light from the fire illuminated the burgundy carpet like a river of hellfire.

"Selene, you have to let me in."

"No." The word held calmness and despair.

"I can break this door down."

"You wouldn't." She sounded certain. I backed up, but I recognized the futility in the action. She'd been traumatized twice over that evening, and she needed gentleness, not force. And I really needed her to attend to my wounds. It would be just my luck if an opportunistic microbe killed me, not a battle wound or something exciting.

"Selene, I'm changing now, and I'm going to go into the next bedroom and get in the shower. I need help with my wounds or else I fear I'll get an infection."

"Your lycanthropic immune system won't handle it?" Now it was the gentle query of a scientist.

"I don't know. It depends on the maker of the bomb and what they put in it."

"Fine, but not here. I can't stay here." And the hysterical note was back.

"Good idea. I'll show you where your clothes are, and then you can take us back to my place."

I CHANGED BACK TO HUMAN—A miserable process—and when I stood, warm fluid dripped down my right butt cheek and leg. I called Garou to process the crime scene and told him what Selene and I had encountered outside of Laird Hall.

"You need to stay there. Dammit, Investigator, I need your impressions."

"I'm injured."

"Fine, I will call Doctor Fortuna."

"That's not a bad idea," I told him. "Tell him to meet me at my place, and you and I can talk tomorrow. Don't argue."

Surprisingly, he didn't, and in half an hour, I lay face down on towels in front of the fireplace in my house. My entire back felt on fire, but I shivered as my nervous system tried to decide whether it would be better for my survival for me to change or stay human. I gritted my teeth Shand suppressed the urge, not sure I would make it if I did transform. One thing both sides of me agreed on: I needed fluids, and Selene gave me ice cubes to suck on while we waited for Max since sips of water made me gag.

Finally the doorbell rang, and Selene went to answer it.

"Thank god you're—oh."

That was an "oh" of "oh, there's another woman here," and Reine's soft voice drifted to me along with Max's deep one. At that point, I seemed to float off the floor, and when I cracked my eyelids open to see if I did, indeed, levitate, the flames licked at the wolf-faced fireback in slow motion. Another shudder racked me, and I squeezed my eyes shut against the urge to change. A sensation of bugs running under my skin covered me, and I struggled to stay tethered to reality in human form.

"Good gods, what happened?" Max asked.

"As I said, he took the brunt of the explosion," Selene said, and I wanted to wipe away the tears in her voice because I imagined them coming out of her eyes as well. I wanted to turn my head to say something comforting, but the wolf's face behind the fire kept me anchored, and I feared I'd lose consciousness if I stopped looking at it.

"How close were you?" asked Reine.

"Too close," Selene said. "We tried to run, but it was too late—they saw us and tried to kill us. He knew. He curled around me and protected me."

A cool finger ran over my back. No, through it. It was a dagger frozen in dry ice coated in ice, and I gasped.

"You're hurting him!" Selene cried.

"Wait in the other room, child," Reine told her. "I'm trying to save him. That was a hellfire grenade, and it will take more than human or lycanthrope magic to mitigate the effects. Then you both wandered through a residual blood magic aura. If he wasn't as old and strong as he is, he would've already died."

A quick swallow and the sound of hair brushing over Selene's shoulders told me she didn't like it, but she nodded. *There's my girl.*

"What do you need me to do?" asked Max once Selene's

footsteps had faded. I wondered where she went, if she was fixing a drink for herself or just curled up somewhere. Curling up, that sounded good, but I couldn't move. My limbs were leaden, and the fire continued its slow, sensuous dance.

"Now it's your turn to hold him, but first we must negotiate a price."

Aw, fuck.

A curtain of sinewy curling white snakes got in the way of my flames, and the fairy's face followed it. Her wide blue eyes held mine with a solemn expression.

"You wolf-men get in more trouble," she said, her lips curling up in a half-joker smile. I never understood the purpose of that card in the deck. It seemed extraneous unless you were playing something needlessly complicated. I never had the smarts or patience for—

"Stay with me, Wolf-man," she murmured, and I blinked, back from the land of floating, sneering face cards. "You know what I want as a price for my healing you."

"I can't," I said through dry lips.

"I don't suppose you'd be interested in offering a child? You can even make it your second if you like."

"No child," I croaked.

"Your name, then."

She held a hand over my temple, and a soft white glow suffused my vision. It soothed and cleared my head from the pain I'd been in. I understood what it would also do: capture my name as it left my lips and allow the fairy to use it however she saw fit. I would be at her beck and call, and she would have power over me.

Max cleared his throat. "You don't have to give it to her, Gabriel. Remember, it won't just affect you if you do."

Right, Selene. If she does have a future with me... But the chances of us being together wouldn't be high if we both ended up dead, and our opponents obviously meant business. A hellfire grenade meant it had been wielded by someone with powerful magic, and I knew I was dead if I didn't accept Reine's bargain.

I took a deep breath and said through clenched teeth, "I am Gabriel Stuart McCord. I give you my name to use once. Employ it wisely."

"All right, then, you are a clever one." She disappeared from my view. "Hold him, Maximilian." Her tone was cold, and I guessed she was not pleased with his interference or my limiting her power over me. "I can sit on his legs, but you need to hold his arms."

"No sticks," I coughed and moved my arms to the side and over my head so Max could easily restrain them. Her weight settled on my legs, and a burning electric jolt shot from my lower back to my neck.

"Oh, darling Gabriel, you're going to wish I was using a stick by the time I'm through."

My name dropped from her lips like a frozen pebble and landed on my sacrum. She murmured words even below my hearing, and each one fell onto my back, chips and daggers of rock and ice, a trail starting from my tailbone and rushing up my spine, sticking into each of those burning, throbbing places. I writhed to dislodge them—*Death would feel better than this!*—but my captors held true. The weight of the spell ground my front into the towels beneath me, and the needles of each little loop and fiber poked me. Searing cold poured through my nervous system, and if Max's cleansing had been a torrent of glacial water, this one crushed me in an avalanche of ice, snow and misery. I thrashed with my head, the only part of me I could move freely.

"Almost there," Reine said through clenched teeth, and I imagined her, face slick with sweat and the effort of the spell.

If the bitch can even sweat.

The sensation turned from crystalline to gel, and it warmed

gradually from the center outward until my entire body had been filled with it. I wondered where my bones went since I couldn't feel them from my neck down, and then a cowl of the stuff grew over my head and face and into my eyes, nose and mouth. I struggled to breathe against its viscous web, but with every inhale attempt, I pulled it further in until it choked my throat.

"Just another moment," Reine murmured. "I have to get all the passages, even the little airways."

My chest worked to breathe, and on what I felt would be my last inhale before I suffocated, the stuff vanished. I drew air into my lungs in deep, desperate gasps.

"Do you always have to make it so unpleasant?" I asked when I could speak.

She laughed. "You boys are the ones who keep finding trouble that requires my kind of intervention."

"Thank you," I said. Max released my arms, and I brought them down to my sides. "I am healed, then?"

"Mostly. The rest is up to your body. The more life-affirming activities you can do, the faster you'll heal the rest of the way," Reine said. She stood, and I rolled to my side and then to my back. It felt sensitive, but closed and no longer raw. Max helped me to sit and then stand and hobble to the couch. Reine brought me a robe, which I put on before collapsing.

"You need food," she said. "And, as I said, life-affirming activities."

"That's the good part of her prescriptions," Max told me with a wink.

She nodded. "But as with Max, you need to recover for a few days."

Max's eyes met mine, and we both seemed to have the same thought: I didn't have a few days to solve this mystery, and he certainly didn't have the extra time. Neither did Selene or her brother. As for the fate of the Institute—my mind didn't want to acknowledge the fact, but with David dead, I'd lost the majority support and possibly the ability to help those who needed it most, the ones who had been turned lycanthrope against their will.

"I'll do my best," I said. "Where's Selene?"

"Selene! That reminds me..." Max stood. "I'll fetch her. Believe me, I have my own questions for her."

I'd half expected her to disappear during Reine's procedure on me, and I have to admit to some embarrassed surprise when she walked in after Max called her. She rushed to sit beside me.

"Are you okay? You were making the most horrible noises."

"Fairy medicine isn't pleasant," I said. "But I'm much better." I put an arm around her. "Max has some questions for you, and you need to finish telling me what you started earlier. I suspect it's all about the same thing."

"Selene," Max said, "we know that the sixth reversal subject Corey Richardson is really your brother Curtis Rial. I need to know what you were playing at and what you've been keeping from us."

She slumped back into the couch cushions. "Gabriel, when I came to you a few days ago and told you Otis's death was my fault, I wasn't lying," she said. "And as much as I've lied, it's because I had to protect my little brother."

"Start from the beginning," I told her.

She pulled away and looked into the fire.

24

"Curtis always had problems," Selene said. "Like, the kind that ends a kid up on medication by the time he hits first grade. Impulsivity, mostly, with a little bit of defiance. It later came out that my mother had an affair, and she never told my father, who left when we were little. Then I found the genetic tests when I was a teenager and pieced it together with information from her diary. She'd written about it in deliberately vague terms, but I knew she carried a lot of guilt with her. It was a relief to find out why my father left and her part in it."

"What did she write about the man who fathered Curtis?" I asked. "We have strict rules about that sort of conduct. Should a child be born with lycanthropy, or what you're calling full-blown CLS, it's the responsibility of the werewolf blood relative to make sure he or she is brought to one of our communities and trained so the child won't accidentally hurt anyone."

"My mother only wrote that she'd made a new friend at the airport, where she worked in marketing. He was a corporate type who flew through often, and she'd caught his eye. Never any physical descriptions, and then a passage about how they never talked any more in spite of everything that had happened between them. If he offered to help with the baby he'd fathered, she must have refused him. Or maybe he didn't know."

"Let's get back to Curtis," Max said. "Does he have CLS?"

She nodded. "Once I learned about the disorder in graduate school, I knew that's what he must have, but the genetic type. He did display the classic behaviors: sneaking off at night even as a preteen, hyperactivity and impulsivity around the full moon, and strong loyalty to friends to a dangerous degree. What is it that parents always ask their teens? If they'd all jumped off a bridge, he would have, too."

"So how did you get it?" I asked. "Or were you also a genetic case?"

"No, just my luck, I had a flu vaccine from the tainted batch when I was on my predoctoral internship at the Central Arkansas VA."

"Maybe the same batch that infected Leo," I said.

"Maybe." She rubbed her eyes. "But I adjusted to it better than Curtis ever did. He struggled in school, even with medications. He hates the changes, which started once he hit late puberty. He didn't tell me about them until he caught me at one of mine. I just thought he'd disappear. It's amazing—he would have been the one per generation that happens in the general population had it not been for the viral vectors. But he can't even hold down a part-time job because the sensory experiences are too intense for him." She blinked, and a tear rolled down her cheek. "He's been my responsibility since our parents were killed. I had to do something, and this was going to help both of us. I am interested in the work, very interested. I understand just how difficult this condition can be for people."

"So you conspired to get a job with us, for him to change his name, and for the two of you to come here." I looked at her silhouette with slumped shoulders against the fire. I wanted to be angry at her, but I remembered the Young Bloods and how they struggled with their lycanthropy. Curtis's case sounded even direr than theirs. Was it fair to withhold something that could help the extreme genetic cases that couldn't function in the real world? Was it any wonder our ancestors who couldn't survive in society took to the woods to become hermits so they wouldn't end up burned at the stake as witches?

"What about Curtis's friends?" asked Max. "The ones who are holding him hostage?"

"As I said, he's overly loyal to his friends. One of them was a Scottish exchange student named Jake. He convinced Curtis to come over early before he was going to be a study subject and hang out for a while. Jake brought him to Wolfsheim, who can look at a person's blood and know things about them. He saw what Curtis had, and worse, who he's related to."

Now her earlier statement that this went all the way up to the Council came back to me. Also the theft of the blood from the Institute's vault. "Who would that be?"

She looked at me over her shoulder. "Curtis is Bartholomew Campbell's illegitimate son."

Reine clapped her hands. "Oh, that's perfect! And does Bartholomew know?"

"I don't know. I suspect so."

"So why did they let you go?" I asked. "What do they want you to do?"

Selene turned away. "Wolfsheim wants me to bring you to him, Gabriel. He wants you to be his spy inside the Council and the Institute. He said something about you not being fully developed, so you're the one it will be most easy to influence." She shivered. "And he is able to influence."

Her words brought back something David had told me, and my gut clenched with anger at what had been done to him. "That was before he killed my friend and tried to blow me up."

"He's powerful, Gabriel," Reine said, the syllables of my name dropping like two diamonds and a pearl from her lips.

"As powerful as you?" asked Max.

"No." She shook her curls, and I thought I saw little white rabbits hopping through them. "But he is very old and has lost what little humanity he had. What motivates someone like that? Power, and then the choice becomes whether to save or to destroy because humans cannot do both. He has always wanted to eliminate your kind."

"He will not do so through me," I vowed, "and I have to destroy him before he tries with someone else."

Selene gazed into the fire, and her silhouette reminded me of an ancient pagan priestess, which made her words that much more frightening. "He has his fingers in all aspects of your life and organization. He will find a way, or one of you will die with his attempts."

"Is that what Otis's death was?" Max asked, and his normally cool tone even icier with anger. *He must have learned some tricks from Reine.* "An attempt to influence us?"

"I don't know."

"But your friend was there," I said. "The one with the scarred cheek."

"Rhys," Selene and Reine said at the same time.

I shook my head to clear the bell-like tone that echoed after their less than perfect harmony. "So when you said Otis had a question for you, it wasn't to ask you out. It was about your brother."

"Yes," she said. "He'd found out somehow through his research that Curtis and Bartholomew were related. All the applicants had to submit initial blood samples to confirm their CLS diagnosis. He went digging."

"And the Institute also had blood samples and profiles on the Council members, their mates, and most of the Institute staff as a show of good faith in the blood magic process and to start a database," Max told us. "But not Bartholomew Campbell. He abstained from the project."

"What if someone got a blood sample from him and slipped it to LeConte?" I asked. "Garou's report said there was no sign of a struggle. What if Campbell's secretary had been working with LeConte all along?"

"Why?" asked Selene.

"To gain access to the rest of the blood."

"Can you prove it?" asked Max. "LeConte was fanatically curious, so I'm not surprised. But that doesn't tell us who killed him."

"He wasn't supposed to go digging like he did, and he would never have betrayed us." But Selene didn't sound so sure. "I can tell you Rhys didn't kill him. Rhys doesn't have that kind of magic. As for who did..." She shrugged. "He won't tell you. His secrecy is a price for working with Wolfsheim, and he's not going to go up against his boss. He told me he doesn't even know a name."

"Did he give you a description?" I asked.

"No. He told me not to worry my pretty head about it and focus on my objective, which was to snare you."

Selene's words hung in the air between us. I knew she spoke the truth, and she'd previously admitted it, but it still stung my male ego. I wanted to inspire her pursuit, not have it dictated. On the other hand, I'd believed her when she said she was truly attracted to me—and her kisses confirmed her words.

"So we come back to an unknown assassin," I said. "But at least there's a clearer motive. I need to talk to Bartholomew Campbell again."

"He's likely at his Solstice gathering," Reine pointed out. "My kind makes complaints every time his filthy pack descends on the islands. He in particular disturbs the selkies."

"I can probably get him to come back," I said. "I just need to find my phone and call his secretary. She owes me a favor, and we need to talk again, anyway."

MAX AND REINE left with the admonition that even if I wanted to go after Wolfsheim and Bartholomew Campbell, I needed to wait until the rays of the coming dawn allowed the last of Reine's cure to work. She didn't compel me, but the possibility hung in the air between us, and I felt the resentment from my toes. Or maybe it was whatever was growing within me to bring me to my full power. However it worked, I agreed to be a good little doggie and sit and stay.

Or maybe not so good. Instead of leaving with the other two, Selene stayed and looked into the fire as I said my good-byes. Her face held a neutral expression, and her posture, while contemplative, didn't indicate the valence of her thoughts. Her still, closed aspect reminded me of her profession as a psychologist, but I wanted to ask her the questions. Did it feel good for her to have the big, ugly secrets off her chest? Or did she feel more vulnerable and conflicted now that she'd revealed what she knew? How would this affect her brother?

As though she read my mind, she said, "We can only have tonight, Gabriel. I can't lead you into danger, and I have to go to Curtis and use what little influence I have to protect him against Wolfsheim."

Her words chilled me, and I moved to stand behind her at the fire. "Let me help you."

She turned and wrapped her arms around me. Her body radiated heat and chased the vestiges of the sensations from Reine's spell away, and I bent my head to her copper hair, which reflected the color of the flames. It smelled of my shampoo—she'd taken a shower while Reine worked, apparently—and I stifled a growl of satisfaction at the small scent indicating possession.

Where the hell did that come from?

I didn't want to become a totalitarian alpha like Bartholomew. I wanted to be more like David, who did his own thing and held his enemies at bay with the promise of strength rather than the brute force use of it.

David. Now when I pulled Selene to me, it was as much for my own comfort as for hers. I closed my eyes and called to mind how he'd looked mocking me in his kitchen for pursuing her and his good-natured teasing, but the image of his bloody demise tried to intrude. I opened my eyes and looked at the flames instead, wishing I had some sort of talent to divine what I should do.

"Gabriel, I'm loving this, but I'm getting hot," Selene said, but she didn't pull away. Instead, she snuggled in. "You've had a rough week."

I let her change the subject, but I vowed to convince her to let me help her. "You have, too," I said. I picked her up and carried her to the sofa. We sat with her on my lap, and I asked, "What shall we do about our weeks?"

"I can think of a very effective kind of stress relief." She traced my jaw with her hand, and she allowed her fingernails to rake through the stubble under my chin, bending my head to hers. The sensation and sound went directly to my groin, and I had to acquiesce to her command.

Our lips met. Now there was nothing between us, no secrets, and we found a rhythm underscored by the crackle of the fire and the howl of the wind outside. I slid one hand up the outside of her leg while holding her close to me with the other one. She put her hands on either side of my face and ran her fingertips down my neck and across my shoulders under my robe.

"This isn't fair," I murmured. "You're wearing many more clothes than I am."

She pulled back with a wicked grin and stood. I reached for her, but she eluded me.

"Sit, stay," she said, and I growled, but I didn't have much of a choice.

"You don't know what kind of beast you're messing with, my dear," I said.

She laughed. Unlike Reine's, Selene's chuckle had depth and sunshine, and it spoke of chases through the dappled sunlight of the trees. I found it preferable to the icy wind chimes of the Fey's.

"Just watch," she said, and I did.

She turned to face the fire, gathered her long, red-gold hair, and pulled it over her right shoulder. The set of her shoulders and the movements of her elbows told me she unbuttoned her shirt, and I moved to stand, wanting to see the fire flickering over her pale skin and to count her freckles with my lips.

"Stay," she whispered. She opened the shirt to the fire and slid it down off her shoulders and back. It fell to the floor, and she held out her arms so I could see her silhouette. As most of us do, she had good proportion and muscle tone, and who am I kidding? My eyes immediately went to the hint of the curve of her breasts at her sides, and my mouth went dry at the realization she wore no bra.

"Care to help me with my pants?" she asked with an over-the-shoulder glance that brought me to my feet and to stand behind her before my brain could command it.

"You bewitch me," I said, my breath swaying the little hairs by her ear. The view of her pale front was even better than I had imagined, and I cupped her breasts and lightly caressed her pale pink nipples with my thumbs.

"Pants, Gabriel," she breathed, but she leaned back into me.

"In a moment. Sit, stay."

I nibbled and play-bit her neck on the side opposite where she'd gathered her hair from her ear lobe down to her shoulder. As I'd hoped, she had a light dusting of freckles across her skin, and I kissed every one I could see and a few the flickering light hinted at. All the while, I savored the weight of her breasts in my hands and the hardness of their tips. She ground her butt into my front, and I feathered my fingertips over her ribs and slid my hands down her belly until I found the button of her jeans, which I unfastened. I hooked my fingers over the straps of her panties as well and slid the whole mess to her ankles. She tangled her fingers in my hair for balance and stepped out of them.

Now she stood completely naked in front of me, and again, she reminded me of a pagan priestess, strong and in command. Only her eyes, the slight *o* of her lips, and the flush of her skin told me she was mine for the taking. I pulled her to me.

"You're sure about this," I said. "This is you wanting it and no other."

"You could've asked me that before I got undressed," she said, "but gods, yes, Gabriel. I want you. And it's just me."

I pulled a condom out of my robe pocket and allowed the flannel to fall to the floor so we stood with nothing physical in the way. She tore the packet open with her teeth, and I had to tamp down the desire to just pick her up and take her without protection. To make matters worse, she grabbed my cock. The feel of her light, slender fingers wrapped around its ruddy length nearly made me lose control.

Finally, she rolled the condom over me, and I picked her up. It showed my weakness from the evening's events that I couldn't hold her up, so I gently kneeled and laid her on my robe in front of the fire. She was more than ready when I slid into her, and again we picked up nature's rhythm. The flames roamed over her skin along with my tongue and hand, and she explored my body as well, her touch sending shivers to my core and driving me to more intensity. We cried our release simultaneously, and it felt that even the fire was quieter for a beat after.

I rolled off her, and she snuggled up to me with her back to my front. We dozed there in front of the fire, our heads pillowed on her clothes and my robe over us.

"I'm not letting you go," I murmured in her ear.

"Please don't," she replied, her eyes closed. "At least not 'til the morning."

"Not even then. Sit, stay."

I wish I had some sort of explanation, maybe the remainder of Reine's magic folding over us or some other influence, but all I can say is that I fell into a deep slumber. When I woke to the tingling sensation of the first sunbeams of dawn, my head rested on a throw pillow, my arms were empty, and a ghost watched me.

25

———

"**I** *used to find you like this in our bedroom closet, asleep on a robe,*" he said as I scrambled to cover myself. I felt like a teenager who got busted making out with his girlfriend—or worse—by his parents.

"Haven't you heard of knocking?" I asked. "Waiting for an invitation? Good gods, were you watching?"

"*I gave you your privacy, but you know I didn't teach you like this, son. Do you and the young lady have some sort of understanding? Are you at least engaged?*"

I turned to him, open-mouthed with shock and feeling all of fifteen. "What do you mean you didn't teach me like this? You died before I was even looking at girls."

"*But I always taught you to respect women.*"

"Oh, I do respect her even though she drives me crazy. Now, do you have something important to say? I need to go after her before she sacrifices herself to some crazy *vargamore* who wants to use her as bait!"

"*Find him. Find Wolfsheim. Expose the influence of the Silver Arrow and what they did to destroy me. Then I can find peace.*"

With those words, he was gone. I ran my hands through my

hair and tried to get my brain to calm down enough to make a plan. The doorbell and the phone rang simultaneously.

I grabbed the phone and padded to the door. The peephole showed me Rhys, the scarred Fey, standing on the other side. *Great.* Even worse, when I answered the phone, it was Morena. *Even better.*

"Emergency Council meeting in one hour," she said. "No excuses."

"How can we have a Council meeting? Cora Campbell is in the Hebrides with Bartholomew."

"They're both back. Be there, Gabriel. More rides on this than I can say." And she hung up.

I flung the phone into the study and opened the door. Now that I was finally faced with the witness to the murder, I didn't have time to talk to him.

"What do you want?" I asked.

"I warned you to stay away from us," Rhys said. He stood with his hands in the pockets of a black leather jacket, and I shivered when the chill breeze hit my bare legs.

"I'll ask again, Rhys. What do you want? Unless it's to give me a description of the man who killed David Lachlan or tell me where Selene Rial is, I'm not interested in talking to you."

"T'waren't no man," he said, and his mouth twisted into a smug grin. "T'was a woman. Thin with short black hair. Kinda green, if you know what I mean."

"Jade?" I gasped, the pieces of the puzzle shifting and my world along with it. "That's impossible! She's not strong enough to have done that." But my mind catalogued the clues that pointed in her direction, specifically her interest in the cure, how she posed as a broker between me and the Young Bloods, the killer's smell in the basement of the Campbells' company headquarters, and the likely person to have gotten a sample of Campbell's blood to LeConte...

"Physically she int. But the girl's got some magic to 'er."

"And Selene?" I asked, both pleased that all roads seemed to lead to Bartholomew Campbell and annoyed that they might go past him.

"The boss said to give this to you." He pulled a braid of copper-colored hair out of his pocket. It was woven into a love-knot, and it tingled with power. "Be at the ruins at sundown. He said you'd know what it meant since you been snooping around there in your wolf form. There you'll be able to make a deal to save your ladylove." He nodded toward the coil of hair in my hand. "Or I'll be bringing you her scalp next."

I BARELY HAD time to take a shower before I had to leave for the Council meeting, but there wasn't any reason to let the rest of them know what I'd been up to. Another problem with lycan-thropy I now thought about in a different way. Did the Young Bloods know when their friends had been hooking up more than they wanted to? In this social media-driven society, it would be one way to stay ahead of the flow of information and know things before their friends did, but perhaps they balked at the unintentional invasion of privacy.

In spite of the chill, I drove with the top down to allow the storm-cleansed air to clear my head. The same questions chased each other in a maddening circle: why wouldn't Selene let me help her? Why did she leave? What were they going to do to her? What could I do to stop them? Why was I going to the Council meeting instead of chasing down Rhys and Wolfsheim and getting her back?

Because there was something that needed to happen first. It wasn't just the timing of the summons from Wolfsheim, but something else. If I was going to take him on, I needed to be at full strength, and my instincts told me that would happen after the Council meeting. No, I didn't know why—something in my blood older than my weight of years just told me to, and I obeyed it.

Sit, stay, prepare...

I first noticed the difference when I walked into Lycan Castle. Formerly the tapestries had seemed faded and old, but today they blazed with color and gore as they told the story of our lycanthropic heritage. While I'd spent a lot of time studying them as a young werewolf, I had no idea what I looked at, only battles with men and other creatures. Now one drew me in particular: a battlefield spread over five of the hangings. In the forefront, a grisly scene worthy of Bosch, where humans and hairy demons fought against other humans and wolves. There was a sense the hairy demons were going to win. In the background, a gaunt figure raised a sword toward an army of wolves, and I'd always thought it rallied them, but perhaps it held them back. Could it be Wolfsheim had become immortalized in tapestry, and I'd been studying him all along?

"Don't dawdle, McCord."

I turned with a snarl to see Morena standing behind me, her crossed arms enhancing her fireplug appearance.

"This could be important," I said. "Who is that, and what is he holding?"

She squinted at the place on the tapestry where I pointed. "That is the foul *vargamore* Wolfsheim." She shook her head. "Of all the tapestries for you to notice... The others tell of our victories, but this one is a reminder of our greatest defeat."

"No one told me about it."

"We don't like to talk about how our kind failed Bonnie Prince Charlie at Culloden. He counted on us, and we didn't show up." She pointed to Wolfsheim. "The tales vary on how he managed to influence us, whether it was a poison that made the soldiers sleep through the short battle or some more sort of direct magic, but whatever happened, we let our guard down and failed. This tapestry is cautionary."

"What can one do against a *vargamore*?" I asked. "Neither wizards nor we have been able to control a creature who has all our talents."

"They don't have full wizard or werewolf abilities, only a subset. All you can do is hope to outsmart him before he influences you. The element of surprise is best."

I looked again at the battle. "What about bringing a second one?"

She smirked. "You're thinking about Lonna Marconi-Fortuna, aren't you? She is young and untrained."

"But powerful, or at least that's what I'm told. Plus Max is in danger of being captured and tortured by the other wizards."

"Those are all little moving pieces in this great big chaotic mess, Gabriel." She moved toward the hallway to the Council Chamber, and I followed. "The worst of which is David Lachlan's death."

I bowed my head to keep the lump in my throat from expanding into tears. "He was a great wolf."

"Who got too close to something that wanted to stay hidden," she said. She stopped just before we entered the hallway and put a hand on my arm. In a low voice, she warned me, "David's charge was to investigate the Order of the Silver Arrow and try to keep track of their activities. Someone tipped them off that he was doing it, and that's what caused his death." Her gaze bored into mine. "Tell me it wasn't you, that you're not the leak."

"Morena, I swear by both my parents' graves that I didn't speak of it to anyone, on or outside the Council. I didn't even know until two nights ago that he had information of that sort. He told me he knew they had something to do with my father's death."

She nodded once, curtly. "I knew it wasn't you. That leaves five others. That's why we're here. News of David's death hasn't gone out publicly yet. You're to help me flush out our snitch, and potentially our murderer."

"Look to the Campbells," I said. "Too much points in their direction to be a coincidence."

"I hope it's that easy, but sometimes the most obvious answer isn't the right one."

Just before we walked in, my phone buzzed with a text from Lonna: *Looked through LC's analyses further. Found another surprise. Call me.*

"You might be right," I said to Morena. "My *vargamore* has an interesting piece of news for me. I'll join you in a moment."

"I'll wait." She crossed her arms and planted her feet. But then Dimitri Corvair rounded the corner. His narrow features lit when he saw her, and his heavy black brows rose.

"Ah, Lady Morena," he said and took her arm. "Just the person I hoped to see. Do you have time for a word before the meeting?"

She allowed him to steer her away from the Council Chamber but looked over her shoulder at me. "Don't forget," she mouthed. "I need to know."

I waved her off and called Lonna. I followed them away from the chamber but took a different turn to bring me to a parlor we used as a waiting room for visiting dignitaries. It smelled of little-circulated air, and I sneezed just as Lonna answered her phone.

"Gabriel? Is that you?" she asked.

"Yes," I said and sniffled. "Sorry, dusty parlor. What's up?"

"Well, it took me, Max, and Iain looking through Otis's charts and figuring out his code—the key is on the laptop Garou has—but we came up with another interesting connection between the Rial family and the Council."

My toes grew cold in spite of the stuffy room. "What?"

"Selene and Curtis—both of them—are related to Dimitri

Corvair through their mother. Closely. I don't know what it means, but—"

"But Morena is in danger. Sorry to interrupt you, Lonna, but I have to run." Indeed, I already ran down the hallway and followed Morena's and Dimitri's scents to her offices. As the leader, she was the only one who rated a nice suite on the ground floor. Their voices came to me in the hall.

"This is irrelevant!" Dimitri yelled. I'd never heard him raise his voice before, and here he was almost snarling.

"Why did you give your blood to be tested?" asked Morena. "You could've abstained."

"How was I to know my great nephew was a test subject and my great niece would be an Institute employee? I had to manage appearances."

I flung the door open, but they stood with no weapons other than their words. "I think this would be a better discussion to have with the Council," I told them. "They need to have the entire story."

Dimitri gave me a smile that chilled me to my core. "Oh, I agree, Investigator. Lead the way."

26

———

Once we'd all assembled in the Council Chamber, Morena started with a call to order. I looked around as she read the minutes of the last meeting—which I'd not been invited to, but which didn't mention me or my situation. I still felt that power coiled at my solar plexus, my third chakra, some would say, but it lay quiet like it waited for something. I, too, waited and dreaded the words that would make the previous evening's horror real. Finally they came.

"As you know," Morena said, "David Lachlan was investigating the Order of the Silver Arrow for the Council."

"Where is he, anyway?" asked Cora Campbell. "I cut a trip short to be here. He should be more considerate."

"I'm sure he would have been here," Morena told her, "had he not died in his home last night."

Cora's mouth fell open in genuine shock. I hung my head in sorrow but watched the reactions of the others. Dimitri's face drained of color, making his black hair, stubble, and eyebrows even starker against his skin. Everyone looked truly horrified and saddened by David's passing, but it made my job harder. And then things got worse.

"Why doesn't Gabriel look more shocked?" asked Cora. "You two were friends."

"I was the one who found him, so I already knew."

"And I assume you've talked to Garou?" Dimitri said. "Morena, will the detective be here today to give us a report?"

"He will," she said, but she shot a helpless look at me.

"I have not yet spoken with Garou about it," I said. "I was injured and had to seek medical attention, and then Morena woke me this morning."

Dimitri sniffed. "I'm not sure what kind of attention he was seeking, but I can tell you it wasn't medical, at least not all the way."

Dammit! "My personal life is none of your business," I told him.

"But the Council and what happens to its members is," Dimitri pushed. "Let me guess, you were with that pretty little redheaded scientist, weren't you?"

"Again, that's none of your concern."

"And who did you seek help from? We know that Maximilian Fortuna, the wizard wanted by his own Tribunal for use of questionable magic, and that silver Fey visited you last night. Was that your 'medical attention'?" He stood and pointed a finger at me. "Lady Morena, I submit for consideration that our own Council Investigator has been consorting and possibly conspiring with enemies of our kind."

The other members jumped in on the uproar, and it was impossible to tell who as for and who was against me in the din.

"And what about you, Dimitri?" I asked when I could break into the shouting. "What secrets have you been keeping from us? Or trying to?" I stopped. I couldn't say anything about Selene and Curtis's involvement with the Order of the Silver Arrow without endangering all of us.

"You've been withholding information just as you are now," he sneered.

My temple gave a little throb. I should've guessed the tension would blossom into a migraine, or would try to. "I can't share all the information without jeopardizing the investigation," I told him. A couple of people nodded, but the rest sat in stone-faced silence, their expressions neither accusatory nor supportive, but more curious. It was then I understood the dynamics at play.

How could I be so stupid? David was dead. He'd been the senior male member of the pack, and although Morena was our leader, the remaining males would then be vying for alpha position. Not Keith, a firm beta who had never shown any desire for leadership and whose graying temples and rounded features watched with curiosity. That left Dimitri, whose behavior suddenly made more sense beyond his hiding his connections to the Institute. I wondered if finding out his niece and nephew were so close made him change his vote. He would be reprimanded for not acknowledging them since it was important for us to keep track of our own kind so we could protect the human population.

"I would like to propose a replacement for Council Member Lachlan," Cora said. Her mask of clueless observation melted away to reveal a shrewd expression. "I would like to propose Bartholomew Campbell as our new male council member."

I raised my eyebrows. "He has no genetic link to the Council."

"Ridiculous!" Dimitri said. "He has not demonstrated the moral fiber necessary to sit at this table. Need I remind you of his infidelity?"

Instead of recoiling from the harsh fact, Cora leaned in. "You call it infidelity, but is an alpha male not permitted to take whatever female he wants from his pack? His actions have all been with my consent."

"Even his actions abroad?" I asked. "With those outside of our knowledge and kind?"

Her features drew in like I'd just forced a very sour pickle into her mouth. "I don't know what you mean."

Damn, I would have to reveal one of Selene's secrets, but I didn't know how to get around it. "He has an illegitimate son by an American woman, a boy who manifested the full spectrum of CLS symptoms."

"Preposterous!" Cora sputtered. "Prove it."

"Otis LeConte was going to prove it. He was working on making genetic connections between known werewolves and found something indicating one of our first test subjects was related to Bartholomew."

"How? Bartholomew refused to give a sample."

"He got one somehow."

She smacked the table. "There must be some sort of mistake. Let's get back to the matter at hand, not airy-fairy accusations." She pointed at Morena. "These are dire times, and we need a full Council to take a vote on the abomination that is the Institute before it further endangers us and our kind."

"The Institute is only a building, Council Member," Morena said. "It cannot threaten you any more than this table can."

"Then the people who make it up." And, with a poisonous glance at me, "And those who advocate for it. Even beyond its stated mission, which in itself is an abomination to 'cure' people of this gift. First it brought danger into our midst, then it risked exposure of our secrets to the humans, and now it is the vehicle for unfounded accusations toward our businesspeople."

"Investigator McCord, can you produce the sample from Bartholomew Campbell that LeConte analyzed?"

"I wish I could, but it was stolen along with all the others from the Institute."

Another uproar, this time with fear.

Keith's quiet voice cut through the chaos. "Garou's latest report mentioned a theft of samples, but it didn't say of what. We should have pressed further."

"Now we're all in danger," squeaked Tabitha, the youngest female Council member. With her short brown hair, small mouth, and big eyes, she looked like a frightened rabbit. "Whoever has it can use blood magic against us."

I wanted to argue and negate the fear, but I couldn't. Was that what had allowed whoever it was to kill David in so gruesome a manner? I swallowed around a choking feeling.

"I promise I have leads, and I am following them," I said. "It's not necessary to take precipitous action or fill a lifelong position out of fear. That would be the worst mistake of all."

"Oh, come now," said Dimitri. "It seems that the more you 'investigate,' the more danger we all end up in. Are you finding out true facts or just uncomfortable family secrets that may or may not be true?"

He, of course, seemed relieved to find out the blood samples were gone because there went the proof of his deception as well. The more I discovered and pieced it all together, the more it seemed that the murders at the Institute and the theft went above me.

Everyone has their secrets, Reine had said. I'd discovered Selene's, but it seemed the Council had an ugly secret of its own with full complicity of all except...

I looked at Morena. She closed her eyes, sighed, and said, "I had hoped it wouldn't come to this."

"Come to what?" I asked.

"Don't do it, Morena," Tabitha whispered. "Oh, gods, don't."

"Do it," Dimitri snarled. "Let him show what kind of wolf he is since he cannot prove he's an honest man."

"I am an honest man," I said. "But I am not trusting, especially of wolves who conspire against fixing a process we allowed to go on too long to begin with."

That got their attention. "What process?" asked Cora. "What sort of new distraction is this?"

I spoke over my heartbeat, which sped up in time to the incrementally thickening tension in the room. My fingers and toes tingled like when I walked into Veronica's shop, and I became aware of the cool weight of the fluorite around my neck under my shirt.

"We knew of the sudden increase in full CLS in the States, and you sent me to investigate. Then you sat on my report and refused to allow me to proceed."

"You got distracted," Dimitri said. "By Landover's granddaughter. And then her friend. Who you brought here to head up the Institute. See? We did allow you to proceed."

"You allowed me to set up the Institute because you felt guilty. Had you heeded my warnings of the small colonies of werewolves popping up in the States earlier, it wouldn't have been necessary. We could have stopped the epidemic."

"This is all irrelevant," Cora put in. "We need a full Council to deal with this new threat, whatever killed David Lachlan. Bartholomew is waiting just in the other room."

"The Council killed David," I snarled at her. "How do I know you didn't have anything to do with it? I smelled Otis LeConte's killer at your husband's company headquarters. Perhaps you and he set up David in a similar fashion so you could force him onto the Council."

"I won't have you slandering my wife in that fashion!" Bartholomew Campbell strode in, fists clenched.

"No one has slandered anyone," Morena said. "Mister Campbell, this is a closed meeting, and you are not on the Council."

"Yet," he said. "Allow me to make my case. According to your bylaws, any related member of a current or former Council member can apply for a vacancy, and it's obvious things have gotten out of control. Consequently—"

"Council bylaws," Morena put in, "state that the application may be made verbally or physically at the discretion of the Council Chairperson." She rapped the table. "I choose physically."

"As in combat?" Bartholomew flexed his broad shoulders. "Fine. I'll take on any of these flyweights." His gaze fell on me.

I glanced at Morena, and she nodded.

"What? McCord?" he asked with a sneer. "You'd have me fight the pup?"

"Not a pup any longer," she said. "Gabriel Stuart McCord, I hereby summon forth your full alpha. Fight for the honor of the Council and your pack."

27

———————

The sensation that had been simmering under my skin and centered in my solar plexus burst inward and outward simultaneously. I dropped to my knees and shook my head to clear the roaring from my ears. Then I recognized the roar for what it was and picked it apart into individual sounds—the heartbeats of the Council members, their chairs scraping across the stone floor under the rug, the rug fibers as they bent and straightened under the weight of chair legs and shoes, and underneath it all, the satisfied growl of Bartholomew Campbell.

"Do you know what he will be?" Tabitha's frightened whisper floated to me on the stream of other sounds.

"I'm hoping he will be like his father, who was a phenomenal fighter," Morena's reply came next.

"Yes, Simon McCord was a fine specimen," Keith agreed. "But shouldn't we hold this in the arena?"

"It's still closed due to flood damage," Morena said. "They'll just have to make do here."

The sounds then faded in favor of the sense of touch, each nerve ending tingling. Now I felt all the little stitches in my clothing and the pressure of my belt and watch. All my senses went through that enhancement, then fading to let another one through, until they all fit together and concentrated on one thing: my heartbeat.

It beat, and I breathed, and it thudded, and I breathed, and with each throb, something expanded outward from it and transformed me physically. This wasn't the painful transformation of most of my years. Nor was it the easy quick ones of the past few days. I felt the strength of boulders, the persistence of ice, the passion of flames, and the freedom of the wind. It made me into a creature of the elements, but especially of earth, with which I felt a bond like I never had before. When I opened my eyes, I saw not brown fur, but gray, and bigger paws than I'd ever transformed into previously.

"Magnificent," someone breathed.

I stood and shook off the remnants of my clothes. Veronica's fluorite hung on a chain around my thick neck, and it buzzed with power I'd not been able to sense before. When I looked around the room, I ticked off who people were: Keith—no threat, Tabitha—no threat, Morena—co-alpha, Cora—threat, but not too big of one, Dimitri—threat to keep an eye on, Bartholomew—

Bartholomew had also transformed into a large wolf, this one all black, and he watched me with shrewd eyes. Now with human niceties stripped away, we could regard each other as the enemies we'd always been.

"You clean up surprisingly well," he said. *"Not the ball of scruff I expected you to be."*

I wanted to respond, but I was too busy analyzing the combination of scents he was putting off. I smelled his surprise and a little fear. Perhaps it had always been there.

"I'm glad I can keep you on your toes," I finally replied. *"You're about what I expected. Tell me, did you leave your little traitor back in the Hebrides?"*

"Who? Jade?" he asked. *"She was the one who insisted Cora and I return. She said she had a vision something had gone terribly wrong."*

"I'm sure she did." Now we circled each other, teeth bared, but the human part of my brain latched on to his revelation. *"You do know she's a wizard, right?"*

"No, she's one of us. I smell it on her. I smell it with her." He licked his lips, and I gave him a disgusted look.

"You would say such things with your wife in the room? Can't you see, Bartholomew? You were set up. We were set up."

"What, are you afraid of a fight?" He switched direction, and I almost ran into him. He nipped me on my rump. *"No matter how big you are, you're still a pup,"* he growled.

"And you're an idiot. You've been sleeping with a vargamore. *She orchestrated all of this."*

His stride faltered. *"To what end?"*

"To destroy us. To create dissent within the Council. To gain control of the reversal process. She's going to use it against us or is going to sell it to the Young Bloods."

"I don't have time for your conspiracy theories!" He launched himself at me, and he knocked the wind out of me. I twisted away before his hind claws could find my abdomen and backed up to regroup. He gained his feet and came directly at me again.

"How did you meet Jade?" I asked and dodged him.

"Is this a fight or an interrogation?" he snarled.

"Why not both?" This time I nipped his shoulder and leaped away, but I misjudged and knocked into a chair. I found myself needing to become accustomed to my new, larger wolf body. What I lacked in maneuverability, I had gained in strength, but it was taking time to find my balance.

"Fine," he growled. *"I'm happy to point out how stupid you've been."*

*"As long as I get the information I need, I'll take whatever you

can give me in whatever form." He lunged at me, and I leapt over him, grazing his back with my claws. *"First blood."*

"You're not fighting fair," he said. *"Sit still."*

My hackles rose at his command. *"I think not. Now my question—how did you meet Jade?"*

He huffed and circled me again. *"She came to the office with resume in hand looking for a job. Nothing interesting."*

"Who hired her?"

"Probably one of the HR people." He dodged my feint.

"And how did she become your personal secretary?"

"The girl who was my secretary had an"—he stopped and blinked—*"accident. No one could prove it was foul play, but there was talk. It happened about a year ago."*

"When we were first talking about the Institute." This time I took advantage of his mental confusion and made a full direct assault. We rolled in a mass of fur and teeth and fangs, and I finally had him by the neck. A whimper came from the other side of the room—Cora.

"Do you give in?" I asked and bit harder such that a little trickle of his blood came into my mouth.

He tried to wriggle free, but with each movement, he sank my teeth farther into his throat. Finally, he said, *"I surrender."*

I let him go and backed away. He lay on the ground panting, blood on his ruff. I sat back and looked at Morena, who nodded, but then her eyes widened.

"Gabriel!" she said and gestured to the floor in front of me.

A mass of black fur toppled me, and I snapped at the face that tried to maneuver to grab hold of my throat. I heard jaws clamp around something and waited for the suffocating sensation of Bartholomew cutting off my air, but he backed up, shaking his head and wheezing. Finally he coughed up the fluorite sphere Veronica had given me. It rolled across the carpet to land at my feet.

"Just like a sissy boy to wear a necklace to a fight," he sneered.

"That was a dirty play, Bartholomew," said Morena. "You surrendered. We have no room for that sort of thing on our Council. You are hereby banished from Lycan Castle and Lycan Village as well as a ten kilometer radius from the Castle itself."

He flattened his ears but nodded.

"What about me?" asked Cora. "What if I don't feel safe being here without him?"

"You can always abdicate your seat on the Council," Morena told her. "I've half a mind to banish you as well."

Cora's eyes widened. "You can't do that! This is a hereditary position."

"And we have just learned of two people who are related to Dimitri."

Cora stood. "You have no idea what you're doing, Morena," she said in a low voice, all traces of her helpless female act gone. "The Lycanthrope Council is a relic of the past, and new forces are coming into play."

Morena tapped her pen against the table. "Are you threatening me, Cora? Threatening us?"

"I'm just making a promise of what's to come." Cora smiled. "Very well, then. I abdicate my position on the Council. I see no reason to continue to support this hidebound organization, particularly if you're going to allow a half-blood to become a full member. That's not what my father would've wanted, and it's surely not what I want."

She stalked from the room followed by Bartholomew, still in wolf form. All eyes then turned to me.

"Welcome to full Council membership, Mister McCord," Morena said. "I suggest you change back to human form. We have a lot of work to do."

"What if I want to challenge him?" Dimitri asked. "Without jewelry, of course. I am still not convinced he is right for full Council membership."

"One does not refuse gifts from a witch," I told him. *"As for your challenge, ready when you are."*

"No," Morena told him and me. "Mister McCord will be keeping his position. He has already proven his ability to maintain focus on the important aspects of a situation in spite of his animal instincts. Now we need to concentrate on our most pressing problem: another *vargamore* in our midst."

Keith grabbed the remnants of my clothing, and I followed him into my tower office, where I changed back into a human and attended to the scratches I'd gotten from my fight with Bartholomew. Thankfully I had more clothing there, and I slipped the fluorite into my pocket. When I returned to the Council Chamber, I found it empty except for Morena.

"They've taken a break for lunch and scattered to their respective offices," she said. "I suggest we do so as well."

She led the way to her office, where the castle staff had laid out a lunch of chicken, salad, and bread. And steak and potatoes and haggis and an assortment of other things in pots and on platters, even chocolate-dipped shortbread. My stomach growled.

"Most of this is for you," Morena said. "Your first alpha change tends to deplete your resources. You likely could have taken on Dimitri, and you may need to eventually as we sort out our new hierarchy, but you need to save yourself for the battle that is yet to come. I wanted to caution you to wait until you've achieved your full strength, but I have heard from the Wizard Tribunal—they're taking Max tomorrow if we don't solve this mystery."

I nodded and chewed the bite I'd just taken. "I don't think there's another *vargamore*," I said once I swallowed. "I think this is just one form of the one we've been dealing with for a while."

She raised her eyebrows. "You mean Wolfsheim?"

"Yes. Tell me everything David found. He showed me some

of his materials, but whoever killed him destroyed many of them." *And I will avenge his death.*

As I ate more than I'd ever dreamed of consuming, she related the highlights of David's research and the investigation the Council had engaged in before he picked it up. As he'd mentioned to me, Wolfsheim had come to Scotland to eliminate the lycanthropes as some twisted way of denying and suppressing the werewolf side of himself. Consequently, he'd jumped in on the side of every war that did not include the endorsement from the Lycanthrope Council, typically losing, but doing much damage to our numbers in the meantime. David had gathered the evidence as part of a case to bring to the Wizard Tribunal in hopes that an alliance could be forged, and together we could bring him down. My father had gone to the Continent looking for him and for evidence of his involvement in the second Great War, for Wolfsheim had been rumored to be in Belgium.

"We suspect he somehow lured your father to meet him at the edge of the Moerbrugge battlefield," she said, "and that's where he used his blood magic to destroy him."

"And how am I supposed to combat that?" I asked. "So far, no one has been able to stand up to his magic."

"You will have to use your wits, not your brawn, I'm afraid." Morena poured a cup of tea for each of us. "Unless you have some sort of protection you can bargain for with Reine."

"I've already given her all the power over me I feel comfortable with."

She raised her eyebrows. "How so?"

"Selene and I encountered Wolfsheim or one of his or her henchmen outside of David's house last night. He hit us with a hellfire grenade. I shielded Selene and took the brunt of it. Reine saved my life in exchange for the one-time use of my name."

"Risky," said. "Even just once. No telling what she'll make

you do. There are other things you could offer her. Your first-born, for example."

"Never. I wouldn't do that to anyone, especially not a child."

"Desperate times, Gabriel. Remember the legend of the Boar King."

"Right." I leaned forward. "Why is that legend so important?"

"It's one of our oldest, mostly a cautionary tale to keep our pups out of the woods at night, but I always suspected it was a map of how to deal with a *vargamore* because another name for them in our old language was torc, or boar, which got confounded with the word for necklace, and of course Latin for twist."

I thought about what I had seen. "I can understand that. It seems that having one of those around your neck will make your vessels twist and explode. Why did you not tell me of this before, particularly since my father was destroyed by him?"

She looked away, and pink came to her cheeks. A blush? "I wanted to, but the rest of the Council, particularly Dimitri and Cora, wanted to wait for you to reach your majority and find your inner alpha. That Wolfsheim lives is not common knowledge among our kind. The others think he died in the Napoleonic wars."

"Right. And now he has Selene captive and the Council by the bollocks. He has issued an invitation for me to come plead my case for her this evening."

"Nighttime is when he is most powerful," Morena said. "Are you sure that is wise?"

"As you said, we have to finish this tonight. We can't lose Max, and I can't give up Selene."

"And you're positive she's to be trusted in this? She's lied to you before."

I nodded. "I would be able to tell if she wasn't, at least now."

"Then let me give you two things. The first is a piece of

advice: don't try to be a lone wolf in this. I've watched you and know you prefer to work alone, but Wolfsheim will be too powerful for you to take on by yourself. Even if it's the fairy, you need to accept help. She likes you, and you may be surprised how willing she is."

"I'll consider it."

"Good. I wish you had more time to adjust to your alpha wolf form and discover what other talents you may have."

"Like what?"

"For example, some of them can aim their wolf-mind speak so their intended target can hear them, but others can't."

"Interesting. What is the second thing you want to give me?"

"Follow me. We're going to the storage room."

We went through the Council Chamber, which was still empty, and I wondered if Morena had dismissed them all. It concerned me that we wouldn't be acting as a pack, at least not for now, and it made the Institute's initial unanimous vote that much more suspicious. Who had been pulling the strings at the time? If—no, when—I made it out of this evening's encounter with Wolfsheim, I would have to do some investigating of his or her connections to the Council. It would be time for some deep house cleaning since he or she had had centuries to manipulate the course of events.

"Good, no one's here," she said. "Guard the door while I open this."

I did as she asked, and she stood in front of the fireplace. She pressed one of the gray bricks and put two fingers in the middle of one of the carved Celtic knots on the lintel. The hearth rumbled, and she stepped back before it opened under her feet to reveal a staircase.

"Quick, now, follow me."

"Great, another dungeon."

28

Of all the dungeons I'd been in, this one was the creepiest by far. The narrow stairwell wound downward, and the trap door above closed with an echoing thunk that sounded like it sealed our doom.

"You're sure we'll be able to get out?" I asked Morena in hushed tones. My whisper bounced off the stone and seemed to tumble into the darkness below. We relied solely on our non-sight senses to lead the way. Morena's scent was manly with the palate of modern "unscented" personal care products with a little sweat and Scotch thrown in. She'd never had a romantic partner as far as I knew, and I wondered—not for the first time—whether she would choose a man or woman as a lover.

"Of course I know how to get out," she said. "If it will make you feel better, there's a torch at the bottom of the stairs."

"I would like to see where we are. This is an aspect of Lycan Castle I'm not familiar with." The texture of the wall under my fingers changed from rectangular stone with crumbling mortar in the cracks to natural stone with all its imperfections and seemingly random bumps and grooves. Morena stopped, and I hesitated on what I hoped was the bottom step.

"Ah, here it is," she said.

The setting made me expect to hear the hiss of a match and see the bloom of a flame, but all I got was a boring "click" and the beam of an industrial-strength torch that swung over the walls to reveal shades of black and gray.

"Did the builders of Lycan Castle dig the dungeons out of the natural stone?" I asked.

"No, there was a network of caves here first. It's difficult to tell with the twists and turns of the stairs, but we are actually just beyond the edge of the castle walls and under the hill." She shone the light on a spot to my left, where someone had carved a series of numbers, possibly a date.

"Do you know what that is?" she asked.

"No, although it looks like it should be familiar."

"You likely learned it at the Council School when you were there decades ago. The first Lycanthrope Council met here on the Summer Solstice of 685. At that point, it was a gathering of clan chieftains who reluctantly recognized their need to ally with each other to preserve their lands and their people from those who didn't understand us and our abilities. That carving commemorates the date and occasion."

"Ah, right."

The light swung back and silhouetted her. "Now on to the stores."

"Who knows about this place?" I asked and lengthened my stride to keep up with her determined steps.

"Only the Council Chair and her second-in-command," she said with a meaningful look.

Her words caught me off guard. "Thank you," I finally said. "Although I'm not sure what I owe this honor to. I'm but a newly minted full Council member."

"Yes, but you've proven your worth as the Investigator, which is a role I'll ask you to keep for the time being." She then echoed my thoughts from earlier. "We're going to have to look very closely at the others. I doubt that the Campbells are the only ones who have been influenced by Wolfsheim and his organization. I know you are trustworthy, but as of now, everyone else on the Council is under suspicion." Another glance in my direction. "Everyone."

What is she telling me?

Morena stopped at an extra dark place on the wall, and when she turned, the beam from the torch sliced through the darkness inside to illuminate shelves with metal and wooden boxes. Each had a tag, some of them brown and cracked with age. Words sprang into view, but the light passed over them too quickly for my brain to sort the handwritten letters into words.

"It's in here," she said and marched straight to a shelf in the back of the roughly rectangular room. "Hold this." After handing me the torch, she reached up and pulled down a metal money box with a dented lid and covered in rust spots. The tag was so faded as to only show spots where the letters had been. By all outer appearances, it looked like it probably held nothing of value—or was disguised to look like it did. The fluorite in my pocket let off a little jolt of static when she opened the container and I had to grit my teeth to keep from squirming at the sensation so close to my sensitive bits. *Damn these spells,* I thought, but all other grumblings disappeared when I saw what lay inside.

A Celtic chieftain's torc, or necklace, lay inside on a bed of black velvet cloth. In contrast to the appearance of its box, it shone dark gold like ripe wheat nodding in the late afternoon sunlight and glowed even when Morena placed the torch on the shelf and directed its beam toward the ceiling. The ends of the torc were wolf heads, and the one on the left held a dark stone in its mouth. The one on the right was empty.

"Do you have your fluorite on you?" she asked.

"Yes." I handed it to her. She gently fitted it into the empty mouth of the wolf, and it stuck. She then placed the torc around my neck under my collar. It warmed more quickly than it should have, and the stones pressed into my collarbone, but only in a "so you know we're here" way.

"Whose torc is it?" I asked in a hushed tone. Part of me felt like I had a sleeping golden snake coiled under my shirt—exciting and powerful, but also potentially deadly.

"In the legend of the Boar King, the boy who defeated the demon was a chieftain's son who later grew up to assume the leadership of his clan. The Fey, happy to have the evil influence out of their lands—not because of their innate good intentions, but because they didn't like the competition—made that and gave it to him." She put a hand on my shoulder. "Those who tried to wield it in the past have failed, for legend has it that its power can only be harnessed by a direct descendent of that chieftain, but due to the loss of oral tradition and the many battles, the gnarled roots of the family tree have twisted and turned into the thick soil of obscurity."

"And you think I am that descendant."

"The only thing we know with certainty about the chieftain is that his nickname was the Gray Wolf. You know how rare it is for one of us to change into a gray before our human hair turns, and you did today."

"What happens if I try to harness the power of the torc, and it's not meant for me?"

"Then may whatever god you believe in have mercy on your soul."

BEFORE I COULD ATTEMPT to rescue Selene, I had one more stop to make in an attempt to gather more information. Laura said ghosts like to talk. Maybe they'd been gossiping with a certain little clairvoyant.

Alexander's father Paul opened the door and looked at me with surprise.

"Investigator McCord," he said, his tone cool but not unwelcoming. The sound of a football game came from the room behind him.

"Mister Taylor," I said, "I apologize for bothering you and your family on a Sunday afternoon, but I would like to speak with Alexander."

He nodded, and his mouth worked before spitting out the words, "He said you'd be coming by."

It was blatantly apparent he wasn't happy to see me, even more so that his son had predicted my appearance, but he stepped aside and let me enter. I followed the noise through the small house to the living room in back. Alexander sat up and hid the book he'd been reading between the sofa cushions, his young face a tight mask of pretend concentration on what was on the television.

"Hello," I said. "I heard you were expecting me."

He looked up with a broad smile and stood. "Investigator McCord, the soldier said you would come."

"Alexander," his father said, his tone tired. He rubbed his eyes. "Why not take Investigator McCord out back?"

Their narrow yard was littered with toys, mostly balls of various sports. Alexander nudged a football out of his way and wrinkled his nose.

"Is everything all right?" I asked him. He looked up, and his face shone hopefully before it settled into its usual neutral expression.

"It's fine," he said, but it was apparent that "fine" was a four-letter word for him.

"Is that what your Da says to tell people?"

He ducked his head so his blond bangs hid his eyes. "Yes."

I knelt in front of him and put a hand on his thin shoulder. "But it's not, is it? Does your Da hit you?"

He shook his head vigorously. "No, he mostly ignores me, but I have friends."

"I suppose you don't mean kids your age."

"No, my other friends." He did that disconcerting looking over my shoulder thing. "You have a new one. He's wearing old tartan and a necklace?" He squinted. "And not much else. And he's dirty, but he's excited."

"Is he talking to you?" Again I listened for something, but I only heard the breeze stirring the leaves on the trees.

"He's a warrior, and he's happy you have his favorite weapon." He spoke hesitantly with the effort to translate spirit-speak as he went along. "But he's also worried about you because you are alone, and warriors need their fellow soldiers like wolves need their pack."

"I don't have that many I can call on," I told him, and I found myself speaking to him like I would to an adult. "The only other *vargamore* I know has a child to consider, so I can't put her in danger, and I can't trust my fellow Council members. My other friend died." I stopped. What had my life distilled to —the Council and nothing else? If I were to be killed that evening, would anyone miss me besides Morena and Troy the bartender? And maybe Lonna and Max, but if I failed, they would have bigger problems to concern them.

Selene would, but would she only miss me temporarily before turning her attention to rescuing her brother? Or rescuing herself along with him. She'd made the sacrifice to save him, and family was her priority—as it should be—but I found myself wanting to be part of that or something like it. Since my father died, I'd been tossed out and knocked around on my own before taking his position on the Council, but in spite of the long lycanthropic history, I didn't have anything or anyone to anchor me. Sure, that had stood me in good stead when I was away on assignment as Investigator, when I could take risks I might otherwise not have if I'd had a family at home, and they'd paid off.

"I would miss you," Alexander said. "You understand me.

So would Miss Reid. She smiled a lot when you were about to visit the Council School last week and was sad after."

That would be an unnecessary complication in my life. "She would only miss me a little bit, though. We're only acquaintances. That's different from friends."

A heavy hand landed on my shoulder, and I looked up to see David Lachlan standing there, his flat, cold eyes upon me. His skin had the gray pallor of death, and his throat hung open in a jagged parody of a grin. Alexander's eyes widened, and I stood to put myself between the apparition and the boy.

"David, what do you want?" I asked.

His words came into my mind as a ghostly wail. *"I cannot rest until you have vanquished the Boar King. Nor can the others."* He waved over the empty lot behind the house, and I saw row upon row of soldiers in the garb of all eras of warfare from Highland clan warriors wrapped in scraps of tartan to modern-day soldiers in pixellated camouflage. And the murdered scientist and security guards from the Institute, yet three more victims of this crazy creature. What did Wolfsheim want? Did I even know it was a he?

"Can you tell me who, exactly, Wolfsheim is?"

But he remained silent.

"Are any of the others telling you anything?" I looked at Alexander, who hunched over on the ground, his hands over his ears. His mouth opened in a silent pained scream.

"Get out, all of you!" I yelled. The ghosts disappeared in a fog, and Alexander's father ran outside.

"Who the hell are you yelling at, McCord? You're as daft as the boy." He knelt by his son, who still covered his ears and panted. "Alex, son, what is it? What did he do to you?"

Alexander moaned.

"Go. Get away from him!" He stood and shoved me with both hands.

I backed away, palms facing him. "I'm sorry. I didn't know that would happen."

"I'll be telling the Council about this, McCord," he snarled at me, and his eyes flashed like he was going to change right there. He grabbed his son's shoulder and hauled him to his feet. "Are you okay, Son?"

"I'm fine, Da. There were just so many of them," he whispered. The little clairvoyant flinched away from his father's touch.

"I'm sure the Council will be very interested in all of this." I wanted to reach toward Alexander, but I held back. "In fact, I'll put a call into the Council School's headmistress this afternoon and tell her about what happened."

"Tell her she's done a terrible job of toughening up my son." He pushed Alexander toward the back door. His hand curled into a fist.

"Where's your girlfriend, Taylor?"

"At the market, not that it's any of your business."

"I need to borrow Alexander for the rest of the afternoon," I told him.

He turned, slowly, his face a mask of anger. "Haven't you done enough? The neighbors are probably already whispering about my daft boy and his daft friend yelling at nothing in the backyard."

"It's Council business," I said, hoping that appealing to his inner sense of hierarchy would overcome his anger. Also that giving his son some importance would protect him, not backfire on him.

He looked down at his son. "Fine, then. His bedtime's nine. Have him back by then."

I held out my hand, and Alexander walked to me and slowly took it. He looked up at me with big brown eyes with smudges underneath them, and I noticed how thin and bony his hand felt in mine.

"Come on, I'll have you back by dark," I said.

He nodded and wouldn't look at his father, who grabbed his chin when we walked by and made him look up at him.

"Behave yourself and don't disappoint me, hear?"

Alexander nodded. We preceded his father into the living room, and I grabbed the book he'd been reading out of the cushions and put it in my jacket pocket.

Once we'd settled in my car and backed out of the driveway, he turned to me. "Do I get to help with the ghosts?"

"Only as much as you can while staying out of danger."

"You need my help. I sent the guard into the blue club when you went in when I told you not to."

"Thank you. That was very helpful."

"I meant it. You need help. Tonight too."

"And what about you? Do you need help?"

He pulled his sleeve over his wrist and the darkening red mark from where his father had grabbed him roughly. "I can take care of myself."

His words confirmed what I had suspected: he'd seen more horrific things than dead soldiers, and he was trapped in a, abusive situation. I gripped the steering wheel and took a deep breath to calm down, and he shrank into his seat, his gaze wary.

Dammit. I need to calm down.

"I won't hurt you, Alexander," I said. "And I won't put you in harm's way. I'm going to take you to a friend's house. Maybe they can figure out how to help you."

29

———

I drove Alexander to Lonna and Max's. She settled the boy in the kitchen with a piece of pie.

"He's so thin," she said when she joined me and Max in the parlor.

"Look, I know that you're already overwhelmed with what's going on," I said, "but I had to get him out of his house." I related what had happened and my suspicions.

Max nodded. "The boy's energy field is off. He lives in a lot of fear, and not of the spirits."

"Can you do something for him?" I asked. "He's technically one of you even though he has lycanthrope parents."

"As far as you know," Lonna said. "He could be adopted or from a previous marriage. Or his father could suspect he's not his. It's extremely rare for two wolves to produce a little wizard, especially one so strong and talented."

"The mother's boy is dead, so we can't ask her."

Max ran his hand through his hair. "We're limited in what we can do for him right now since we're at odds with the Wizard Tribunal."

"What about your friend Arnold?" I asked. "Surely he'd be interested in a little clairvoyant like Alexander."

"Still missing. Leave the boy with us," Lonna said. "At the very least, I can fatten him up, and Max can maybe show him some shielding techniques so he'll have more control over how much the spirits communicate with him. As for his home life... I'll kick in some of my social worker training and see what options are available for him."

We all looked at each other, feeling helpless, but even our sketchy plan felt better than just leaving the boy there with his brute of a father.

"And what are you going to do?" Max asked me when he walked me to the door.

"I have a date with a *vargamore* tonight. He has Selene." I gave him a summary of what had happened the night before.

"My condolences for your loss. I didn't know him well, but David seemed like a good guy."

"He was." *And now he's relying on me, too.*

THE WEIGHT of all those counting on me for help—David and my father, Selene and her brother, Max and Lonna, and now Alexander—pressed down on me along with the heavy torc around my neck. Morena and then Alexander had urged me to seek help, but I didn't know where I could find it. Morena hadn't volunteered, and I was pretty much out of options unless one dropped into my lap.

I drove to David's estate and parked outside the main house. I thought it was empty, but Garou came out of the front door. He looked even thinner and less rested than the previous time I'd seen him, and I suspected he'd been up all night.

"Burning the candle on both ends again?" I asked him.

"If my witnesses would only cooperate, I wouldn't have to,"

he replied. "I don't suppose I'm fortunate enough you came to give a statement."

The soft breeze and sunlight on my face mocked my irritable mood, and I couldn't help but bait him. "I hadn't planned on it, no."

"Fine. I will file an order with the Council." He ran a hand over his face, and I could almost hear my mother scolding me. My mental voice wasn't as gentle as hers would've been.

Stop being an ass, Gabriel. He's just trying to do his job.

"Look, I have a few hours to kill, and I need to fill you in on what I've found," I said.

His expression of surprise turned to one of suspicion. "What's the catch, Investigator?"

"No catch. Honestly, I may need your help." It surprised me to say so, but now that David was gone and Morena had essentially stepped aside after warning me and giving me the torc, Garou was my most reliable ally.

Now he looked even more skeptical. "Are you healed from your injuries last night? It seems you may have hit your head."

"Let's just say I've finally started listening to what the universe is trying to tell me."

He neither argued nor gloated. He only nodded. "I am at your disposal. Shall we go inside?"

The front door hung open like the mouth to a den of horror. The images of my father and then David flashed through my mind. "I can't go in there. Grab one of the bottles of whiskey and a couple of glasses, and we'll talk on the back patio."

Because that's how we Scots prepare for battle.

He gave me a strange look but went inside and closed the door. My father's picture, the one the commander took on the battlefield, nudged the edge of my consciousness, but I pushed it away.

I have to focus on the present now. And my future.

. . .

"Mind if I smoke?" Garou tapped a box of cigarettes against the wrought-iron table. It seemed ridiculous, the two of us sitting there sharing a decanter of whiskey like gentlemen of leisure. I checked my watch. Seven o'clock. Three hours until sundown...and my showdown with Wolfsheim. A long time to wait and a short time to figure out whether Garou would be a useful ally. Not that I wanted to put anyone else in danger, but the overwhelming chorus seemed to be in favor of me not doing this alone.

"Go ahead," I said. "How very continental of you."

He lit one. "Why have a long lifespan if you're not able to enjoy it?"

The combination of the smells of cigarette smoke, summer air, and Scotch brought old memories to the surface. I struggled to hold on to my sense of time and place. "How old are you, anyway?"

Garou leaned back and squinted at me before putting on his sunglasses. "Old enough to have known Agatha Christie."

"No kidding? You're older than I thought. I'd ask if you were her model for Hercule Poirot, but you're French, not Belgian."

"No, I am Belgian, albeit a Walloon. But no, I wasn't her model. I did help her with some of the finer details of her stories."

"Interesting." Had I never really looked at the guy before? Or had I been seduced by the "old family, Council member" snobby mentality I detested so much? That thought made me squirm.

"And you?" he asked.

"About eighty. And feeling every year." I looked into my glass, where the amber liquid reflected the still strong sunlight. "Kind of makes it ridiculous that you and I were arguing over Selene last week. She's just a pup."

Garou shrugged. "Does age matter, Investigator? The young

are full of impulsivity and passion, but that's what keeps us old dogs alive."

His words tickled the back of my brain and returned me to the question of how Wolfsheim had managed to live for centuries.

"What do you know about Wolfsheim?" I asked. "If you've been around that long, surely you've heard of him."

"Yes, I am aware of the Order of the Silver Arrow, but I thought they were a legend. I could never understand why the Council was so obsessed with them."

"It's very much alive, but in a way no one expected." I leaned toward him and lowered my voice. "What if these organizations we've been watching closely, the Young Bloods and the Purists, weren't their own gig, but rather were the new face of the Order?"

"How many of them could possibly be involved?" Garou asked. "You're talking about a huge conspiracy."

"There's no way to determine the entire scope of it. I can't help but wonder if there truly is a Wolfsheim or if it's a title that's been passed down. Secret societies have outer rings and inner ones. It could be that there are so many layers that there isn't a true center anymore."

"Oh, no, there is a Wolfsheim," a young male voice said. I turned to see Robert MacLemore and his wife Alice, the leaders of the Young Bloods, standing at the edge of the patio.

Garou and I leapt to our feet, but they both drew weapons before we could reach for ours. Not that I had one. The menacing firearms in their hands seemed at odds with their golden, sun-kissed stylish appearances. The thought crossed my mind, *But hippies hate guns! I guess hipsters don't. Remember the era you're in.*

"And he wants to see you right away," Alice added. "You should've stuck with us, Investigator. We would've made your capitulation a lot more pleasant."

"I'm sure you would have. Tell me, do you drug the objects of your interest often, or just the ones you really like?"

"Just the ones we think might fight back too hard."

Rob kept his gun on us while Alice patted us down for weapons. She took Garou's service weapon and the knife he kept strapped at his ankle.

"Of course we can't confiscate your most dangerous weapons, your wolf selves," Rob said. "But we can dampen them for a while."

Alice took a syringe out of his pocket. "Just one?"

"We were only instructed to bring in McCord," he said.

She sighed, obviously exasperated. "I told you to bring two just in case."

"I didn't have an extra. You forgot to pick up the refills. We used the other two last night. Just inject McCord."

"I'm not going to let you," I said.

Rob turned his gun on Garou. "If you don't, I'll kill him. The boss doesn't care whether he lives or dies."

"I bet you know what this is," Alice said in a singsong voice and came toward me with the syringe in one hand, her gun in the other. "If you try anything, Inspector Garou gets it."

"Let me guess, Luridatone?" I asked. An atypical antipsychotic, it cut off our ability to change by short-circuiting the reward and motivation pathways in the brain, making our bodies not want to go through the effort. Its effects were temporary but potent.

"Very good," Rob said. "Now inject it into his quad, Alice. Either one is fine."

I sighed, frustrated that they had Garou hostage. Alice took the top off the syringe and injected the clear liquid into my left thigh. It burned, and my knees gave way beneath me.

"As for you, Detective," she said, "I'm going to have to make sure you don't get found for a long time. Lead the way inside."

"*Act like you don't want to go in the dungeon,*" I told him with my telepathic wolf-voice, hoping I had the talent Morena had mentioned earlier. Theoretically it shouldn't have worked with us both being in human form, but he nodded slightly as she walked him away. *"There's a hole with a grate at the very end. It leads to a tunnel in the woods. Follow my trail to the ruins. Wolfsheim's lair is underneath."*

They disappeared into the house. Rob checked his watch, but not for long enough that I could distract him or get away.

"Aren't you millennials supposed to be addicted to your phones or something?" I asked. "You know, there's a pause in the action, so you need to tweet about what you had for lunch. Or Facebook—'OMG holding Council Investigator hostage. Hashtag gonnagetputaway.'"

"Very funny," he said but didn't laugh.

After a few minutes, Alice reappeared. "All right, I knocked him out and locked him in the dungeon."

I cursed under my breath to sound like I wasn't happy about it. Hopefully Garou wouldn't be out for too long or get lost once he woke up. As for me, a heaviness spread through my limbs, and my vision narrowed.

"There might've been a little something else in there." Alice's voice floated above me like an oil slick on the water—opalescent in color but not pretty. I sank into the blackness away from the blue sky and everything that was safe and pure in my life.

I woke in a cave. A single torch—a real wooden one this time—flickered in its sconce on the wall above me, and a stalactite dripped cold water onto my face. I rolled to my side and then to my knees, noting how dry my mouth felt. Scraping my tongue against my teeth only brought a little relief, and I dared not try the water dripping in the cave for fear of microbes and parasites.

Speaking of parasites, where did Rob and Alice go?

I stood, careful not to bump my head on the ceiling. Trying to close my eyes and start the change didn't produce any effect. *Dammit, that's right, there was Luridatone in there. On the other hand, maybe if I'm in human form, I won't be as susceptible to Wolfsheim's spells. If I'm lucky.*

I grabbed the torch and followed the corridor. In Celtic legend, caves were supposed to be places sacred to magical creatures like wyrms and fairies, and I wondered if Reine could be lurking about somewhere. I came to a widening and entered a room covered top to bottom with shining crystals. They reflected the light of the torch like a million little flames. In the middle, a stone throne held a young man. He gestured for me to come forward.

"You are seeking me," he said in a surprisingly deep voice. "I am Wolfsheim."

I looked around for guards or other signs of human life. It made sense he was powerful enough to sit without guards, but something felt off.

"I don't think you are," I said.

He nodded and vanished along with the crystals, leaving me alone with my torch.

"Well, that was one," I muttered. "Fairytale things happen in threes, so here we go."

My steps next brought me to a cave where the walls seemed to be assembled from planes of black mirrors. Again the light from my torch filled the room in a blaze like the walls were on fire. In this room, a wizened old man with a long gray beard sat on a black throne made from a material that looked like obsidian. The flames from my torch reflected in his eyes, and he looked like a centuries-old wizard.

"I am Wolfsheim," he said. "You and I have business to discuss, young man."

Although they were merely reflected, it seemed the flames

in the walls emanated heat, and a bead of sweat dripped down my face and pooled underneath the torc, which still sat on my neck. Again, I couldn't name what it was, but something told me that this was not he.

"You are not Wolfsheim," I said. He vanished, leaving me to blink the after-images of the flames from my eyes.

"And that was two."

I walked through that cave into a third. It was just a cave with what at first glance looked like stalagmites and stalactites reaching toward each other from above and below, but too regular. Further examination revealed them to be Roman statues staring at me with blank eyes. The thought of the ones behind me watching me made my neck and back muscles twitch. The throne stood large and faced away from me. I circled it slowly, ready for any surprise. When I could finally see its inhabitant, I nodded. This, finally, made sense.

"Did you miss me?" asked Jade. She puffed on her cigar, which smelled like a combination of pipe smoke and kerosene. Yes, that was the scent of the killer. She waved her hand, and my torch went out, leaving us in blackness.

30

B linking in a cave didn't do any good, but I couldn't help it. It was reflexive to struggle to see in the pitch darkness. When the cave was once again illuminated, I squinted tightly.

"Damn, Jade, you're wreaking havoc on my retinas."

"Jade is gone." The voice held the softness of velvet and the old stone smoothness of the Roman statues that surrounded us. A well-dressed man sat in the throne. He seemed ageless and ancient at the same time, like he'd cultivated his wrinkles for show. Gray-streaked white hair fell back from his temples.

"Jade is you."

"No," he said. "Jade is my daughter. Or did Morena not tell you?"

His words landed like a punch to my throat, and I swallowed. "No, she left that little detail out."

He studied his nails. "She never wanted to claim me, to confirm we were lovers. She thought she was playing a game for information about my activities. I found it to be an entertaining seduction."

"There go my assumptions," I said.

"Not necessarily. It has been a constant source of shame for her that she succumbed to my charms and lost my game. Hence why she is not here at your side."

"So you used your daughter to infiltrate the Purists and the Young Bloods," I said.

"She acted on her own, but I accepted her help." He gazed at me, and I found I couldn't look away from his eyes, which were slitted like a snake's. "People tend to want to help me, Gabriel."

I shook my head and forced my gaze away from him. "I will not willingly do so, Wolfsheim. I wouldn't give you control of the reversal process even if I had that power."

"But you can bring it to me, all the instructions, once they've perfected it. I can supply my own blood magic. And first I will play with your useless Council and control them with their own blood, and then humanify them."

"Again, I wouldn't do that."

"Ah, but I have a bargain for you."

I sighed. "Fairytale villains always do."

"First, there is the easy offer." He gestured over my left shoulder, and I saw Rhys and the young man from the first throne room holding Selene by her arms. Her hair was now chin-length. "You are rather attached to Doctor Rial, are you not? She had hoped to offer herself in exchange for her brother's life, but as you can see, he is more than willing to serve me. A pity because I do love redheads."

"You've spelled him," I said. "Like you're trying to enchant me."

"And then there is your second choice." This time, he pointed to the space beyond my right shoulder. Jade posed like a game show girl with the racks of blood samples that had been stolen from the Institute. "The proof of your accusations to the Council today, both regarding Bartholomew Campbell and Dimitri Corvair. To sweeten the deal, I have the paper trail showing how they conspired to hire Jade to kill Otis LeConte."

"Okay, fairytale stuff happens in threes. What else have you got?" I asked and turned back toward him. He held a manila envelope.

"And choice three: the answer to what happened to your father all those years ago." He caressed it with his long fingers. "I have the letters that didn't make it out, the mistakes that told me his position and what he was after. Once all comes to light, his soul will finally be allowed to rest in peace. You may only pick one. Which will it be in exchange for you handing over the formula and procedure for the lycanthropic reversal process?"

He had me pinned between love, duty, and family. *What would an alpha wolf do?*

The answer came to me immediately: *Take control of all of it.*

Wolfsheim stood and circled me. The torc grew cold under my shirt collar. I tried to keep my eyes on the *vargamore*, but as he moved around me, my muscles tightened and grew numb beyond my control. When he stood in front of me again, a spark arced between the two stones.

Dammit, this thing is supposed to help me!

Fog filled my vision, and a roaring in my ears warned me I'd lose all conscious control soon. Wolfsheim swept his arm in a downward gesture, and my knees buckled. The torc's temperature dropped further, keeping me focused and most of the fog at bay. I tried to move my arms, but they stayed glued to my sides.

Small fingers tangled in my hair, then tightened and yanked my head back, bringing me in eye contact with Jade.

"Can I keep him, Father? He's pretty and tried to save me from that mean man." She caressed my cheek, and I tried to pull away, but she and her father's magic held me fast. The capillaries in my left cheek burst under her thumb in little spurts. She licked her thumb, and my stomach folded at the thought of the power she might now have over me. She released me, and I swayed but didn't faceplant on the cave floor.

"So what will it be?" Wolfsheim asked. "Your ladylove—although Jade might have something to say about that—saving face with your Council, or finally allowing your father's soul to have peace?"

One of the shadows at the edge of the cave moved, and I bowed my head as though defeated. I opened my senses as I had in the Council room to determine who was there and what threat they posed to me. My suspicions confirmed, I looked straight at Wolfsheim.

"I choose to challenge you," I said. "For leadership of the Order of the Silver Arrow."

"You would challenge me?" Wolfsheim shook his head. "I never took you for suicidal. Very well, then. I admired your strength and cleverness, but now you're going to make me kill you."

I couldn't help a glance over my shoulder at Selene. *"Are you okay?"*

"Gabriel, be careful!" Selene's mental voice came to me even though she stood perfectly still and stared straight ahead. Rhys and Curtis stood back against the cave wall and watched the fun. I wondered if they'd made wagers as to how long I'd last against their boss.

Wolfsheim flicked his wrist, and I flew backward and smashed against the cave wall. I wanted to think the crunch I heard hadn't been my body and the blooms of pain that snapped open along my bones and especially the wounds on my back didn't belong to me.

Come on, healing. I staggered to my feet in spite of every joint's protest. I reached inside and found my inner alpha wolf. The Luridatone must have worn off, or maybe they had dosed me wrong.

When I changed, the dead skin and scabs from my exposure to the hellfire grenade sloughed off. I lost my clothing, but the torc remained around my neck and fit better in my wolf form. This transformation was even larger than in the Council fight, and I stretched to give my brain a better idea of my dimensions. Even so, another hit like the one he'd given me, no matter what shape I took, would likely finish me. I had to do something to make him let down his guard. As for Jade, I could only hope the ally I sensed was truly there and would help neutralize her rather than decide this was a good time for payback for the frustration I'd caused him.

"By the ancient laws," I said and staggered a little to give the impression I was still reeling, *"I demand to choose the form I battle with."*

"Oh, this gets better," he said. "Very well, I will humor you. All my forms will be stronger and more powerful than your little lycanthrope one."

The repeated warnings not to take him on without help played in my mind, and I remembered the story my father had written to David, the one he had told me as a child. In it, friendship had defeated the villain. *"I challenge you as the Boar King."*

"Ah, yes, my favorite. Well, you will be a tasty little wolf. So will your lover." He stretched out his arms. An invisible wind blew his garments, and he tilted his head back. Now the flames from the torches along the walls elongated and raced to the middle, enveloping him in a dozen fiery ropes.

Thankfully I'd correctly estimated Wolfsheim's penchant for drama. He reveled in his fiery form. I got the impression of an elongated lower jaw, tusks, and coarse hair. A harsh, snorting laughter filled the cave, and the torches snapped their flames back. I had one shot at this, a fleeting moment of vulnerability or he would eat me alive—literally.

"Now!"

I guessed at when his moment of disorientation would occur, leapt for his throat, and closed my jaws around it. He grabbed for me, but when his hooves met the metal of the torc, a sizzling sound and bacon smell told me it still had some magic and found me a worthy wearer. I held tight in spite of his hooves raking my tender back and used his thrashing motions to sink my teeth deeper into his neck.

"This will not work," he said and dropped to all fours, pinning me under him. "My neck is too thick."

"Lies," I said. I struggled to breathe but held on and used the opportunity to have my back claws go to work on his underbelly while scratching at his face with my front ones. His thick, leathery skin resisted my attempts, but I kept at it in spite of the soreness in my digits. I hoped he had to direct enough of his resources at me that he would release the spell on Selene.

The sensation of bubbles racing along my limbs warned me that someone was using blood magic on me, or trying to.

"Selene, is Jade still in here? She's magnifying his power with the blood."

"I'm stuck! I can move, but Rhys is holding me."

Anger surged through me, and I wanted to go to her aid, but I couldn't let go of the Boar King, or all would be lost. Then I remembered my ally who had snuck in.

"Garou, help!"

A crack like that of stone on bone reverberated through the cave, and the internal fizzing stopped. Wolfsheim wheezed, and the iron taste of blood seeped into my mouth. A lethargy seeped into my bones, then, and the thought occurred to me that his blood was poison, and it was killing me, and I should let—

The two stones in the torc shocked me before I followed the compulsion to release him.

"Nice try, Wolfsheim," I said.

He roared and tried to slam me against the floor, but he didn't have the momentum. I rolled and gave a vicious shake with the last of my strength. His throat tore open. I leapt away and lay on the floor, panting.

He flopped to his back and shrank to his human form, but instead of the vibrant older man he'd been, he looked like the creature that represented the wizard race among the gargoyles on the Council School: emaciated, bald, and with bulging eyes and fangs. He clawed at the air, and his thoughts floated through my mind—destructive ones—and then the resignation that this was how it would end after seven hundred years. Finally, even those faded, and the ugly, broken body on the stone floor lay still, its limbs up like a dead roach's. His blood flowed light pink down his gray skin, the faded colors a measure of how his blood magic had drained his own life force.

Mindful of my father's warning, I spat his blood from my mouth, at least as much as I could. A shout brought my attention to the side of the cave, where Curtis, now released from his compulsion, struggled with Rhys. Selene slumped against the wall, dazed. I ran to her and lunged at Rhys, knocking him away from Curtis. I growled at him.

"You picked the wrong guy to mess with."

"Gabriel, stop!"

Reine's words halted my lunge for Rhys's throat. He glared at me, but the stain of a vindictive smile spread across his face. "The slavery Wolfsheim offered you would have been nothing compared to what you will experience with my sister."

"Don't be ridiculous. He was too smart to give me unlimited power." Reine looked around with a shudder. "Ugh, it smells like dead wizard in here. I only wanted to make sure he wouldn't hurt you, dear brother."

"You're his sister?" I asked. *"Why were you helping me?"*

She gestured to Selene. "The girl can tell you. Sometimes you have to rescue your younger siblings when they take up with the wrong crowd. He wouldn't listen to reason, and I am limited as to how much I can interfere in the affairs of other races, so I had to act indirectly. Plus I like you, Wolf-man."

Selene scooted closer to me and put a hand on my head. "I do too," she said.

"Likewise."

Jade lay on the floor behind the vials of blood, and I couldn't tell if she was dead or merely unconscious. I trotted over to her and was relieved to see a slight fluttering of her chest.

"That one will have to be locked up."

I looked up to see Garou standing there. He had blood on his temple but otherwise seemed to be fine.

"I'm glad you're here."

"You had better be. Someone had to neutralize the guards outside the chamber and this one. Otherwise, you would have been in trouble."

"I was wondering. And thank you."

MORENA WOULDN'T MEET my eyes at David Lachlan's funeral. She slipped out before the bagpiper played the final strains of "Amazing Grace." I wasn't up for a confrontation, anyway. My handkerchief had gotten soaked with my quiet weeping, which I tried not to let Selene see. Of course she noticed and didn't seem to mind, only offered me one of her paper tissues, and her gesture reminded me that these modern women had more tolerance for their men showing emotion. Or at least the ones in psychology did.

I didn't see any spirits, and Alexander, who accompanied me, said he didn't either, only the normal ones that hung about Lycan Village's big stone church. He told me it was a good thing —that it meant they were at rest. "If you don't finish something a ghost wants you to start, they'll let you know," he said.

I nodded and touched the torc around my neck. Since

Morena had avoided me, I hadn't had the chance to return it to her, and it felt like a link to the important past we didn't know enough about. Who had been the chieftain to wear it? How had he defeated the Boar King, and more importantly, why did the creature come back? I only had his name—Connell. If his spirit visited, I didn't know, but I told Alexander to look for him and ask him if he got a chance. I suspect the torc, like many magical objects, endured because evil spirits were never truly destroyed —they just were vanquished and then gathered their power to return.

As for the Order of the Silver Arrow, I technically won leadership of it, but the only member who stuck around was Curtis Rial. The rest had scattered, and the leaders of the Young Bloods went into hiding to avoid being arrested on kidnapping charges. I trusted Garou would find them—he was a good detective, after all.

Curtis found me at the pub after the funeral reception. Troy gave me a whiskey before I ordered anything.

"For the old man," he said, his eyes red-rimmed. "It was his favorite post-funeral dram."

"*Slàinte,*" I said and raised the glass before knocking it back. It burned all the way down, but this time in a good way. It also gave me an excuse for the tears in my eyes, and I had to take a moment to compose myself.

"Mister McCord?" The young man's voice beside me brought me back to the present and out of my spiral of "what if?"

"Yes, Curtis?" I didn't mind the kid, but I'd sent Selene home and wanted to be alone, or as alone as one can be in a pub. I sought the anonymous alone with the occasional understanding nod from the barkeep.

"I just wanted to say thanks for saving my sister. I was stupid, and I didn't mean to put her in harm's way. He promised he wouldn't hurt her."

I thought about scolding him, but he looked like he was doing a just fine job of beating himself up. I knew the feeling. My mind wouldn't let go of the sense I should've done something to save David. Instead I asked, "What did Wolfsheim promise you in exchange for allowing him to get to her?"

"That he would show me how to manage my CLS so I wouldn't have to go through the reversal process." He looked at me with an expression of hope. "There are some things I like about it, but I don't have the knowledge or control you do. What you did in the cave, how you kept things from happening too early or late, how easily you changed, how you manage among all this stimulation—that's what I want to learn."

Anger flared at Dimitri for allowing his great nephew to struggle for so long, particularly as it had put him and Selene in danger. Just as David had taken me under his wing, I could do so for Curtis, and I nodded.

"So you don't want to be a reversal candidate anymore."

"Not if I can learn how to deal with this."

"Fine, I'll teach you." I gestured to my glass. "We'll start with the important things tonight. The first step to becoming a Scottish werewolf—how to use that enhanced sense of smell to choose your favorite whiskey."

He grinned. "I think I'm going to like this training program."

Finally, when I got home, I opened the manila envelope Wolfsheim had taunted me with. I had to bury one father figure at a time, and even though the ghost had bothered me leading up to the confrontation, it was hard to say goodbye.

I slit the edge, and several letters and telegrams spilled out. Words floated up to me from the letters as I skimmed through them. *Hot on the trail of the torc... Getting close... Tip he's in Belgium...* Double crossing, betrayal, and lies.

And then there was the picture of my father's body on the battlefield with wounds I had assumed were shrapnel, but now I saw for what they were—blood magic eruptions. This time I could look at it without shuddering. As horrific as it was, knowing exactly how he'd died and at whose hands gave me some peace. Knowing I had the information in my possession and intended to complete David's collection of letters and other information about the Order seemed to have allowed his soul to rest as well.

I put it all away.

31

———

S *ix Months Later*
       I sheltered Selene from the cold wind as much as I could, but it blew with bitter persistence and nipped at our noses and any other exposed parts.

"Why do you live in this part of the world, again?" she asked once we reached my office suite, which had moved to the ground floor at Lycan Castle after Morena resigned her position as Council Leader and the others had voted me into the position. We unwound our scarves and shed our coats in front of the roaring fire.

"Because the women are so gorgeous," I told her with a kiss.

"I'm not Scottish, you ass," she said and smiled up at me.

"I'd rather attend to your ass." I pinched her adorable behind. "And you've got Scottish blood in you."

"It's a good thing I'm giddy about the news I have for the Council. Otherwise you'd be in big trouble."

We tried to sober our expressions before entering the Council Chamber, but I had to avoid eye contact with her so I wouldn't break out in a grin. Finally, after our call to order and approval of minutes, we moved into business.

I looked around the table at a different set of faces than I'd faced when getting approval for the Institute. Of course Cora Campbell had abdicated her position, and she'd moved with Bartholomew to Oban. They were trying to keep a low profile since Garou and I unearthed evidence that Bartholomew had inappropriately used his influence to seduce female cult members who worked at his company, which allowed us to employ sexual harassment charges. There was also questionable use of charitable funds, and I suspected they'd both be in jail before the end of the following year.

Of course Morena had left. She said she wanted to take time to work on her relationship with and care for her daughter, whom Wolfsheim had brainwashed. Dimitri had "retired" after I assumed leadership of the Council, no doubt in protest and to hide from the charges of conspiracy to murder Otis LeConte. Replacing his bloodline had been an easy task.

Also present were former members of the Young Bloods and Purists, both young relatives of the previous Council members, and I hoped they would represent the interests of modern werewolves. Finally, Selene attended occasionally as the Institute liaison. She was so excited I allowed her to speak first.

"I am happy to report that our first experimental reversal appears to have been a success," she said. "Genetic tests are showing no evidence of CLS in that participant's cells, and all symptoms have been remitted for weeks."

Everyone burst into applause with cries of, "Bravo!" Once the room settled down, one of the new members, a young woman named Lacey, asked, "What's next, then?"

"We have to see how the other four subjects fare, although their cases are looking hopeful as well, both with regard to physical reversal and psychological adjustment."

"But will it be available to genetic lycanthropes?" Lacey persisted. "Will you include some of them in your next phase?"

"We are currently working on a protocol, which will have to be voted on by the Council, of course. We anticipate the psychological burden on those participants to be higher, as it has been part of your identity since adolescence. Plus, we need to develop an assessment tool to determine what reasons are strong enough for someone to make this major life change."

Lacey nodded. "I'm just glad this discussion is still open."

While I admittedly had mixed feelings about it, I trusted Selene and her colleagues. The rest of Council business moved quickly, as we all had Winter Solstice celebrations to get to. But, as always, we read the Lycanthrope Creed:

Our lives are long and full.

We watch the cycle of life and death, death and rebirth, the wheel of the seasons.

Taking responsibility for our bloodlines and vowing to teach our pups.

We act in accordance with honor no matter the adversity.

Standing guard over those whose lives are shorter than ours, saving them from themselves and dangers they can't even imagine.

Standing alongside humanity, we are shadows that come to life under the moon.

Standing together with our pack.

SELENE, Curtis and I had all been invited to several Solstice gatherings, but there was no question as to which one we would attend.

"Blessed Solstice!" Max announced when he opened the door. Then he shivered. "I don't know why you people live in this cold part of the world."

We got inside as quickly as possible.

"It's because the men are so handsome," Selene said with a wink at me. She kissed Max on the cheek and hugged Lonna. Iain was there, and we shook hands.

"Was the Council happy?" he asked.

"Very. Of course there are questions about the next part."

He nodded. "Equal opportunity for all, eh? Come in and have a drink. I'll pick your brains about it later."

A tug on my pants leg made me look down into a pair of emerald eyes. "Gabriel, up!" I picked up Abby and carried her into the living room.

"There she is," Lonna said and took her from my arms. "I've tried everything to get this kid to stay in her crib, but she keeps getting out. Even through the locked door."

I pinched Abby's nose, and she giggled. "Maybe it's all right for her to stay up this once? Selene loves her. I do too."

Lonna sighed, but happily. "I wonder how wizard mums do it."

"If I meet one, I'll ask for you."

I moved with the flow of the party, Selene by my side. I greeted Garou, whose sour expression had melted into friendliness, and the more we worked together, the more I respected him.

Eventually Selene and I ended up under a sprig of mistletoe. I took her into my arms.

"You did good, Investigator McCord," she said and snuggled up to me. "This wouldn't have happened without you."

"What, me being under the mistletoe with you?"

"No," she said and gestured to the party. Most of it was Institute staff and guests. Alexander, now an adopted brother to Abby, played with the little girl. With the Council's help, Lonna and Max had been able to get him away from the abusive Paul. "All these people together in the same place enjoying themselves. You're even getting along with Iain now. And the program is a success."

"It's all because of you doctor types. I'm just a humble werewolf."

"And a smart politician."

"That reminds me," I said. "I think it would be smart for you and I to have some sort of formal arrangement. It took me a while to recognize it, and I don't say it nearly enough, but Selene Rial, I love you."

Her mouth dropped open. I knelt beside her, took her hand, and said, "Will you marry me?"

She looked around. A few people were smiling in our direction, and soon silence fell over the party as the guests realized what was happening.

"About time," Curtis grumbled, but others shushed him.

Selene didn't allow him to distract her. "Yes, Gabriel, I will marry you."

Everyone cheered, and I pulled a velvet box out of my pocket. The ring fit her perfectly, a two-carat diamond surrounded by little ones. We kissed.

"Now we're going to have to get you to learn to drink whiskey," I said.

She wrinkled her nose. "So that's how you survive these winters..."

"By the way," I said, "now that we're engaged, tell me what you see when we sniff."

She grinned. "I see a Scottish warrior with the torc standing by a waterfall. He's you and not you. We don't need genetic tests to tell where your bloodline comes from."

She squeezed my hand and moved away with the flow of the party to show the insistent female guests her ring. I looked outside at the snow swirling from the sky. No spirits disturbed us tonight, and I knew whatever may come, I wouldn't face it alone. I hoped that wherever my father and David had ended up, they were also celebrating the longest night of the year with family and loved ones.

The snow swirled into the shape of Reine, who blew me a kiss and mouthed the word, "Congratulations" before disappearing.

.   .   .

DEAR READER, thank you so much for reading Blood's Shadow! It would be really helpful for me if you would please leave a review for the book on the site where you bought it. Retailers count the number of reviews a book has in its overall rank, which means that leaving reviews and telling your friends about this book are the best way to help others discover it. Plus I always appreciate the feedback, both positive and negative. Thanks! - Cecilia

A MILLION SHADOWS - PREVIEW

Witches, werewolves, and murder - oh, my

A Million Shadows
© 2017 Cecilia Dominic

The Lycanthropy Files, Book 3.5

Former model and heartbreaker Kyra Ellison is accustomed to making trouble, not being on the receiving end. When she's kicked out of her family's Ozarks cabin where she's been taking refuge - okay, hiding - after a wicked ancient syndrome wrecked her old life, she's forced to go to Salem, Massachusetts.

Yes, that Salem, where a murder, witches with secrets, and a handsome billionaire make danger irresistible. Kyra finds she's not the only one with secrets and skeletons in her family closet, but some are more deadly than others.

A confrontation with ancient danger and a new foe forces her to choose between the old life she's been craving and the new love she can't resist.

A Million Shadows is a supplemental novella in the Lycanthropy Files, an urban fantasy series with the bite of a medical thriller. If you like magic, compelling mysteries that keep you up past your bedtime, and hot wizards who make you want to stay up all night, then you'll love *A Million Shadows*.

Enjoy the following excerpt from A Million Shadows:

A moonbeam found its way through the blinds and speared me awake at around three o'clock. I rolled away from it, but my movement was echoed by a thud downstairs. I sat, all senses alert, and heard a scratching sound like boots scrabbling in sand.

I pulled the T-shirt I'd slept in over my head just before my hands curled into paws. My fingernails turned into claws, and the change came on from my extremities. It felt like I curled inward and folded into shapes no human body should endure. The fur itched as it pushed through pores I hadn't had before, but I couldn't control my paws enough to scratch it.

The final thing to change was my face, and that was the worst sensation, of someone taking my nose and pulling so hard it brought my skull with it.

Then the pain stopped, and a sense of strength, grace, and deadliness unfurled like a flag in my middle and filled me with purpose. To my wolf eyes, the room seemed awash in daylight —not moonlight—and my lips curled.

There was an intruder in my house, and I wanted to tear him or her apart.

No tearing apart, I reminded myself. *Not unless I want a visit from that nice policeman later.*

I jumped off the bed with as little noise as possible and slunk into the hallway and down the stairs. My fur was the same color as my hair—almost black—so I knew I would blend into the shadows.

Whereas the sulfurous smell had dissipated to my human nose, it was still very strong and present to my wolf nose. But that wasn't what made me stop, all fur on end, when I turned toward the front hall. The sand I had stepped in glowed an opalescent blue, and I saw it was in a circle shape about three feet in diameter. I could see the panes of the front door through the ghostly figure that struggled in the middle of it.

My wolf brain, eminently practical, noted that I couldn't do anything about a ghost because it wasn't solid enough to be afraid of me, so I should just turn around and go back to bed.

But then I heard my name.

My ears perked up, and I moved closer, sticking to the darker patches. Why was the ghost calling my name? Was it a deceased family member visiting for the Festival of the Dead? What was I supposed to do about it?

"Kyra, where are you? I'm trapped. I just want to talk to you."

The ghost pushed against some sort of invisible barrier. When I got close enough to make out its features, I gasped, which came out as a canine huff.

Jared Steel was the ghost trapped in the circle.

"What are you doing here? Are you dead?" I didn't know if he would hear my mental voice, but he spun around.

"Where are you? I can't see you."

"I'm right here. It's nighttime. Why are you here in my parents' house? Are you dead?"

"No, I don't think so. I think I'm dreaming." He looked at his hands and grew more solid. I moved out of the shadows to sit in front of him, and he tried to back up, but he bounced against the back of the circle.

"Kyra, wherever you are, go! There's a wolf."

He looked so bewildered I wasn't sure whether to laugh at him or comfort him. I still didn't know whether he was dead, but I suspected not. If some wolves could spirit-walk, then I supposed some humans could, too.

I did want to know who had made a binding circle in my foyer, but I guessed it wasn't my confused astral projection house guest.

And if he was projecting while he was asleep, I could have some fun. My instincts told me he didn't realize he had this ability and would just write all this off to a strange dream in the morning.

As he came more into view, his attire resolved itself into shorts and a tight-fitting T-shirt that hugged the muscles of his upper arms, shoulders, and chest. Dark hair showed above the rim of the v-neck collar, and I licked my lips at the sight of his lightly fuzzed and nicely shaped legs.

Yes, Jared Steel was quite nice out of his work clothes, and I found myself disappointed that he didn't sleep naked.

If you'd like to read more about Kyra and Jared grab your copy of A Million Shadows *from your favorite online or local retailer. You can have your local bookstore order it from Ingram Spark with ISBN* 978-1-945074-48-6

DO YOU WANT TO KNOW MORE ABOUT REINE THE FAE?

Sometimes even a Fae princess has to agree to an impossible bargain. Unfortunately there's no "fair" in Fae.

The Shadow Project

© *2020 Cecilia Dominic*

Fae Files, Book 1

Exiled Fae princess Reine has gotten comfortable in the Earth realm, but she'd drop it all in a heartbeat to return home to Faerie. When her scornful mother proposes a pact, Reine knows she better be careful, because Fae bargains are always loaded with tricks...

On the same day she agrees to help smoke out a traitor on a team of scientists, an invisible shifter attacks her in her supposedly ultra-secure home and a teleporting kitten adopts her. She suspects it's all connected, but time is running out for her to figure out how. After discovering a shadowy manipulator is intent on seeing her fail, Reine must confront a deadly conspiracy that reaches into the Fae realm and could spell the end for her kind.

Can Reine unmask a sinister cabal before she loses her ticket home...or her life?

The Shadow Project is the mesmerizing first book in The Fae Files urban fantasy series. If you like snarky heroines, memorable creatures, and thrilling mysteries, then you'll love Cecilia Dominic's spellbinding story.

*The Shadow Project i*s available in most online retailers and can be ordered from any physical bookshop with ISBN 978-1-945074-59-2
Grab your copy and pierce the veil today!

ABOUT THE AUTHOR

Cecilia Dominic wrote her first story when she was two years old and has always had a much more interesting life inside her head than outside of it. She became a clinical psychologist because she's fascinated by people and their stories, but she couldn't stop writing fiction. The first draft of her dissertation, while not fiction, was still criticized by her major professor for being written in too entertaining a style. She made it through graduate school and got her PhD, started her own practice, and by day, she helps people cure their insomnia without using medication. By night, she blogs about wine and writes fiction she hopes will keep her readers turning the pages all night. Yes, she recognizes the conflict of interest between her two careers, so she writes and blogs under a pen name. She lives in Atlanta, Georgia with one husband and two cats, which, she's been told, is a good number of each.

You can find her at:
Newsletter: http://www.ceciliadominic.com/newsletter
Web page: http://www.ceciliadominic.com
Facebook: http://www.facebook.com/CeciliaDominicAuthor
Twitter: http://www.twitter.com/ceciliadominic
Instagram: http://www.instagram.com/randomoenophile

WOULD YOU LIKE A FREE NOVELLA?

Claim your copy of Noble Secrets today!

"I could not put it down! Cecilia Dominic has a new fan..." - 5-star Amazon review

Discover the Aether Psychics series, in which science has no limits and love overcomes even the highest boundaries, in this 94-page prequel novella (no cliffhanger).

A dangerous man from her past. A handsome duke in her present. Secrets that threaten their future.

After tragedy hits and danger moves in, Pauline Donahue flees London, searching for sanctuary and a way to start over. A job at a small university provides the escape she needs. Keeping recalcitrant professor Edward Bailey on task after a shattered heart renders him broken and destroyed becomes her daily routine. But when the same vicious man from her past sets his malicious sights on Pauline, her safe haven comes crashing down.

Duke of Waltham, Christopher Bailey, never counted on the gentle commoner, Miss Donahue, to save his brother--and himself--from broken pasts and a lifetime of mistakes. But she does just that. As their love blossoms, danger closes in, threatening Pauline and Christopher's lives. Together, they are forced to face their biggest fears, revealing secrets that could ruin them both.

Go to www.ceciliadominic.com/booknewsletter to grab your copy in exchange for signing up for my newsletter list. I promise to keep your email safe and secure!